Mush On And Smile

Klondike Kate — Queen of the Yukon

MUSH ON AND SMILE

Klondike Kate — Queen Of The Yukon

— A Novel —

by
Val Dumond
and
Babe Lehrer

Muddy Puddle Press

First Edition

ISBN 0-9679704-2-3

Cover design: Sands Costner & Associates, Tacoma, WA
Cover Photo Courtesy of University of Alaska, Fairbanks

It's easy to know where your
heart has been,
but how can you know where
it's going?

—KATE ROCKWELL

RED RED RED RED RED

KATE STANDS ALONE ON THE STAGE, SHROUDED in a cape of white ermine. She stares straight ahead, her violet eyes blank, unseeing.

Look at me, damn you, look!

Not yet! Not until you're quiet.

Quiet down, fellas. Your Katy is here. I'll just stand still and stare at you until you settle down.

That's better. Now you've got the idea. Up here. Up here on the stage. Here I am, look at me and get ready for a show.

Every man is silent. No boots shuffle, no bottles clink, not a sound in the packed saloon. The piano player's hands freeze above the keys. Every man holds his breath as Kate's eyes close — just a little.

Then, with a slight shrug of her shoulders, she lets the white cape falls to the floor as a lone shaft of light picks up the glitter of her elegant sequined tights, the colors dancing red, blue and purple over the soft curves of her slim twenty-year-old body.

The crowd, made up mostly of healthy young men, lets out astonished gasps as Kate deftly leans over, takes a swipe at the floor and grasps the wand at her feet. She lifts it over her head, trailing yards of bright red chiffon around her body. The piano players begins the slow steady opening to Ravel's "Bolero." Kate struts about the stage, turning, twirling just enough to keep yards and yards of the diaphanous red material airborne. The tinkling piano moves up the beat as she spins faster and faster, the fiery patterns swirling about her head, winding loosely around her body as she pirouettes.

Faster yet, the piano throbs with the heady tempo, racing to keep up with Kate's tall gyrating body, rotating ever faster to keep the fire in the air. She seems ablaze, the red now clinging to her body, now flowing freely over her bright red hair, always caressing her.

Flames seem to lap about her limbs as they would a burning tree. But this tree undulates, sways, bends and stretches under the fiery canopy.

Her eyes are closed, Kate's head spins with a frenzy she knows is reaching deep into her audience.

They're all watching me. They can't keep their eyes off me. Only me. They love me. I'm the only woman in the world they can think of right now. They love me. They love me.

With one final red flurry and one last pirouette, Kate drops to the floor, arms over her bowed head. The music stops. For a moment, as the reddish halo settles about her prone body, there is a dazed silence in the room. But only for a few seconds. Then, as if by an unseen jolt, the room explodes, every man on his feet, clapping, whistling, stomping, calling out, "Kate, Kate, Queen of the Yukon. Our Kate!"

On stage, Kate lifts her head only enough to throw a smile to her admirers as they begin to toss their gold at her — nuggets, some still in pokes, and pouches of gold dust. She gracefully gathers up the gifts, the chiffon and her cape, smiling and blowing kisses, waving to her audience.

There! That ought to keep you boys happy for a few days back at your mines.

She takes a deep breath, offers a final bow, and instantly the haze of red is gone. Klondike Kate's famous flame dance is over, until the next time.

THE FLAMES DIMMED INTO THE CEILING OVER KATE'S BED. She opened her eyes and blinked. She closed them again, trying to retrieve the vision, then opened them. In those seconds, a half century passed, leaving only the faint smell of cigar smoke, whiskey, wool mackinaws and coal lamps lingering about the room. "Like I was still there, still Klondike Kate, Queen of the Yukon," she murmured.

Kate sat up, swung her legs slowly over the side of the bed and prodded herself with words. "About time you got going, Miss Queen of the Yukon. This is shopping day." She looked at her feet for a few moments, remembering the years of dancing they had accomplished for her, weary feet, tired feet, but strong feet. She pushed them into worn slippers and stood up. *Red, yes I'll wear red today.*

The Queen Buys Bread

FRIDAY WAS GROCERY SHOPPING DAY. IT WAS one of the few excuses Kate Rockwell had for leaving the house. When you live alone, each day becomes special, each holds a special significance or possibility. Thursday you cleaned, Friday you shopped and Saturday you baked. That way you had something to look forward to.

Today Kate chose a sheer dress of red voile. She knew how it set off her white hair and perked up her sagging...well, just about everything. She wore red shoes with a slight heel that added curves to her already curvy dancer's legs, and propped a wide-brimmed matching hat on her head, letting the ribbons fall down her back. As a finishing touch, Kate wrapped a delicate red chiffon scarf around her neck, jauntily tossing one end over her left shoulder. She could have been preparing for the stage, for her audience, as she did all those long years ago, but today she was preparing for another kind of audience, the neighbors. Kate never allowed herself out in public without "dressing."

Her old pre-war Plymouth still managed to get her where she wanted to go, rain or shine, winter or summer. The new 1952 models with chrome and fancy adjectives were being promoted at the car agencies over in Bend. Now that the war was over, it seemed cars had all the gadgets and conveniences a person would want. Yet, as long as this old thing ran...wasn't the car just like her? Wasn't she running with old parts herself? Old cars just go with old women, she'd decided. Let the youngsters drive those fancy new machines.

The trip was only a few blocks, but taking the car meant she didn't have to climb the hill loaded down with shopping bags. Few cars were in the parking lot at the Piggly Wiggly when Kate drove up. She pulled into a spot right in front of the door, checked her list, tucked it into her purse and got out of the car.

"Morning, Miss Kate," a friendly voice called from behind the checkout counter.

"Oh, good morning, er...to you," she called back cheerily. The price of fame is that everyone knows you and you don't recall their names. Or is that what comes when you reach 70?

"Up before breakfast, aren't cha?" the voice continued. "Nice day to get out. Hear you're getting married. When's the lucky day?"

Dang, how'd they find out? Cornered and needing to give an answer, she replied quickly and vaguely, "Next month. Sometime next month."

Another clerk's voice: "Congratulations, or is it best wishes I'm supposed to tell the bride?"

"Thank you." Kate couldn't commit to more just then as she hurried past the checkout counters and into the store. She looked for a basket to carry, she hated those new carts the stores had brought in. Wheels indeed! When you shopped, you carried a basket.

"Good morning, Mrs. Matson." This was the store manager. He always saw her coming and greeted her himself.

"Good morning, Mr. Harley," she returned, moving quickly back toward the fresh produce. She didn't want to talk anymore. Somehow the news of her marriage was getting around, and she realized she wasn't ready to answer the questions just yet. Why on earth did she call the paper to tell them she was getting married? She hadn't decided any such thing. Not completely. Not definitely. What was she thinking about? *Why wasn't I satisfied just to be interviewed for the Memorial Day Parade?*

Kate liked to play "housewife" as she roamed through the store, picking up the necessities. The store personnel called her Mrs. Matson, the name of her last husband. *Wonder what it would feel like to really be "the wife, the little woman, the better half."* The name Matson still sounded funny to her. Strangely funny. She could barely remember the Little Swede, Johnny Matson, that she had married twenty years ago. He had returned to his Yukon mines so fast he was almost a ghost. A letter a year was all she had of him until there were no more letters.

She vaguely remembered what he looked like, short...came up to her chin, not quite as tall as she, or was that because he was so hunched over? He was an old man before he had time to get old. That's what the Yukon did. That's what the freezing winters and hard living did to a man.

"Ready for your wedding?" a voice asked as she reached the meat counter. "Heard you was gettin' married."

"Uh, yes, yes. I'm getting married. How is the chicken today?" She pointed to the fryers in the case. *There was a time we chased chickens around the yard instead of choosing them from under glass!*

"These are fresh this morning, Mrs. Matson."

"Fine, I'll take one, that large one...there."

"Company coming?" He was being friendly.

"Why, yes. My...intended...my fiancée will be here this weekend...for Memorial Day. The parade, you know." She offered nothing more of her life to this near-stranger. After all, she knew him only as the butcher, not her long lost friend. "Also let me have that smaller one. I'll be fixing something for the poor folks' home too."

"You do good things over there, Miss Kate, er Mrs. Matson. They really appreciate all you do."

"One has to share one's bounty." She ignored the familiarity as she put the wrapped birds into her basket and turned to leave.

"Best wishes to the bride," the butcher offered. "You be happy now," he ordered.

"Thank you." Kate smiled politely and walked towards the dairy case.

Shrill stage whispers reached Kate's ears from the next aisle. "Hummph! Mrs. Matson. Mrs.! Who knows if she was actually married, legally I mean." Kate easily recognized the Van Ryck sisters, who owned half the town.

"Now she's found another one," said one Miss Van Ryck. "Is the Matson fellow really dead?"

"I heard he refused to live with her. Went through the ceremony, but wouldn't live with her."

Kate narrowed her eyes and called loudly through the shelves, "Sorry girls, it was me who wouldn't live with him."

Whispers, real ones this time, "She heard us."

"Of course I did. Wasn't that what you wanted?"

"Shhhh."

"It was me who refused to spend another winter in the Yukon," Kate continued to shout through the shelves. Kate enjoyed this needling game she played with the town's rancorous women. "Johnny was still mining gold. And yes, he really died, with a smile on his face remembering me. Ah, but you should see my new fiancé. I never have to look far for an adoring man."

Kate lifted her chin, pulled two cans of peas off the shelf and moved on. As she turned into the next aisle, the two women faced her, cheeks red, eyes startled wide. "Oh, Mrs. Matson...Kate. How lovely to see you."

"Really. I don't have time for town gossips. If you'll excuse me..." she walked around the women who were gasping for air.

The smaller woman reached out and grabbed Kate's elbow. "I'm sorry, Mrs. Matson. We didn't mean..."

But Kate pulled back her arm, looked straight ahead and continued her shopping. *Damn women. Damned gossips. What did they know? Nothing more to do than chatter about my choices, the men in my life.* She had heard it often, the slurs about her clothes, the hints at her life, her reasons for settling in eastern Oregon. Would they never tire of it?

The women of Homestead had tolerated Klondike Kate since she settled there back in 1914. She had worked hard and helped build the town to fit the needs of early Oregon homesteaders, but that didn't matter. The women saw her only as a threat to their marriages, to the sanctity of their homes.

"My Elmer's over at that Kate's house again, fixing her roof," one would complain.

"My Jake spent three days there last week putting in new water pipes," another would add.

"She lured my Wilbur over every day for a week to help her with that new chicken coop," another would try to top their grievances.

"She wears dance hall costumes. I'll never believe they're from Paris. She wears gaudy jewelry. They can't be real. And those shoes, heels much too high for walking. Her hair is always loose. I'll bet she colors it. Nobody's a real redhead anymore."

Kate should have gotten used to it after 35 years, but it still stung when she heard their snide remarks. *Oh, to be just plain old Mrs. John Matson.* But if she was, the newspaper wouldn't print Mrs. Matson's name, clerks wouldn't offer Mrs. Matson the royal treatment. Only Klondike Kate received that kind of attention. And she had to admit that she loved it.

When her shopping basket was full, Kate remembered she needed a new broom and picked up one before she headed for the checkout. The Van Rycks were just paying their bill, trying to rush out before Kate. But they weren't fast enough to miss Kate's departing move.

"Oh dang," she cried in feigned forgetfulness. "I need some toilet tissue too." The clerk reached below the counter and fumbled in a large blue box to retrieve a roll of bathroom tissue. "Just hand it over," Kate shouted at the red-faced clerk who had tried to stuff the offending item into a sack.

"I'll just take it this way," she said loudly. At that, Kate skewered the roll of tissue onto the handle of her new broom, paid her bill and marched out of the store, her head high, her easy dancer's gait drawing attention. Calling over her shoulder, "Mush on and smile!" she carried the broom and tissue like a ship's ensign to her car. The store manager, who made a show of providing special service to his favored customers, scrambled to keep up, carrying the two bags of groceries. The Van Rycks sat in their black Cadillac and gasped. The young bag boys giggled and mimicked the old woman's heads-up walk.

"We'll be looking for you in the parade," Mr. Harley called out politely as he piled the bags in the car, all the while trying to keep a straight face. He snapped a crisp salute as she drove off.

Kate wheeled through the parking lot and pulled onto the road, slowly and without looking. She was barely aware of the screeching sound behind her as an oncoming pickup just missed taking off her fender. "Whyn't you watch where yer goin'?" an angry voice shouted into the wind. The truck pulled alongside Kate's, and the red-faced driver leaned across the passenger seat and rolled down his window, steering with one hand to keep pace with Kate's sedan. "You're a menace on the road, you old hag," he shouted. "You gussied up old broad, whyn't cha sell that pile of junk. You'll kill somebody out here…" He probably continued to yell, but Kate turned onto the next street and left the angry driver shouting into space.

Still she had heard the words…gussied up old broad…old hag…. Whoever that man was angry at, she had certainly taken the brunt. *More new people in town. The place is overrun with boorish outsiders.*

Kate tried to overlook the fact that folks such as the Van Rycks continued to regard her as a show-off, a nuisance and a threat to the good women of Homestead.

They're probably just jealous because they don't get their pictures in the paper as often as I do. Kate smiled as she pulled her car to a stop in her driveway.

Homestead

KATE WOULD BE THE FIRST TO TELL YOU ABOUT Homestead, how it grew from a cluster of small farms and ranches into a booming town. Folks there didn't have to be as big as Bend — it was enough to have the city nearby.

Homestead, Oregon was one of those sleepy towns you read about, the ones that grow from early pioneer roots but never quite make it to become a city.

Its founders were pioneers who moved west early in the 1800s and scratched out a living from wild earth, and built comfortable homes with sweat and nails. Nails were among the supplies these hardy people hauled over mountains and across deserts in their search for seclusion. They were miners, cattle ranchers, farmers, rugged mountain folk. While they prized their remoteness, they craved neighbors, only not too close.

Kate Rockwell found this appealing, the remoteness — and the people. This flamboyant woman needed people for her audience; never mind that she preferred audiences of men. Yet, when she came to Homestead she was seeking a hiding place. When an animal on the desert hurts, no matter how pretentious it may be otherwise, that wounded animal seeks a quiet hiding place to heal its pain.

Kate was in pain and had heard about the Homestead Act that opened up central Oregon. She bought a horse and rode — rode, mind you — from Seattle. Some say the horse gave out by the time she got to Homestead, so that's where she settled. Others insist that it was Kate who gave out.

Homestead itself nestled around a general store that burned down one frosty night and was rebuilt into the new more fashionable grocery story that still is called the Piggly Wiggly. The hardware store next to it provided tools and materials to its hardy customers. The drugstore came later, after the restaurant, Millie's Cafe. Finally, a small hospital was built during the horrendous flu epidemic in 1918, and a fire department followed the burning of the landmark town hall in the mid-twenties.

Millie's Cafe actually belonged to Kate before she gave it up, some time after the Great Depression. All during those lean years, Kate fed her profits to any soul who wandered in looking for a free meal.

That's what began the gossip about just who this woman really was. While she whirled around her cafe wearing brightly colored dresses that once served as costumes for her stage performances, she whirled around providing sustenance to those who needed it. When the Depression finally picked itself up, Kate had exhausted her resources. She retired to her home and her love of river rock art, earning occasional fees from appearances at anything from a parade to the annual Sourdough's Celebration.

The talk around town was split into two camps. There were those who lauded Aunt Kate for her generosity and there were those who clicked their teeth and let you know that "Kate was once a dancehall entertainer, you know, *that* kind of girl."

She kept up with news of her entertainment friends and stage opportunities through her subscription to *Variety*, which the post-master always read first before delivering it. When Kate came by to pick it up, he'd call to her, "Mush on and smile!" To which she bowed gloriously and swept out the door.

"Mush On and Smile" was Kate's motto. It was written all over everything Kate did. It was painted across the door of her cafe. She had postcards made with her picture and scrawled the words across it. The words also appeared on the stone monument she built down by the river to remember the great loss of life during one of Homestead's tragic floods. The words soothed her aching heart when the other tragedies struck, those bad times when love failed and there weren't enough other words to quiet the pain.

The words belonged to her, but she shared them with the town that both welcomed her and shamed her. The words appeared at length over the big sign at the firehouse in response to the request of the volunteers, who loved her.

The Newspaper People

GUESS WHO'S LEADING THE MEMORIAL DAY Parade again?"

"Naaah! Really? Well, *there's* a big story for this week's front page.

"She's getting married again, too."

"No. Should I be surprised? Aunt Kate is just full of news this week. Tell me, who is it this time?"

"Some guy named Warren something. Probably another sourdough."

"Aren't they all? What's she trying to do, out-marry Doris Duke? What's she up to now? Number Four or Five?"

"You should be keeping track. You're the reporter."

Annette pushed her chair back from her desk.

"Paul," she pleaded, "why don't you take a crack at the interview this time. She's different with men."

"Sorry, Annette. Klondike Kate's your beat. Besides, she likes you, thinks of you as her daughter. Isn't that what you told me after the last interview?"

"Uhhhh. They're all the same, Paul. I could write it now — without the interview." Annette picked up a copy of the Homestead *Courier* and pretended to read, "Klondike Kate, Queen of the Yukon at the turn of the century, recalls her days in Dawson City, the heart of the Gold Rush country. 'Life was fun in those days,' she says. 'The sourdoughs came into town with their pokes full of gold dust and they spread it around wildly. Easy come, easy go,' said the still-beautiful former mistress of Alex Pantages, theater kingpin..."

"She wasn't his mistress. Didn't you say she hates being called that."

"Well, one word or another, Mr. Editor. She mooned over him long after he done her wrong."

"A little respect here, sweetie. He was a married man."

"Hmmm." Annette turned her head so Paul couldn't see her. She lit a cigarette and ran her hand through her thick dark brown hair as she inhaled deeply. "A sweet young thing in love with a married man. Isn't that a strange one?"

"Please don't get cynical on me. You know where we stand. I'm not free...yet. Let's get back to the subject here." Paul straightened up and tried to look like he was in charge. "We want an interview with dear old Aunt Kate about her upcoming marriage — for next week's *Courier*," he said.

"Yes, boss," Annette answered, swinging her chair around to face the typewriter. Under her breath she murmured, "With or without the interview."

The editor, his white shirt sleeves rolled up to his elbows, peered at her across a desk littered with news stories that he was sorting for the next issue. He leaned back, stuck a grease marking pencil behind his ear and scowled.

"And don't get cranky, Annie. I hate it when we quarrel."

"Well, I hate it when…when you call me Annie," she finished the sentence lamely. Then she picked up the phone and dialed Kate Matson's number. She knew it by heart.

That afternoon Annette Whittier drove to the edge of the small town called Homestead, a community founded the first time after an 1851 gold strike. The village had survived that brief Oregon Gold Rush, weathered Indian uprisings, but succumbed to frequent range wars between cattle barons and lumber interests. It became a ghost town in the late 1800s and had dissolved back into the desert when Kate discovered it. The government opened it to homesteading in 1914 about the time when Kate, just back from the Yukon and mourning the loss of her beloved to *another woman,* had swapped some land in Seattle for the homestead she still called home.

Annette pulled up in front of the lonely little house that stood on a hill nearly two blocks from its closest neighbor. The porch was lined with river rocks and sagged near the steps. Parts of a wood railing needed paint. One section looked like a rotted part had recently been replaced by new wood. Next to the door a small stone pot held a frail plant that needed watering. A neat foot scraper and welcome mat lay directly in front of the screen door, as if placed there by someone who knew that miners' boots often were caked with mud.

The reporter left her purse in the car and carried only a note pad and pencil. Two extra pencils peeked out of her jacket pocket. She knocked on the door and waited. One more interview with Kate seemed repetitious. *My life is turning into repetition. Am I getting stale at this job? Is it time to move on? Will Paul ever make up his mind to stick with me?* "I'm beginning to sound like a soap opera," she said aloud. She shook her head to clear it as she heard the footsteps inside and the frail voice call out, "Is that you, Annette?"

"Yes, Kate. How are you?"

Beautiful long fingers pushed back the screen door. Kate had changed into a stunning green dress that brought out the depth of her gray eyes. "I'm just fine, honey, did you hear? I'm getting married." Kate smiled and led her guest inside.

"Yes, that's why I'm here."

But Kate was teasing. "Come right in. We can sit in the parlor. That's where Warren proposed to me. At my age. Just a week ago. He was so precious. He even got down on one knee — or almost. He's younger than I, but after years in the Yukon, a man's legs...well, you know all about us old folks, don't you? This man is different, Annette, he's gold, solid gold. I mean, he's one of the rare ones that stashed away his diggin's, made something of himself and still has a fair amount in the bank. Good investment for me, don't you think?"

Kate rattled on, asking an occasional question, but not leaving room for Annette to respond. "Don't you think every woman ought to marry a few times? One man won't do for a lifetime," she preached. The older woman, only her white hair giving away her age, led the younger woman into the parlor. It wasn't exactly dark, just not bright, a parlor that reminded Annette of her grandmother's old house in Spokane, small with few windows. Dark furnishings almost hid the worn places.

In Kate's parlor, the gold wallpaper and rose-patterned drapery set the tone — there had been money once, but it ran out. The dark gray upholstered chairs had been well used. Kate took in boarders from time to time, sharing her need for company with an occasional drifter or single school teacher. The banker's son stayed there once for a few months waiting out a family rebellion. Then there were all those homeless men during the Great Depression, homeless and hungry. During the war years — the first World War — she even had had women boarders; one was a soldier's lonely wife who was waiting for her baby to be born, and another was the first woman teacher who had come to Homestead.

"Every woman should marry young for love," Kate went on, "…then marry again for kids, then a third time in middle age for security and finally in old age for companionship. Looks like I'm at the companionship stage…"

"But you skipped a couple of stages, didn't you, Kate?" Annette broke in. "You skipped the marrying for love and the one for kids…"

"Wait a minute, miss. I was…Alex and I were…he was going to marry me…legally…but that young hussy got her nails into him while I was off in Texas — carrying on *his* business. We were partners, in business and in love. We were…" her voice trailed off and her eyes looked way into the past, moving into a time when flowers bloomed behind picket fences, birds sang soft songs to lovers in a sunlit field and gentle clouds shaded the sun over their glorious moments.

Annette knew how to wait. She made a note of Kate's bright green dress, her matching jade earrings and green high heel shoes. Green had become a favorite color for redheads ever since Maureen O'Hara wore it in some movie in the '40s. Kate's hair had been red once, but that was years ago.

The young reporter noticed a red handkerchief tucked into Kate's pocket. "Tell me, Mrs....er, Kate, did you mean to carry that red handkerchief with that beautiful green outfit?"

"There's a story here, if you have a minute." Somehow Annette suspected there was. She sat back. "Years ago," Kate began, "when I was dancing in the Yukon, I had a famous number that the miners insisted I dance for them. It was called the Flame Dance, and it included swinging around fifty yards of red chiffon — and sort of wrapping it around me like flames lapping at my body. It was all very sensuous and, as I said, the men of the Yukon loved it. Well, when I came to Oregon, it didn't appear that I'd be doing much flame dancing, so I took out my scissors and cut that red chiffon into a bunch of smaller scarves and boas and handkerchiefs. I even made bows for my hair and a sash for my waist. That red chiffon has sorta become my trademark; I always carry a piece of it."

"I heard that you used to wear your gowns when you were homesteading here," Annette commented.

"Of course I did. You see, when I came here, straight from the Territory, I didn't have a penny. All I had was my trunk full of dance costumes — and of course my gold jewelry. So when I started farming, the only things I had to wear were those costumes. High heels and all." Kate threw her head back and let out a laugh. "Boy, was I a beauty. You should have seen me out there clearing land in my fancy costumes with matching shoes!" She closed her eyes for a moment, remembering the days when she had to learn about poverty the old-fashioned way, from riches to rags.

The reporter scribbled a few doodles on her notepad and waited for Kate to resume her story. She wished that she had a cigarette. She finally prodded the older woman, "You were talking about marriage, Aunt Kate."

Kate's eyes opened and she continued, "Alex Pantages and I were...almost...married," she chose her words very delicately. "And no, I never found the man to have children with. My sour-doughs were my children, I guess. I took care of them the same way I'd...but they're different. Sourdoughs may think they can take care of themselves, but they really need a woman's care." Kate began to retrieve her momentum as she launched into more of her tales of the Yukon. "It was what we called the Gay Nineties, the splendid years as one century ended and another began. Those were the years of the gold strikes in the Yukon Territory." She leaned forward, "They're making it a state — Alaska."

"I heard."

Another pause. Kate pulled out her bag of tobacco and pro-ceeded to roll a cigarette with one hand, a bit of business she liked to use to entertain reporters and strangers.

"On Christmas Eve, 1900...Annette, I know you've heard this story before, but it bears repeating..." Kate paused again as she lit her freshly rolled cigarette. The effect was just what she wanted.

Annette stared, fascinated. "Where are my manners? Would you like a cigarette?"

Annette fumbled for her purse then remembered she left it in the car. "No thanks," she said. She wasn't willing to risk a hand-rolled cigarette just yet.

Kate continued her story, "…on Christmas Eve the sourdoughs made a crown of tin that held candles and they placed it on my head. My hair was very red and curly then." She touched her white hair and smoothed the soft waves. "They stuck fifty candles on that crown and it couldn't have been more beautiful if they were fifty diamonds. When I entered the room with that thing on my head, every eye turned my way. The men gasped at the sight. I must have been a knockout, as the kids say."

"I'm sure you were."

"Oh, how we reveled that night. We ate caviar and drank champagne and danced, and all the time I balanced that flaming crown on my head. By morning, my hair was so tangled with wax that I had to cut off most of it. Gave myself a haircut at four in the morning. But it was worth it, just to see the looks on their faces. There were only a few of us girls in Dawson City then and all those men coming in from their stakes, pokes full of gold dust…."

Kate peered into the past, almost purring the memories. Then she leaned forward again and continued, "Do you know, they tossed gold nuggets and dust at us on stage. We could only carry off so much. There were some enterprising guys who actually tore up the floor boards to gather up the dust that sifted through. Made their living that way. We made ours on the nuggets they threw to us. Or the pokes of dust they used to pay for their drinks. We had to get them to drink lots of whiskey and champagne, then we'd push the bottles away before they were empty and get them to order more. We got paid very well for the extra bottles we got them to buy."

"Your marriage…" Annette tried to cut in. She'd heard Kate's stories before, and often. She wanted to record the current story and return to the office. Paul said he'd get away for an early evening and she didn't want to waste a minute of their precious time together.

"I'll come to that. You have to know what things were like back then, in the Yukon."

"I have a pretty good idea. How did you meet Warren? What's his last name?"

"Thompson. Warren Thompson. I met him in Portland in…1932, just before I married Mr. Matson. He says we met earlier, but I don't recall. He's been with the same firm for many years and I consulted that law firm since the time I filed my homestead papers back in World War I." Kate stared out the window, looking at pictures from the past. "I met Warren after that altercation at Alex's trial…when I was a witness. Alex and I had lived together, we were going to be married…when that gold digger got her claws into him." Kate was rambling again. "You knew that Mr. Pantages and I owned theaters together. I put up the money and Alex opened them — you've heard of the Pantages theaters. Those were his, all over the country. And I staked him."

Annette shifted in her chair. *Dear God, what have I done? Now she'll carry on about Alex for another hour or so.* "Could I have a glass of water?" she asked carefully. *Maybe if I change the subject, she'll forget where she was.*

"Of course, my dear." Kate carefully put out her cigarette, stood up and walked slowly into the kitchen, her tall dancer's body slim and regal. Annette watched her. Like many another woman, Kate had given her man everything she had — her money, her talent, her time, and probably even her body — and he tossed her aside when it pleased him. *It's not as if she fell in love with a married man and tried to take him away from...wait a minute. That's dangerous territory. Let's stick to Kate's story.* Annette caught her breath as she glimpsed some young reporter someday asking her questions about how she met Paul.

"Would you like some iced tea?" Kate called from the kitchen. "I made some fresh this morning. Sun tea, like the Indians make."

"That would be nice," Annette called back.

Kate carried in a tray with two glasses and a plate of cookies. "I bake these for the neighbor kids...and the firemen," she said simply, placing the tray on the table next to their chairs.

Annette took advantage of the break in Kate's memories. "Mr. Thompson is an attorney then?"

"Yes. His firm represented us, Alex and me, at the turn of the century when we were negotiating for theaters in Portland. Warren was new at the firm when I went back to file my homestead papers, let's see, that was 1914. He was a new young lawyer...then. Well, weren't we all, new and young? I recall that he knew very little about theater life and I, well, educated him."

"He was married then?"

"Yes, I believe he was."

"And his wife..."

"Oh, she died a few years ago, about the time my…Mr. Matson died."

"And did you like Mr. Thompson…back when you met?"

"I really didn't get to know him then. He was just my lawyer. Didn't know beans about vaudeville and the theater. Taught him that we were real people, even if we performed…I performed…on a stage. Alex never performed. His only real talent was making money. And he made lots of it. Put together a fortune…but mostly of other people's money. I lent him thousands from what I made in the Yukon. I put up the money for his first theaters in Dawson City, then in Seattle. Did you know that?"

"Yes, I believe you mentioned it." Annette sipped her tea and wondered how many times she would hear this story again. At least once, she surmised. At least once more today.

"I gave him money to open a theater. Then more of them. Until that fiddle-playing floozy got her claws into him." She paused and grinned at Annette. "That's pretty good, don't you think? 'Fiddle-playing floozy.' That about says it. She was only a kid, not even twenty, when she went behind my back and enticed him into her bed. I got back from…Houston, or wherever…and they were already married. Must have been carrying on behind my back for months. I thought he loved me."

"But you were young too. You can't beat yourself up for missing the signs."

Kate stared off into space, then half to Annette and half to herself, she said, "Oh, what I'd give to be able to talk to that silly 20-year-old me…"

"What would you tell her?"

"I'd warn her about that man, let her know how he was hood-winking her. He did love me, I know it. It was that woman…" Kate's voice trailed off again and the two women sat in the dimly lit parlor, sipped iced tea and let their minds drift into reverie about the wrong man.

A Young Affair

TWO HOURS LATER, ANNETTE RETURNED TO the office. She scanned the room as she pushed open the door and noticed it was past five o'clock. The office clerk had gone home, but where was Paul? Maybe back puttering with the press. The old offset press worked very well for its age, but Paul liked to tinker with it. He called it his thinking time — tightening bolts, cleaning off ink rollers, oiling gears, setting pieces forward or backward. He found it was the best way to clear a muddled head.

What could be bothering him today? Is he getting ready to confront Isabel? Is he going to ask to get out of their marriage soon? Is he "hood-winking" me like Alex did to Kate?

Annette tossed her note pad and purse on the desk, pulled her chair towards the typewriter and rolled a clean sheet into the machine. She opened her purse and found her cigarettes, lit one and leaned back to consider her opening line. A well-trained reporter, she always sat down directly after an interview and combined the notes in her mind with those she had written. She began her story:

"Kate Rockwell, known for years as Klondike Kate, Queen of the Yukon, has announced her upcoming marriage to Warren Thompson, a former sourdough, now an attorney from Portland…" The story carried some of Kate's all-too-familiar memories (Annette would hear about it if anything was left out) as well as a few notes about the current bridegroom — as much as Annette was able to worm out of Kate.

After three pages, the young reporter finished her story, typed the imperative "30" at the end and yanked the paper from the typewriter. She had seen Rosalind Russell do that in the movies and considered her the authority on how women newspaper reporters should behave. "Done," she said aloud. "And just in time." She turned to greet Paul coming through the door.

"You always look so good to me," he sighed, removing his print apron and brushing a kiss across her cheek.

"And you always look so handsome walking through that door, almost like opening a box on Christmas morning. I found you…how many months ago? Six, seven? And I still shake inside when I see you."

"Oh god, Annette, you're beautiful."

"Thanks, but we shouldn't talk like that here."

"Nobody's around. I've been thinking about you all evening. We've got to be together…soon."

"Patience."

Paul went to his desk without touching her, although both wanted to cling to each other forever. Still, they were in the office, and had gotten used to playing it safe. Only when they were sure they were alone would they even use intimate language, and then very carefully. They both wanted to protect Isabel from as much pain as possible, they told themselves often. They weren't out to hurt anyone. They just needed to be together, just needed to enjoy each other's company.

"How's Kate?" Paul called quietly from his desk.

"Oh, you know Kate. She's...just Aunt Kate. Always Klondike Kate. She's still in the Yukon, if that's what you're asking."

"Surprised?"

"No. And this new 'love' — and I use the word loosely — seems more of a routine for her, something to do, rather than some need for a husband. I didn't hear anything about love, even *like*. They've known each other a long time and they're just *getting married*."

"Maybe it's a legality. He's a lawyer, I hear."

"Yeah. Maybe. Alex Pantages has always been the great love of her life and still is. It seems more like anyone else is just...a husband."

"You say that with envy."

"Of course I do. She couldn't marry her great love. At least not legally. And she can't get over him. She's still carrying the torch after all these years."

"Can you imagine carrying a torch for fifty years?"

Annette sat silent for a long time before answering very softly, "Yes."

K ATE SAT STILL IN THE OVERSTUFFED CHAIR FOR A LONG TIME after Annette left. The interview had stirred up the dream again, or more accurately, the memory. "Those were the good times," she sighed, taking a sip of what remained of her iced tea. "Those were the good days."

Kate had read an article in *Family Circle* about how old people talk to themselves for company. "Of course we do," she had said aloud. "Who else do we have to talk to?" Now she talked to herself more often, convinced it was as healthy for her as the article said it was. Helped her vent, according to the author, a well-known psychologist. Helped her keep from feeling alone.

Kate bent over from her chair to replace the glasses on the tray. "I'll just take a moment, then carry them into the kitchen." She leaned back and rested her head on the soft upholstery, her eyes closed to the parlor and opened to the past.

Too many years, too much living had tired her out. Stimulated by the talk, she was feeling nostalgia…loss…regrets? "No, not a single regret," she said. "Well, maybe one or two. Oh, Alexander, why did you leave me?" She would begin to cry soon if she didn't do something.

What fools we women are, to chase after men we can't have. "He hurt you, Kate," she whispered. "He hurt you and still you miss him, long for him."

Kate opened her eyes, raised her head, then leaned over and picked up the tray. Slowly, after all she was past seventy, she stood up and turned toward the kitchen. She felt the ache in her neck, the tightness of her legs after sitting so long, the vague sense of being somewhere she didn't belong — but then, she had never felt she belonged anywhere — and she knew it would all end soon.

She passed the mirrored sideboard in the dining room and stopped to address her image. "How'd you get so flamin' old? Your eyes look all watery and dim. Where's that mop of red hair? The sweet soft face? You've still got your legs," she looked down below the green rayon skirt. Yes, her legs had remained shapely. "God gave me great legs and let me keep them," she smiled at last, "even if that old knee hurts most of the time.

"You're going to be okay, old girl," she told the image. "Warren will be good to have around. That's all you need now, isn't it? Someone to be here when you get to feeling low, someone to talk to, someone who'll talk back once in awhile. Warren will talk back."

Hearing his name, Warren picked up the phone on his desk in his Portland office and dialed. Kate's new phone rang just as she set the tray down next to the kitchen sink. She walked quickly into the dining room and picked up the receiver, glanced at the clock and knew who it was. Warren usually waited until the rates went down after five.

"Hello," she called into the mouthpiece. How anyone could speak in one place and be heard miles away still remained a mystery to her. "Hello. Who's there?"

"Evening, Kate," came Warren's voice. "How's my best girl?"

"Warren? That you?"

"What other man would be calling you his best girl?" Now that was a dumb thing to ask. He was afraid there'd be an answer.

"Warren. Warren." Kate couldn't think of anything else to say, so she repeated his name. "Warren."

"I was just sitting here thinking about you. I always think about you."

Kate listened, not speaking.

"Hope everything is going well there. Have you talked to the minister about the church? Are you busy getting ready for the wedding? What date have you set?" He hoped.

"Warren, I'm so glad you called. I had a reporter here today. She stayed all afternoon and we just talked and talked. She's doing an article about me in the *Homestead Courier*. They always treat me so well in the paper…"

"Kate, I'm happy for you. Did they ask about the wedding?"

She couldn't escape that question. "Yes," was all she said.

"And what did you tell them?"

"You'll have to read the article when it comes out, probably in next Friday's paper. Will you be down for Memorial Day?"

"What a question! Of course I'll be down next weekend. I'll come Friday night, my darling, should be there about eight. I'll take you over to the hotel for dinner if you'd like."

"No need to fuss, Warren. I'll fix you something here."

"Oh good. I'd like that. Oh say, Kate, I saw something the other day I want to buy for you, a necklace, all gold, twenty-four carat, very elegant. It looked just like you. And it's set with sapphires, I know you like them. It will go with your eyes…"

Kate glimpsed those eyes in the sideboard mirror again and closed them. All she could say was, "That's nice, Warren. Then you'll be here about eight next Friday."

"Yes, my dear. And I can hardly wait to see you. We'll have a nice weekend and I'll stay over for Memorial Day. Let me look at my calendar here…ummm…yes, Memorial Day will be Tuesday."

"Yes, Warren, a nice weekend. Nice Memorial Day. Time to hang up now. Don't want to waste your telephone money. Nice of you to call."

After she had hung up the receiver, Kate stared at her reflection in the sideboard mirror. *Old woman. Old woman. Why would anyone want to marry you?*

"Because you're a high flyer, Kate of the Yukon!" came the answer. "Because you're a stunning looking woman…with a past. You've lived high, you've lived well, you've lived! And those who haven't lived — like those old biddies in the grocery store — find you fascinating."

Kate continued to stare at the mirror. "And I want to marry Warren." She repeated the words, as if to convince herself. "I want to marry Warren. He's a good man, he loves me, and he won't hurt me." That last seemed important. "He won't hurt me. I want to marry Warren."

The pep talk worked and Kate clicked approval out the side of her mouth, tossed her white-maned head and returned to the wash-up in the kitchen, humming. She sang as she slathered the dishes in suds and rinsed them in hot water. "Hello my honey, hello my baby, hello my ragtime gal…" With the tea glasses neatly cradled in the drainer, the dancer-singer turned to the refrigerator for her supper.

Maybe I should eat that frozen dinner tonight. During her trip to the grocer's a week before, Kate let herself be talked into buying one of those new frozen dinners — Salisbury steak, mashed potatoes and peas. *All you have to do is heat it in the oven. What'll they think of next? The war was good for something*, she decided. Someone turned K-rations into a dinner she could cook when she wanted it. Kate pulled a match from the box and lit the gas oven. As it heated, she read the instructions on the box, dutifully tore back one corner of the cardboard cover and set it aside until the oven was warm. "It's got to be better than cold potatoes and sourdough bread," she said aloud, her mind back in the Yukon. "God, it got cold then, and nothing to heat up food with." Then it hit her, the irony, and she threw back her head and laughed, a hearty loud laugh that she felt all the way down into her stomach. "Hell, *all* our food was frozen back then!"

Kate usually went to bed early. That night she sat up, lights off, smelling the soft spring scent of lilacs and listening to the sounds outside the parlor window. The breeze felt warm and her head was clear. *This feels like mid-summer in Alaska, when Alexander and I would walk out into the fields at night, lie on the grass and watch the moon come up, the stars shining bright. He'd make wreaths of daisies for my hair and he'd crown me like I was a real queen. Only it wasn't exactly night, it was early in the morning, after the last show. He had such energy; I felt so excited, so alive. We had to walk, run, skip about in that meadow. What must the birds have thought seeing us out there to wake them up? Poor critters. Poor little critters.*

*Yes, that night, that Christmas Eve, when they put that crown of candles on my head, I was Queen of the Yukon. I was...*but Kate had nodded off, sitting in her chair in the dark next to the open window, watching herself wearing a diadem of daisies and cavorting with the love of her life all those years ago in a Yukon meadow.

The next morning Kate shifted in her chair as the sun came around the corner. All night in the chair had cramped her tired old body. She rose and stretched, slowly and long, then went to get a glass of water. She caught a glimpse of movement in the garden outside her window and rushed outside to shoo away an early scavenger, probably a raccoon or a rabbit. Returning to the house, her mind skipped to Warren's question. When was she planning her wedding?

She felt the mischief and spoke aloud, "Dear me, that reporter forgot to ask for our wedding date. Maybe I ought to set a real day and call the minister." She plodded up the back steps, into the kitchen. "I want to marry Warren," she remembered the mantra from the previous evening. "He's loony over me and he has a good heart. Giving me gold necklaces. Whoo! Doesn't he know how much gold jewelry I already have? And good stuff, not that glitzy ditzy store-bought stuff. My pieces all custom-made from gold craftsmen, the real thing.... But his heart is trying, Aunt Kate," she added, pouring water for her coffee.

After a breakfast of oatmeal, toast and a cup of fresh-ground coffee...she mixed it half with milk like they do in France...the woman climbed the stairs to her bedroom and lay on the bed for a few minutes. Her bones felt the night spent in the chair. *Warren will be good for me. I'll have someone to talk to. Maybe I can get him to move his practice here. Surely ranchers have legal problems that he could solve.*

A knock at the back door roused Kate from her day-dreaming. "Aunt Kate, Aunt Kate," came a tiny voice.

"Ah, Beatrice," Kate half-called out. "My darling little Beatrice."

Kate tried to hurry down the steps, holding tightly to the handrail, and calling out, "I'm coming, Beatrice. I'm coming."

She opened the door and bent down to greet the eight-year-old from down the hill. "How's your granny?" Kate asked.

"She's well, thank you, Aunt Kate," the child answered. "How are you? Gran asked me to come see how you are."

"You tell her that Aunt Kate's just fine. I'm about to bake up some wonderful oatmeal cookies. Can you stay around a bit?"

"Oooh, yes, Gran said I could stay for one hour."

"That's just enough time. I'll light the oven and you bring over the oatmeal box. Can you handle that?"

The two spent most of the next hour measuring, mixing, grinding, chopping, stirring, and spooning out dough on the cookie sheet. Beatrice watched the clock and announced the time to open the oven. Aunt Kate sheathed her hands with oven mitts and brought out the steaming cookies. The little girl oh-so-carefully scraped each cookie off the pan and placed them in rows on waxed paper.

"They sure smell good, don't they," Beatrice hinted.

"Sure do. Suppose we ought to try one to see if they're fit to eat?"

"Uh-huh!" The crispy pecans in the cookies crunched happily inside Beatrice's mouth. "We did it right, didn't we."

"You bet we did."

As they chomped cookies, Kate asked, "How's school? Learning anything good?"

"Aw, it's not so bad."

"What's your favorite subject?"

"Baseball."

"Baseball, eh? They teach that now?"

"Not exactly, but we play during recess. Sometimes I get to play with the boys, but not much."

The chomping continued without talk for a few moments.

"Aunt Kate…"

"Yes, darlin', what's on your mind?"

"Well…" Beatrice stalled.

"Come on, out with it. You got a boyfriend or something?"

"Oooh, no," Beatrice wrinkled her face in disgust. "I'm too young for boyfriends. Mama says so."

"Well, what then?"

"In a way, it's boys, but not thaaat way!"

"Which way then, sweetheart?"

"They tease me…sometimes…about being a boy. They tell me I'm a tomboy and say I'm going to grow up and wear trousers and ties and stuff."

"Do you think you're a tomboy?"

"Well, yes, kinda, I guess."

"And that's not good?"

"No. I mean, yes. I mean, they say it isn't good, but I sometimes wish I were a boy."

"Really?"

"Yeh, then I could play baseball all the time and wear knickers and run fast and grow up to be somebody instead of just a mother."

Kate took a deep breath. "Did you know that I did stuff that people called being a tomboy?"

"You? Naw, not you?"

"Yep. Me. I had a boy cousin who let me wear his pants and I'd pull my hair under a cap and run around with the boys."

"Oooh." Beatrice breathed a deep sigh of wonder.

"And I even disguised myself as a boy to get to Alaska. Had to. They wouldn't let women get on the boat that went to the gold fields. I had to fool them."

"Wasn't that scary?"

"Sure, but that's the point."

"What do you mean?"

"If you're not feeling something, you might as well lay down and call it quits. You gotta stay in there and do those things that make you happy — even if other people don't like it. You gotta smile at them and mush on."

"What's that mean, mush on?"

"It means keep going. When you're out in the snowy places in Alaska all alone with only a bunch of sled dogs, the only way to get where you're going is to call out 'mush, mush.' That tells the dogs to keep on pulling, and they do. It kinda keeps your own spirits going too. Many's the time I felt like I was stranded out there in the icy wilderness and…"

But the hour was up. "Oh, Aunt Kate, I got to get home." Beatrice skipped off happily back to her gran's house down the hill, carrying a bag of Aunt Kate's cookies and a small doll that Kate had picked up…somewhere…just for such an occasion. Aunt Kate kept toys to give away to children. Like the goodies she kept in her cupboard to offer occasional guests.

No matter she didn't have a family to bake for, no matter that visitors were rare, no matter that Warren wasn't due to arrive for a week, this was Saturday, baking day. So Kate continued to bake after Beatrice left, first a lemon pie (her favorite) for herself, then her famous Kiss-off Chocolate Peanut Pie for the boys at the fire station. While another batch of cookies baked, Kate busied herself preparing the chicken for the old folks' home, frying succulent pieces that she had dredged in her famous seasoned bread crumbs. She liked sharing her bounty, as she called it. *I may not be as rich as I was once, but I can still reach out to the less fortunate.*

For years, Kate had helped feed the community, even during the years she could barely scrape together two onions and a squash. She was an excellent cook (who needs Swanson's frozen whatever-it-was?) and enjoyed cooking large quantities she could parcel out to "the less fortunate."

She had learned that from her folks back in Kansas. She and her dad used to carry food down to the railroad station and hand over discreet packages to raggedy looking people. "I haven't thought of that in years," she said aloud. "I must have been three or four then." Kate stood in the center of her kitchen, hands in her apron pockets. Kate's dad had been a bookkeeper for the railroad and was gone a lot, but when he was there...ah yes, Kate remembered the father who disappeared from her life just as she was getting to know him. Always jolly. Always happy. "Why shouldn't he be?" her mother had told her, "he was always drunk."

Then he was gone.

Kate rested her hands on the side of the sink and stared out the window.

Through the glass she saw the little girl whisked up in her father's arms, saw her tighten her grasp around his neck. "I'll be a good girl, Daddy. Let me stay with you?" she cried. "I'll be good."

The smallish balding man held his daughter close. "You *are* good, my darling. You are the best. Don't ever forget that. You are the best."

Then the man turned into the elderly judge who encouraged the girl, "You can call me Father, or Judge, whichever you prefer."

"You're not my father. I'll call you Judge. Mother wants me to."

"Kathleen Eloise," her mother scolded. "If you act up again, the judge is going to throw both of us out. Then where will we live? What will we do? You must behave." The judge's wife must, after all, keep up appearances.

"Will you throw me out too, Mama, like you threw out Daddy?"

Kate shook her head to free thoughts that were becoming entangled with cobwebs and visions of what used to be.

Respectability! Is that what it's all about? Queen of the Yukon, Klondike Kate! Or sweet old Aunt Kate? Just which is respectable?

The old woman held up an aluminum pan and enjoyed the reflection of a feisty red-haired teenager dressed up in feathers and silk, parading boldly down the staircase and through the assembled guests of the judge and his new wife at a party so long ago. Most definitely a queen then, and still a queen.

"There's your answer," Kate murmured, placing the pan onto the shelf.

Stones and Circles

On Sunday, Kate delivered the bounty of her cooking and baking to the firemen and to the old folks' home, then turned her old Plymouth towards the high desert. While Kate's spiritual life had been formed around the Catholic church of her youth, it had been merely a place to exercise her own freedom, an education in creating space for herself in this world. As an adult, Kate found great spiritual uplifting out in the high desert. There was no place to hide there, where she could touch base with Earth, center herself, pull meaning out of her daily existence. There she escaped the critical eyes of her neighbors and found room to nourish herself. There she could straighten out daily dilemmas, calm doubts and make necessary decisions. Because the desert held no distractions, that is where she dared to daydream, where she had time to think about Alex. Alexander. Alexander the Great Pantages.

Not a day went by in Kate's life that she didn't think of him. What could have been. What was. Still, she confined her thoughts to home. Here in the desert, memories were given free rein — and they galloped around her like wild ponies.

What was seems so far away now. How many times when he was still alive did I think...believe...he would come to me, marry me, settle down somewhere and have a houseful of children...live the happily-ever-after of fairy tales?

He loved me. Of that I have no doubt. I can still feel the touch of his hand, the smell of him, the taste of him. I can still see those huge brown eyes, the tinge of a smile on his graceful mouth, the sculptured classic Greek look of his face.

Kate often *saw* him...or thought she did...walking that easy swinging gait of his, standing tall and pensive in front of a store window, hurrying through a crowded street, entering a restaurant in Portland, or Seattle, or...he was everywhere. Was everywhere, now nowhere.

Kate loved to hike out to the high desert after a trip to one of her...their...cities, after the noise and rushing of the Outside. Much as a sourdough retreats to the frozen stake, so Kate retreated to her space where she could see the stars, hear...nothing...nothing but the rustle of wee animals in the sage, the whisper of wind looking for trees, the sound of herself breathing.

That Sunday she slung her rock bag over her shoulder and headed for a nearby mound. She spent an afternoon collecting rock specimens, some because she hadn't seen any like them before, some because they appeared to be semi-precious, and some just because they were pretty. Periodically, she'd carry the bag back to the car and the campfire, stop for a cigarette, a tug from the water bottle and a snack from her knapsack. She'd rest a moment, stoke the fire and then gather up her rock bag and move off in another direction.

She often sought rocks in the giant crevasses that interrupted the flat desert. That day she discovered an interesting cliff that promised a clear white crystallized stone she hadn't seen before, and spent hours chopping away at the surface to free some samples to take home.

By evening she had collected several bagfuls of bright rocks of all sizes. She'd use these in her next garden decoration, maybe add some to a special monument she was planning for the old folks' home, and put the best ones on her fireplace mantle to enjoy every day. Rocks told the story of life from the beginning, the very beginning of time when there weren't people, or critters or troubles or loneliness.

What a way to talk, Eloise, she scolded herself. *If you go that far back, there aren't joys or singing or people who matter, or flowers or...she was running out of high spirits. Can't let that happen.* She threw back her head and began to yodel at the stars, "Deep in the desert there lived a young cowboy, yodel-o-de-odel-o-de-ay!" Country singing was something she had picked up in eastern Oregon and she loved it. Such emotion! Such round notes! Such aerating of the soul!

She put fresh tumbleweed on the fire and hungrily finished off her sack supper. Exhausted by the day-long rock hauling, the exuberant singing and the mindsong of memory, Kate sat back with fresh coffee and a cigarette. She lounged near the campfire and watched the sun drop behind the far-off mountain peak, the western sky emblazoned first with reddish gold then fading, slowly, slowly. Kate lay on her back with her head on the bedroll. From there she could watch the spectacle of the three hundred sixty-degree day's end. In the west, the sun was casting its final glow of orange, yellow and pink over The Sisters and Mt. Bachelor. And in the east, indigo grasped the flat horizon and shaded itself upwards into purple and blue. Here in one great ring around the sky were all the colors of a giant circular rainbow, while directly overhead the sky had taken on a colorless cast — not white, not blue, not gold nor silver.

"Isn't this what a river trout must feel like lying in the skillet?" Kate spoke softly to herself. "You can see what's up there all around you, but you know it won't last!" Kate chuckled at the image and drew her greatcoat closer around her. "Yeh, just like…a…trout…" She quickly drifted off to sleep, missing the twinkling diamonds that began to appear in the darkening spring sky. The fire smoldered beneath the logs as Kate's body gave way to weariness. As the campfire died into embers, the dreams crept into her soul.

She woke just before dawn and lay still gazing up, feeling the refreshing vastness of life, the smallness of it. She sat up and mindlessly pulled out a pack of ready-made cigarettes, lit one and stoked the campfire. In the chill of an early May morning, she felt the warmth of the wool-lined coat around her shoulders and the heat of the growing fire before her.

Great thoughts wandered through Kate's head when she was

alone like this. They seemed great to her. Great in that she felt closer to herself when the stillness of the desert offered its protection. The very flat land that stretched to the horizon in a perfect circle seemed to offer a sanctuary that she could enjoy nowhere else. Here she could discover parts of herself that seemed lost in her daily world...the parts where she was a girl, a very small girl, before she grew into a queen.

"It's warming up. Spring's here," she spoke to the distant mountain peaks that poked at the edge of the protective shield. *You know...the shift in the wind that turns it from a chill to a warm embrace? I felt it this morning. I feel it now. Never mind that the bulb flowers are poking up in town; never mind that the birds are returning; never mind that children forget their jackets at school, jackets they need in the morning, but can do without after classes.*

The boarding school suddenly came into view against the blueness of first light in the morning sky. There she stood, alone on the playground, the new kid, the outsider. "That didn't last long," Kate reminded herself.

"Hey, Eloise, did Sister whack you one this morning?"

"Naw, we had a talk. You know one of Sister's talks."

"Betcha she whacked you one."

"Didn't.."

"You mean she didn't cream you for writing that stuff on the blackboard?"

"No. No, she...well, maybe a little whack."

"I knew it." The intruding child turned to her friends. They all grinned at the new girl with the red pigtails. "You'll do," they said and crowded around her.

Kathleen Eloise Rockwell always needed to prove herself in a new school. And then the proving would send her away to another school. Still, she wanted to be accepted. Little Eloise did not like to be alone.

"You've come a long way, my girl," Kate spoke the words as if to a small child. "You've made them look at you. You won't let them pass you by without noticing. Never again. Like those biddies in the store, they're jealous. They notice and they envy the attention I get. When reporters come to my house, the biddies wish they could attract reporters. But dull people live dull lives. And I won't do that."

Little Eloise had fashioned herself into Kate, Queen of the Yukon. And the Queen had created Aunt Kate, a favorite of the newspapers, her public, her admirers. "Hell, Kate, be honest for once. You don't do it for them. You do it for Eloise, so she won't have to hide in the corner anymore."

Kathleen Eloise Rockwell tossed her cigarette into the fire and stood up slowly. Darned old bones, she complained to a critter that skittered past her. She turned her body in a circle, her head tilted back to scan the vast space above.

The dawn light always reminded her of Homer and his "rosy-fingered dawn." Only above the flat Oregon horizon, orange, purple, reddish, pink, silver, gold — radiance seemed a better description. So many shades of yellow, red and blue that she would cry at the sudden beauty that replaced the glorious carpet of stars. This morning, stretched out before that almost sacred ritual, Kate felt the awe deep inside her. Awe at what made it happen every day. Awe at how she was so blessed to be able to see it. Awe at why the entire world wasn't out there watching with her. Awe at the...*stuff*...she loved that word...the stuff in her head. A lifetime of stuff.

She returned to her bed on the warming desert floor and snuggled into her greatcoat, wishing only that she could understand, could make her life what she wanted. Ah, but that was the tricky part. What was it she wanted?

And the answer was always ready, always the same. Alexander. Even though she knew she couldn't have him, "God, he's been dead fifteen years!" Still, a corner of her heart was still yearning for the man who made her life hell, who also made it heaven, and she didn't know why.

"You'll always love me, won't you, Kitty darling," the words with the heavy Greek accent echoed across the desert the same way they had echoed in the frozen air of Dawson.

"Of course I will. You know us Irish girls; we stick with our man."

"Don't toy with my heart, Kitty darling. I watch you with other men."

"That's just show business. You know that, Alex."

"Then get out of it."

"I can't."

"Yes you can. Come live with me. Be my right hand. Help me build my empire. That's all I want, Kitty, my love, just you and me, we make the world sit up and notice."

"Yes, Alex, just you and me...and the world standing to applaud us."

"You. I want them to applaud you."

"But you wanted the other rewards, the riches, Alex, my love. You wanted too much for yourself. You didn't know that I could help you get it, if only you could have given me some of yourself. Just a bit."

"You're right, Kitty, I wanted too much. There was no room for you. If I keep you by my side, I lose my eye for what I really wanted: the attention, the wealth, the fame, the limelight. You took away some of that light; I no could risk that."

"I'd have shared it with you. We'd have shared it — together. But you couldn't see that."

"I saw it, my darling, and I no could accept it."

"So you tossed me aside."

"Had to, my girl. Had to. That's show business."

"But I loved you...love you so."

"Love doesn't help when you hungry, when they come take away your home, when you don't have money for shoes, when you have to dig in someone else's field for food."

"You did all that?"

"And more, in the old country, in Greece. And I decide that when I come to America that I never do that again."

Kate looks at her love's shoulders sag forward, his chin droop. He no longer appears the highly successful, tall and splendid king of the vaudeville theaters. He no longer imitates his idol, the man he had named himself after, Alexander the Great.

Very softly, she begins: "When we met, my sweet Alexander, you were waiting on customers at Charlie Cole's Saloon in Dawson City. You had no money, barely enough clothes to keep you from freezing, and you were smiling. You sang as you poured beer, you joked with the grubstakers, you teased the girls. You seemed happy."

Alexander the great theater magnate scowls back at her. His eyes turn inward for a moment as he tries to remember. "I smile? You sure I smile? I no remember that."

"You smiled, you crazy man. I remember. Maybe I'm the only one left who remembers the days you smiled."

"Don't joke with me. I honestly can't remember ever daring to smile."

"Must've been safe for you back in those icy mountains, tucked away from the rest of the world, where no one could get in for most of the year, where no one could get out. You must remember how safe Dawson City felt."

"Yeah, I guess maybe..."

"Alex, if we had stayed in Alaska..."

"You'd never be as famous as you are now." Alex was teasing.

"And you'd never have opened all those theaters."

"Seventy-two at the top, sometimes one or two more, sometimes less, but seventy-two."

"And you let it all disappear."

"That minx took it all away, the lawyers, the bad press, the embarrassment."

"What, you embarrassed? I can't believe that."

"Yes, me, embarrassed. You forget about the courts, the accusations. Not bad enough I lose much when stock market crash, but then the courts...everything...gone."

"And now…"

"And now I must say goodbye…again."

"Again…goodbye. Maybe this time for good. Maybe this time I can believe that what happened wasn't anything I could change."

"Of course not, my Athena, my goddess, my love."

"Then you did love me."

"Why else would I let you go?"

The Desert Church

KATE SAT UP, THERE IN THE DESERT LAND OF Oregon, and watched the figure of her beloved Alexander fade away as the sun climbed higher over the desert. At last he was gone. Maybe now she could let him go. He had opened his heart to her, without pretense; maybe now she was free to release him and concentrate on Warren.

Kate's stomach grumbled as the morning bloomed. She pulled out a cigarette and lit it from the flame she fanned. She put another pile of sticks on the fire, hobbled to her car and pulled out the tin of coffee. She half-filled the old porcelain coffeepot with a jug of water, spooned out some coffee into the strainer and fixed the cover. She grabbed a brown paper sack and hobbled back to the fire. *My bones feel in the morning like*

I've danced all night. Old age, like they say. For while the world was told that Klondike Kate was in her late fifties, she knew darned well she was closer to seventy-five than she ever thought she'd live to be.

She set the coffeepot atop a makeshift grill over the now-blazing fire, opened the sack and took out a sweet roll. How she loved the fancy Danish pastries her store furnished. Kate had never mastered the art of baking bread and rolls that required yeast. She bit into the raspberry roll, then reached back into the sack and found an orange. She couldn't help but glory in being alive as she peeled the orange, nibbled on the Danish, and watched the sun slowly creep across the desert floor.

No doubt about it, mine has been a most extraordinary life. But then you wouldn't have it any other way, would you, Kate girl? Not a chance! Can't think of how I could have eked any more out of it.

"Well, you could have married that baron in Valparaiso," came a small voice in her head.

"No, no, god no." Kate's shoulders shook as she laughed her great laugh, listening to it cascade across the desert. "No, not dandy, handsome, girl-chasing Juanito, the bull of Chile."

"But the way you were going, you could have become Senora Juanito," returned her mother.

"To be saddled as his wife would have been disaster. To be tied down to the strict society of a small country in South America, never to know the beauty and the drama of Alaska...? No, no, a thousand times no." Kate put it to music: "I'd rather die than say yes."

"Nice music, but it might have been."

"Dear god, I couldn't have been more than sixteen, a mere child.

I will never understand how you, my own mother, could have left a 15-year-old beauty…"

"Beauty?"

"Face it, Mama, I was good looking — how could you leave me in a godforsaken place like Valparaiso, Chile?

"But you got to admit, Katie, you had a good time."

"If you can call getting engaged to seven men at once a good time. Remember how you looked when you came to pick me up at the convent? 'Kathleen Eloise Rockwell,' you yelled."

"I never yelled!"

"You did that day. 'Kathleen Eloise Rockwell. I leave you here with a convent full of nuns for six months and what do I find when I return?'"

"My lovely daughter who thought she had been abandoned."

"A girl of fifteen, a mere child."

"I was distraught. The judge had just died. I was alone again. And you…"

"I was teaching school, just like the Sisters showed me. I helped the little children learn their English lessons."

"So you said."

"And at night I danced. A lot. With many fine young Chilean boys. They fell for me and asked me to marry them. Sure, I was too young. What did I know? I loved receiving all those lovely diamond rings."

"But Chile is a different country, a different culture. In Chile, children marry at fifteen. Their families were thoroughly disgraced when you ran out."

"You mean you'd rather I married one of them and settled down to raise niños in Valparaiso?"

"No, no. Oh, Kathleen. What's to become of you?"

"Well you can see what's become of me, Mother. I went on to conquer the New York stage, a few stages on the way back to Seattle, and then I wowed them in the Yukon! And not a moment that I regret. Well maybe the getting dumped on a try-out in Philadelphia."

Kate always had a good time. Again, she took a deep drag on her cigarette and laughed into the morning desert.

The coffee began to bubble and soon Kate was leaning back, her hunger quieted, to enjoy her strong coffee. She turned to feel the sun on her face as it climbed higher over the desert, and she closed her eyes. "No," she murmered, "I wouldn't have done it any different." Then, after a moment, "Not even with Alex."

Amazed at that idea, Kate sat up and stared into her coffee cup. *Did I just rid myself of that man? Can I be finished with him at last? I'll have to remember to ask myself again tomorrow.*

Kate, who had spent some very cold winters in the far North, sat sipping hot coffee and feeling the sun on her face, the warm sand beneath her. The morning breeze died down and the sun heated up, and Kate didn't move. Her head was a jumble of visions, places she'd seen — Chile, the sea, the Cape of Good Hope with its turbulent waters, the White River of the Yukon with its deadly white foam, happy-go-lucky Manhattan, the scruffy Savoy Theater in Dawson, that detested nuns' school in Spokane, and the rolling beige wheat fields in Kansas. She had lived in Kansas for such a short time, was born there, and she couldn't remember much about it other than the image of golden fields reaching to the edge of the blue sky — just like the desert here, reaching to the edge of the sky.

She did remember Papa, that gentle man who lifted her high over his head and kissed her face over and over, who came home in the afternoon to play with her. *That's strange,* she thought. *I'm not even sure he's alive, though I'm sure he isn't. I wonder what kind of life he led after Mother and I left him. All I remember are some small moments, and even they aren't clear.*

Kate's inner pictures took on faces of people in her life: the jolly sailors aboard the boat to New York, her friend Gloria who taught her the ropes of chorus line dancing, and her pal Flossie who got her the audition in Seattle to join the dance troupe headed for the Yukon and who remained her best friend in Dawson.

And Johnny, dear sweet Yonny, my yam and yelly man. Kate smiled at the memory of the dear man who carried a torch for her for thirty years before he married her.

"But enough of this meandering down memory lane," she spoke directly to a critter that slithered past, moving quickly to avoid the embers of Kate's dying campfire. She leaned over to dump the last of the coffee onto the coals, then dropped her cup into the empty paper sack and scooped handfuls of sand over the remaining fire.

She carried her gear back to the car, trudging slowly, very slowly, feeling every bone and aching muscle in her body. "I just can't spend these cold nights out here anymore," she promised her body. "Gettin' too old."

She started the motor and turned the old Plymouth towards home. *Let's see, what must I do today? Maybe pull a few weeds in the yard. Maybe clean out that hall closet. Maybe…why? Why clean out a closet? I'll be moving soon. Warren wants us to live in western Oregon, down in the Willamette Valley, when we get hitched.*

The thought of Warren surprised her, seemed to intrude on her memories, her all-night reverie. She had never shared her desert with her new fiancé!

The car swerved as it bounced over the crude desert road which was rather more like a path, and headed, uncontrolled, through a patch of sage and across a stretch of desert dunes before the engine hissed to a stop.

"Dag nabbit!" she yelled as she pounded on the steering wheel. "What've you gone and done now?"

The Savoy Shack

KATE PRESSED THE STARTER BUTTON WITH her foot and listened with a sinking feeling as the ignition ground for an instant, whirring and buzzing. Nothing happened. She tried again. Then, not one to sweat the bad stuff, Kate opened the door and got out. As she did, she spotted a cabin, more like a lean-to, a shack. *Funny, I don't recall any buildings out here. Must've been out of sight from the road.*

The sun was hot now. *Figure a body could stay cool in there,* she thought, reaching back to grab her water jug. *Reckon I could stay there until the sun gets lower before heading back to town on foot.* While she didn't look forward to the walk back home — her knee never fully recovered from that fall all those years ago — Kate didn't relish being baked in the scorching desert sun either.

She approached the cabin. *Is that music? Or am I going daft out here?* It sounded like music. She went closer. *Maybe somebody lives here.* Yet, there were no signs of life, no outhouse or remains of a vehicle. No greenery outside, no curtains at the lone window.

The door was closed. *Who would stay inside on a hot day like this with the door closed?* Kate tapped lightly at the door, then reached for the knob, turned it and slowly pushed it back.

What she sees stops her breath. What she sees is the old Savoy Theater in Dawson. Men wearing dingy stained overalls and heavy jackets roam around the bar. A few sit at tables, some with painted girls at their side. A larger table is surrounded by men playing poker, their moose-leather gold pokes lying across it.

Upstairs, in one of the curtained balcony boxes, she knows a sourdough is fishing in his pockets for more gold nuggets to pay the box waiter for a fresh bottle of champagne as the brightly-gowned woman next to him smiles coyly and reaches for her glass. The music pounds from a tinkling player piano, pumped by a dutiful old man whose legs had been made strong by his long walks over mountains of ice to and from his mine.

Stunned at the sight, Kate feels her heart pushing her blood faster and faster through her body, meeting the pulse of the music. She hums the familiar, "Daisy, Daisy, give me your answer true…" She watches the crowded dancers whirl around the tiny dance floor, more a bumping and shuffling than dancing, but she knows the miners only want an excuse to hold a girl in their arms.

"Hey, Kate," someone shouts. "There's Klondike Kate," another calls. "Give us a song, Kate, Queen of the Yukon," comes the cry throughout the room.

Kate lowers her head, pretending to blush, then realizes no one is looking at her. Their eyes are fastened on a small figure who has just entered from a door next to the dance floor. The figure waves gaily at the crowd with both hands. They whistle, clap and shout until the figure moves across the room toward the small stage. From her place near the bar Kate stares at the young woman who sways her hips as she climbs the three steps to the stage, modestly lifting the skirt of her turquoise satin gown as she does, exposing a trim ankle.

"What'll it be, boys?" she calls from her perch. "What'll it be this time?"

"Down By the Old Mill Stream," someone calls out. "Daisy," another calls. Then they all are calling out names of songs. She waits until she hears the one she's rehearsed, then she waves to the piano player and motions for the crowd to calm down.

"Okay, if you insist, I'll sing…"

The piano player gives her the cue chords and she leans back and begins, "Hello! ma baby, hello! ma honey, hello my ragtime gal…" She flounces back and forth across the stage, swirling her long skirt, shaking her shoulders and wiggling her hips, all the time gazing into the crowd, making every man believe she is singing to him. At the start of the second chorus, the dancer bends over, grabs the hem of her skirt and raises it to expose both ankles, then with a tease, first one then both her legs. Even though her legs are wrapped in scintillating blue tights, the men go wild at her audacity.

Whistles and shouts fill the room as the hungry miners gape at her legs. She dances for them, bouncing and gliding about the stage with the steps she has learned in New York. Occasionally she kicks her legs into the air, sometimes she turns and spins to let her skirts show more of the blue tights. No one moves as the entertainer repeats the first chorus and ends with a boisterous, "Tel-e-phone and tell me I's your o-w-nnn!"

She bows low, letting her red locks fall over her white shoulders. She knows she is a knock-out, a beauty, and her audience responds. In a delightful gold shower, nuggets and packets of gold dust are tossed onto the stage and the audience is further treated to the sight of the young dancer bending over to pick them up.

Standing at the back of the room, Kate feels the thunder of their applause, now accompanied with stomping feet and more whistles. Her head pounds too with what she is looking at, what she is seeing with her own two eyes. *What in the world...or out of this world...is happening? What is going on here? I must be losing my mind.* She holds her head with both hands, closes her eyes, shakes her head and then opens her eyes again.

The sound has died down and the stage is empty. Kate's shock has turned to anger. Who is this tart to steal her show? Why is she doing Kate's act...and wearing Kate's clothes? *I paid a fortune for that gown from Paris. And her shoes...she's wearing the wrong shoes. There's a matching pair of turquoise shoes for that dress, and she wore white shoes. I'd best set her straight.*

Kate elbows her way toward the door next to the dance floor. Somehow she knows there's a hallway that leads back to a tiny dressing room behind the stage. Of course she knows; she worked here for months before she and Alex built the Crystal. She wonders briefly if Alex would be down to help tend the bar...but the notion slips out of her head as quickly as it entered. First, she has to take care of that red-headed imitator.

Slowly, Kate works her way to the door. Miners barely notice the old woman. She wears dungarees and a plaid jacket, just as they do. Few even notice she isn't a man.

There is a moment as she reaches out to push open the door that she wonders what the hell she's doing here at all, but that passes too. Her hand on the open door, she squints into the dimness of backstage. She spots the glow of the mirror lights through the half-open door down the hallway and walked towards it. The entire place is familiar now, the two boards that creak, the musty smell of makeup and old wood and dust and stored crates of liquor and more stacks of crates that hold lord-knows-what-else.

Kate's curiosity takes over. What is happening here? Who is this impostor and what is this saloon doing in Oregon? Although, to tell the truth, Kate is beginning to feel the chill of the Yukon winter seeping through the cracks in the wall.

At the dressing room door, she's aware of the heat on her legs from a small stove in the corner. Then she smells the perfume, familiar and sweet, and she sees the turquoise gown draped over a chair before she glimpses its most recent wearer.

"Hi, come on in," a cheery familiar voice calls from behind the door. "Just getting into my next costume," the voice smiles out at the older woman. "Didja like the show? There's more. Wait till you see my flame dance. It's the one they all wait for, and it's just about time. Gotta wait until they've had lots of champagne, ya know. Can't give them all the best stuff first...save it till last. Hey, come on in and take a load off." She amends her words as she notices the aged woman. "I mean sit down, ma'am."

Kate feels very old, more like this child's grandmother than ...what?...who?...herself?

She lowers herself slowly into the chair. "Thank you, Miss... Miss? I'm sorry, I don't know your name."

"Rockwell. It's Rockwell now, but it'll be Pantages soon. Alex and I are getting married."

"Alex?"

"Yeah, Alex...Alexander Pantages. He's a waiter here, but we're considering a business deal where we'll build our own theater and saloon and.... He's a tycoon. Not rich yet, but we have plans." She paused and blushed, explaining, "Alex is my...er...my intended. Can you believe that? Alexander Pantages and Kitty Rockwell, Queen of the Yukon!"

"You're..."

"Klondike Kate. Just call me Kitty. Everybody does."

"Kitty. Kate. Klondike...Kate...Queen..." Kate gropes for words, for the idea behind the words, for some sense out of this crazy moment. "You're Klondike...Kate...you can't be. You just can't be..."

"Well, Kate's my name, but Kitty's what they call me. It's Alex's favorite name for me. What's your name? if I may ask."

Kate pauses before answering. How can she explain this? "Kate. Kate...Matson. Well, actually Kate Rockwell Matson."

Kate has the advantage. She is the interloper. She figures, heck, if she can talk to herself all day, why can't she talk to herself...as a…different self? As bizarre as this appears, it begins to make some sense to Kate. But Kitty stands speechless.

The two women stare at each other, neither of them moving. Kitty stands half-dressed, her cheery smile frozen on her face covered with pancake makeup and bright red lipstick. Her huge gray-violet eyes search for something in the face of this old woman that would give her a clue. "You have the same name. Almost. Are you my mother or something? You don't look like my mother, well, actually you do, but maybe you're my aunt or my grandmother or…who are you?"

"I told you, Kate Rockwell Matson, formerly known as Queen of the Yukon." Kate is beginning to accept all of this, even though the young woman seems to be grappling still with what is happening.

"You can't be. You can't. Why are you here?"

Kate pauses, then remembers the shoes. "Your shoes," she says, "you should wear the turquoise ones with that dress."

"I can't. They're too small and they pinch."

"Oh yes, now I remember. Your feet are swelling."

"Who are you? What do you want with me?"

"What year is this, Kitty?" the older woman asks, moving toward the girl.

"It's, let's see, it's eighteen hundred something. Almost a new century. Yeah, it's 1898, no nine. Yes, 1899."

"And where do you think you are?"

"In Dawson City." She squares her shoulders as she proudly continues, "at the brand new Savoy The-ay-ter in downtown Dawson City, Yukon Territory."

Kate holds her breath. What should she tell her? What *could* she tell this young woman who Kate believes to be herself half a century earlier? How can she explain? Hell, she isn't sure she can explain it to herself.

But she tries. "Kitty," she begins, "Kitty..." then she has another idea. She stands up and takes a step forward in the tiny room. She calls out, "Eloise..." and waits for a response.

The startled girl opens her mouth to speak, but can't.

Kate tries again. "Kitty...Kathleen Eloise Rockwell, whether you can believe this or not, you're talking to yourself...that is, you're talking to me, but I'm you. I...we...god, how can I put this? I've lived about fifty years more than you, but you're me when I was a girl. I can't explain how this is happening, but..." Kate pauses for breath. Kitty stands still, her jaw hanging.

Kate takes her hand. "Sweetie, I'm your future. And you're my past...."

"Look, lady, I don't know where you came from, but I have another show to do and I have to get dressed." The girl turns away to take down a shimmering sequined gown from where it hangs on a nail beside the door. Kate reaches over and grasps her arm.

"Kitty, I can tell you how you got here."

"Down the White River and over the mountains, just like you, I expect."

"No, I mean, I know why you're here in Dawson instead of going to school somewhere back in the States."

"I like it here. School was boring. All the other girls wanted to do was flirt with boys and plan parties."

"And all the teachers wanted to do was make your life miserable."

Kitty has been scowling, peevish, resistant. Now she appears more playful. "Sorta like I'm feeling right now. Fed up with talking to you and ready to go out and dance for...them." She nods toward the door.

"I know."

"You dance too?"

"Of course. I remember how much fun it was to watch their eyes when I began to dance, how the audience melted away as I went along with the music, how I'd get lost in the sound until I was alone, dancing with the wind and the sound and the music." Kate sways as she recalls the special place she experiences in dancing. "I was in a world that was my own."

"Yes, I do that too." Kitty pulls her hand from Kate's and runs it through her dark red curls, patting some, twirling others. Her eyes sparkle as she continues Kate's memory for her. "It's like dropping out of this place, this cold dingy place, and being whisked through the light of a thousand candles into a palace ballroom, and feeling my body move to the music in ways that make me feel warm and loved — all the way to my toes." Kitty twirls around in the cramped room, bumping into the chair in front of her makeup table. "I just love to dance," she sings out as she drops into the chair.

The two women, one young and slightly flushed, the other old and weary, stand looking at each other and know the other understands her completely. They stare, smiling, at each other for a moment, then Kate speaks. "I believe you're the only person I've ever known who could understand me, could know why I came here all those years ago."

Kitty backs away, takes the chair and offers it to Kate. "Sorry, I have only one chair. Maybe I can find another." She turns toward the door, then swings around to face Kate. "But I won't because I'm afraid if I leave, even for a minute, you won't be here when I get back. I don't believe this but I want to talk with you." Kitty pulls at a trunk that stands against the wall, clears it off and sits down, leaning toward Kate. She'll play the old woman's game until she figures out what to do.

"But your dance." Kate nods at the door.

"They'll wait. They always wait for the Queen of the Yukon and her famous Flame Dance." This time it is Kitty who takes Kate's hand. "Tell me, do you still dance?"

"Not much anymore. Once in awhile they ask me to dance a bit, or sing, for some special occasion. I get to lead parades, and during the war I danced and sang for servicemen." Seeing the question on Kitty's face, she explains, "Soldiers, sailors, you know."

"Are we still fighting the Spanish?" Kitty asks. She had seen soldiers the last time she was in Seattle, had heard something about a war in the Philippines.

"No, this latest war covered the whole world. We've had two of them. Our boys went to Europe, to fight in France. In this last one, they fought all over the Pacific too. Wars aren't good and I did what I could to entertain — you know, raise money and show the boys some fun."

Kitty smiles. "Still dancing and singing. I hope I dance and sing my whole life, like you."

"You will. Except, watch the knees. They get tired and achy real fast. I fell a couple times and then had a car accident a few years ago. That pretty much ended my dancing."

"Car? Don't you mean cart?"

"No, I drive a car, you know, a motor vehicle, horseless carriage?"

"Oh yes, I saw a picture of one of those once. I've never seen a real one." Kitty turns toward Kate and braves a point blank question. "What year is this, where you are?" She feels sillier than silly for asking, but she wonders how the old woman will respond.

"In my time it's 1952." She hears Kitty suck in her breath. She has no words. Then, "How do you get on with Alex?" Kate asks, watching Kitty carefully for her reaction.

"Oh, we're very happy. I make so much money in gold that I'm able to help Alex with his dreams. He's moved in with me to save rent while we're getting enough together to open our own theater. I make sure that he dresses well. You know how he loves to look good. Do you know that I paid fifteen bucks each for his shirts? And I keep buying those expensive cigars he likes. After we build our new theater here, he wants to open other theaters at some of the camps that are still springing up all over. And there's been talk of a gold strike in Nome. Alex thinks a theater there would do well."

"I meant you. How does he treat you?" Kate wants to hear it from the young girl.

"Sometimes he barely notices me. But most of the time he tells me how much he loves me. He's staying at my place and we're, well, you know…very happy."

"But…" Should the experienced woman tell this girl what's in store for her? Would she herself have wanted to know?

"But what, Miss Kate?" the girl asks.

"But, don't forget he's a man," Kate finishes. A bit lame, even for Kate.

"If you're me, I mean an old me, tell me what your world is like. Tell me what lies ahead for me." Kitty thinks she'll humor her visitor.

"No, I don't think that would help you at all."

"I knew it. you're pulling my leg."

"Perhaps." Kate can see that Kitty's doubts are wavering. "I think you have to make your own life, as I did. You…I…we make mistakes, but we have some fun along the way. I don't think life is about making mistakes. It's about getting through the best way we can. You know, mush on and smile."

"Yeah, that's good. Mush on and smile. That's pretty much what we do around here. You make a strike one day, hold in your hands more wealth than you can imagine, then bring it to town and spend it, have a whale of a good time for a few hours, then you go back to dig out some more fun from that frozen earth."

"You sound older than your twenty-three years."

"I'm twenty-one."

"Ah, shaving them off already? Remember that I know when you…we were born."

Kitty grins, her gray Irish eyes reflecting green for the moment. She is enjoying this old woman. "Girls get old real fast here, Kate. And the miners like 'em young. I don't suppose I'll stick around much longer. Alex and I are planning to open a string of theaters on the west coast." She forms her fingers into an empire and adds, "Pantages/Rockwell theaters from Nome and Dawson City to San Diego, maybe even South America."

"Ever wish you had married one of those señors in Valparaiso and stayed in Chile?"

"Golly, I haven't thought of them in years." Kitty blinks and takes another breath. After a moment she says, "No, I was just a kid then. Every man looked good enough to get me away from Mama. Every man looked like a way to adventure and excitement...until I got to know him. You get close to some of those exciting looking men and they're very dull. All they want is to own you, lock you up and keep you for themselves. I wasn't ready...in Chile... to be tied down to one man. But here, now, with Alex. This is different. Here I know what I want, and it's Alexander Pantages."

Kate can't agree more. Still, she knows how it will end. She knows of Alex's deceit, his unforgiving greed, the selfish nature of his appetites. She knows the pain that lies ahead for this girl barely started in life.

"I can't quite grasp how young you are. Yes, even at twenty three...er...one. Was I ever this young?"

Kate seems to be talking to herself. She is, but in a different way. What can she tell this young self that would help her as she becomes the older version? But more importantly, what can Kate find out about her young self to help her face her own future?

The two women sit quietly looking at each other through the mirror on the makeshift dressing table. Each considers the other an apparition. Yet, there is a reality about them they both recognize.

"Okay, Miss Kate, if you're me in fifty years...and I'm not quite sure I can accept that...tell me how life is...you know, outside. In the States. Where do you live?"

"I live in Oregon, out near the high desert. That's where we are now..."

"Oh, no, I know where I am. I'm in Dawson City, in the Savoy Saloon...er...Theater, getting ready to do my act again. That is, if I can get rid of you."

"Oh, honey, you don't want to get rid of me. I'm your future."

"You know what I mean. I don't buy this. Somebody put you up to this. My only question is how an old woman like you got here. It isn't easy getting to Dawson."

"I'm here. Never mind how. I don't even know. And you're here too. We've been given a moment together. What are we going to do with it?" Always the one to take advantage of an opportunity, Kate is grappling for insight, no, for reason...understanding. She is trying to understand.

"Well? Are you going to tell me what life is like in...Oregon? Do you and Alex have a ranch or do you live in Portland or somewhere like that?"

Can I tell her about the real Alex? About how he's going to abandon her in a short while? How he's going to make his fortune without her, me, and end up.... No, she has to live it. Just like I did. Or maybe we won't remember this tomorrow. Maybe time has stopped.

Instead of answering the girl's question about Alex, Kate starts to answer an earlier question. "Kitty girl, you won't believe the States in the next fifty years. I told you about the automobile. Well, there are aeroplanes, ships that fly through the sky. I took one and flew from Seattle to St. Louis just last year."

"You're joking!"

"No, I went back to Kansas where I was born and…"

"I wouldn't go back there for all the tea in…"

"Oh, it wasn't so bad. The folks greeted me as a kind of celebrity. Course I had to phone the papers and let them know I was in town."

"Phone?"

"Yes, telephone. Everybody has one now. And some folks put them on a table instead of hanging them on a wall. You can call anyone in the world, anywhere." She sees the amazed look on Kitty's face. "Except in Dawson. I don't think there are phones here yet."

"Aeroplanes that fly, telephones that talk to people anywhere. What else? Sounds like you live in a magic place." Her eyes narrow. "Or are you kiddin' me?"

"In a way it *is* magic. I have a machine that washes my clothes, another that sweeps up dust, another that grinds up food. And I could have an electric blanket to keep warm at night except I'm not sure they're entirely safe. I still like my down comforter and my own quilts."

"Electric blanket? I could use one of those." Kitty's eyes are wide in disbelief. "Will the whole world be electric? They're only beginning to install electricity here in Dawson."

"Yeah. I imagine Alex and I could have used some of that here. Those old oil lamps stink sometimes. And imagine what those gowns of yours would look like in a spotlight that changes colors."

"Spotlight?"

"Yes, spots with electric lights. They have spotlights now that shine directly on performers on the stage. They can turn different colors and keep you lighted while you perform. They're far better than the candles with the reflectors that you use."

"Oooh. Wouldn't that be marvelous? Especially for my flame dance?" Kate hadn't thought of it before, but yes, an electric spot on her during the flame dance would have thrown brighter red and blue lights than the coal oil spots. Wouldn't that have been spectacular bouncing off her sequined gown and red veils? But that was a long time ago.

"Well, if you're from fifty years in the future, my future," Kitty begins, "you must be seventy..."

"One," Kate finishes her sentence.

"Come on, woman. You can't kid a kidder. I know how many years I've already shaved off. And I'll just bet you're passing for fifty-nine or sixty back in the States."

"I don't discuss age. When I am interviewed, I avoid those questions. We know," she winks at the young woman, "and we'll just keep our information to ourselves."

"Well, I gotta say, you look pretty good for an old woman."

"Clean living and fresh air," Kate grins, letting the girl see she still has her sense of humor...and her teeth.

A knock at the door reminds them that Kitty is due to start her act again. "Gotta finish dressing," she says, reaching for the sequined gown.

"The famous flame dance of Klondike Kate, Belle of the Yukon," Kate murmurs. "I always felt so sure of myself in that dress. I could hear the men gasping, see them holding their breath, watching me with their whole bodies." Kate's eyes hold the dress as she dances in her head, spinning and turning wildly sending the chiffon through the air like flames lapping at dry wood. Her body remembers every movement of the sensuous dance, how she moved across the stage as slowly as creeping fire, ending with a blaze of spinning and whirling that caught the essence of flames devouring even the souls of the miners. Kate's eyes remain glued to the dress as tightly as she remembers the miners' eyes affixed to her all those years ago.

"It's my favorite dance too," Kitty says softly. For a moment she feels sorry for the old woman who would dance no more in that glorious dress. Then she shakes her head of red curls, as if to clear it, and reaches inside the gown to slip it over her head. "Can you button me up?" she asks Kate. "I always need help getting into this. Strange that Alex isn't here by now. Oh well, you'll do."

Kate's fingers recognize the soft material as she touches the buttons. "Alex always liked helping me dress," she says aloud.

The younger woman holds her breath. *This isn't real. Having your dress buttoned by yourself standing behind you? It isn't real.* As the last button slips into place, she spins around. But she is alone in the room. "How? What the hell is going on here?"

"Come on, Kitty, your public is waiting," Alex calls out angrily as he bursts through the door. "Need help with your...oh, you look beautiful," his voice softens. "But how? who?..." he sputters as he sees the buttons all done up.

"Flossie came by," Kitty lies. "Come on, it's time." Alex catches up the white ermine cape and steps into the hallway. Kitty scans the room as she closes the door. *Maybe I had too much to drink.*

In seconds, Kitty stands in the center of the stage, the light of the reflected candles bouncing rainbows of color off the luxurious white cape. The miners' talk lowers to a murmur as she stands still, waiting for silence. Another full minute, before the coughing and shuffling stop. Not a whisper can be heard in the room as a couple hundred grizzled men forget about their beer and whiskey and become silent before their Yukon Queen.

At just that moment, Kitty shrugs her shoulders with a soft wave that sends the fur cape to the floor. She nods to the piano player as she sinks to the floor for a few seconds to grasp a long veil of red chiffon that lays at her feet. She turns as she rises, bringing the chiffon out full sail around her, the flaming folds caressing the air around her body, shimmering and fluttering as they go. The music pulses, gently at first, then faster and faster, as Kitty sways and prances about the stage. At the height of the performance, tiny beads of sweat appear on her skin, further heightening the illusion of fire and ice. Then it is over. With a great sigh, Kitty twirls a last time and drops to the floor in a heap of bright red chiffon.

Dead silence for a moment, then the house erupts in wild clapping, shouting and stomping. The stimulated Kitty pants, partly from the dancing and partly from the audience, as she slowly rises from the floor, now covered in her cape. She primly gathers the gold pouches and nuggets around her and fades back off the stage.

Near the entrance, Kate takes a deep breath before she walks back into the heat of a desert afternoon, her body shivering at the sensation.

She started to walk towards her car, but stopped to turn around, to be sure the saloon, the shack, was still there. The ramshackle building leaned a bit to one side, but remained on the horizon.

"It didn't happen," she said to the windshield as she settled behind the wheel. "It didn't happen. I've been in the sun too long." Without thinking, she turned the key and pushed the starter. The motor turned over. "Wha...? Well I'll be damned." Without questioning further — Kate was in a state of mind to accept whatever happened — she turned the car around and headed to town.

Back home, the woman stood at the kitchen window in the midst of preparing a sandwich. She hadn't eaten since breakfast on the desert, but she wasn't all that hungry. Her glazed eyes searched for the picture she'd seen earlier, the hut in the desert. "Just an apparition. You have one wild imagination, Kate."

She wondered silently that if she could conjure up herself fifty years ago, why couldn't she conjure up Alexander? She munched on the buttered bread. She had neglected to put anything between the pieces. She didn't notice.

When's the Big Day?

KATE CHECKED THE CLOCK AS SHE WALKED slowly into the parlor. "Time for 'Perry Como,' she remembered. She turned on the television set, adjusted the rabbit ear antennae, and was settling into her chair when the phone rang. She pushed herself slowly back up and hobbled across the room. "Hello?"

"Mrs. Matson, this is Annette…Whittier… from the *Courier*."

"Oh yes, how are you, Annette?"

"Fine, Mrs. Matson, just fine, thank you. I'm finishing my story about you and I can't recall what you said about the wedding date. Maybe I skipped it in my notes, but I don't have it."

"The wedding date." Kate paused. She knew she was cornered. What date did she tell the grocery clerk? Oh well, it didn't matter. She probably wouldn't remember anyway. "Well, ah, let's see. Just what did we decide? Warren has obligations in Portland and I, well you know how busy I am. I think I have to go to Yakima later this month and...let's see..." Kate knew she couldn't stall much longer. She glanced at the calendar and leaped. "June seventeenth. Doesn't that sound like a lovely date?"

"Yes...but is that the date you've chosen for your wedding?"

"Yes, isn't that what you asked? We're going to be married, Warren and I, on June seventeenth."

"Okay, guess that's all I need right now. Thank you, Mrs. Matson. Bye."

Strange way to approach your wedding, Annette thought as she put down the phone and turned her chair towards the typewriter. *Maybe she's been through this so many times one date is as good as another.*

"Working late?" came a voice from the doorway.

"Just waiting for some prince or other to come rescue me," Annette pulled the sheet of paper from the typewriter and made a note with a pencil.

"Your Klondike Kate story?" Paul walked over and began reading over her shoulder as he gently massaged her neck. "Come on, let's go for a drive. I'll lock up, you get your stuff together."

Annette slipped a sweater over her shoulders and grabbed her purse. "Ready to go, boss," she smiled. All was right with the world now that he was there.

Paul and his reporter worked closely enough to be accepted as a working unit in the small community. Still, whenever they wanted to be alone, they chose to drive out of town. A little roadhouse called the Drop On Inn had become their hideaway.

"Hi folks. Back again, huh? Your booth is empty," Madge, the owner and bartender called across the bar. "Beer?"

"Yes, please," nodded Paul. "And can you make us a couple of ham and cheese sandwiches?" Two construction workers sat with legs wrapped around their bar stools and arms wrapped around beer mugs. In the dimly lit corner the juke box moaned about two-faced lovers and broken hearts.

"Coming up," called Madge as she filled two mugs with foamy tap beer.

Annette slid into the booth. "Thanks, I haven't eaten since...I can't remember."

Paul sat across the table from her. "And some French fries too, Madge."

"You got it." Madge set down the mugs and retreated to the kitchen.

Paul reached across the table and grabbed Annette's hands, both of them. "I just love it here. I love being with you. I love the characters that hang out here. This place has a Runyonesque feel about it."

"Are you writing again?"

"I'm thinking about it. I have an idea for a short story that would follow the lines of a Bret Harte tale, but would have some of the characters of Damon Runyon. Does that sound like a wild mix?"

"The wildest. Are you actually writing? Or are you just...uh...planning?"

"I'm writing. I'm writing. Or I will when I get home tonight. I don't sleep much anymore. I guess I might as well use the time to write."

"Maybe you'd sleep better if you had the right company." Annette smiled at him and turned her hand to squeeze his.

"Annette, my sweet young thing, what are you suggesting?" Paul feigned shock.

"You sound downright Victorian."

"And you sound bold, much too bold for an Oregon news reporter. Or are you really from New York City and just pretending to be a sweet girl from the Northwest?"

"You know me, Paul, probably better than anyone does — including my mother."

"Yes." Paul didn't move for a moment, just watched her face, looking through her eyes, wishing he could claim this girl for his own and knowing the consequences if he did. Tempting as she was, for now, he'd stick with Isabel.

Marge set down a plate of French fries and the sandwiches. "Enjoy," she said as she turned back to the bar.

"Ah, this looks good." He reached for a fry.

"You didn't have supper either?"

"No, didn't go home. Called and said I had to attend that meeting over in Bend. I'll get the report from my contact tomorrow morning. Nobody but you will know I wasn't there."

"Very clever." *If he's that clever with his wife, then how clever is he with me?* The thought flashed through her mind, then disappeared.

As they ate, Annette and Paul went over their work projects, the stories they were writing on their own, the ones they were working on together.

"How was your interview with Aunt Kate?" he asked.

"Nothing I haven't heard before. She told me everything from the flame dance and how to do it to the day she asked Alex Pantages, the famous theater king, for a loan and he handed her six dollars."

"Is she getting married?"

"Yes, and that's the only piece of news — I use the word loosely — that she left out. And when I called her this evening to get the date, she sounded vague, like she hadn't decided on one. Then it sounded as if she just pulled one out of the air. In June, I forget when."

"Kate just likes to see her name in the papers. If I hadn't met Mr. Warren what's his-name, I would think she was dreaming him up."

"You met him?"

"Yeah, a couple months ago. He was in town to see her and he stopped by for a copy of the paper and our advertising rates. Said he was thinking of moving his practice here. Sounds like he's more serious than she is." Paul bit into his sandwich and sat back to chew and look at Annette.

When she noticed him watching her, she smiled, sat back and took a sip of beer. "I like working with you, Paul Benjamin," she said.

"And I love working with you, Miss Annette Whittier," he returned. "We're a great team. The paper is looking better than it ever has. And Dad notices. He called me after last week's paper got to him. Said it was the best one he owns."

"Can't beat that for praise. It's nice working with someone who understands you," Annette said. "And someone who is so…charming," she added. "We make beautiful newspapers together, don't we?"

"If things don't improve at home, we may just have that chance to make more beautiful newspapers together for a long, long time."

"What are you saying?"

"No promises. But it's beginning to look like we won't be able to work things out. She is so controlling, wants to keep me tied so tight. I think she wants another baby. And I'm barely making ends meet now."

"Oh, come on. Doesn't Daddy help you out?"

"No. He as much as told me that I made my bed with Isabel and now I have to lie in it."

"I'm sorry you feel so penned up. I hate to see you hurting. Maybe it'll help to look towards the day when we'll be together. Maybe that's what we need to keep our eyes on."

"Annette, you're so good for me. I love you. I really do. Yes, one day…we'll…" Paul took another bite of his sandwich. "Coffee? Madge, could you bring us two coffees?"

As illusive as the famous Klondike Kate, Annette thought.

THE ILLUSIVE MISS KATE FELL ASLEEP IN HER CHAIR. NO matter that her favorite "GE Theater" was presenting a new play with her favorite actors, she just couldn't keep her eyes open much after dark anymore. As magical as television was, it still couldn't keep Kate's attention very long.

She woke with a start just after midnight to the sounds of the TV test pattern and the pawing of a pair of raccoons at the compost pile. She shuffled to the back door and shined her flashlight at them, but they were so used to it, they barely noticed. Kate went up to bed.

"Must've been a dream. Sun stroke. Heat prostration. Something I ate," she mused remembering her confrontation with Kitty in the desert. *Be good to sleep in my bed tonight. Can't take the desert nights anymore. And I'm damn glad I don't have to contend with those winter nights in the Yukon.*

She fell asleep recounting her conquests in the far North — her shy Johnny and all the other admirers from the gold fields, the young barkeeps who promised her a split of the liquor take if she kept the miners drinking, the audacious Greek waiter who caught her behind the curtain one night and snatched her heart right out of her body. *Alexander, oh Alex. I wish I could convince you not to break that poor girl's heart, but I know you will. That's just how it is, how it was...I loved you so.* Klondike Kate fell asleep in Alexander's arms.

When Kate awoke, she lay watching the spring leaves dance outside her window and listening to the birds greet the early sunshine. Noisy critters. And irresponsible. Nothing to concern themselves with except finding food. And raising babies, the afterthought. *One good thing about marrying after you're fifty is that you won't be bothered with kids.*

Kate took in a deep breath of spring air and rolled over. Her groggy mind wandered. *When you have a secret, one that nobody —*

but nobody — else knows about, you sort of forget it yourself sometimes. Babies. A secret like that seems hard to keep at first, but after the years go by and it's still a secret, well, somehow it tends to get lost behind the today stuff. It's not necessarily less important, it just becomes a part of the life story. Babies. Then comes a moment when, with a jolt, the secret pushes its way to the front and pops up, usually at an unexpected moment.

Kate had held her secret for five decades, pushed it so far back that she only thought of it at Thanksgiving time, that long-ago Thanksgiving when she looked more like the turkey than the bird did, when she was swollen to bursting with new life, when her smooth white skin was stretched and puffed and when her dancer's legs barely could take her across a room.

"Wedding date," she said aloud as she swung her feet from beneath the comforter and into her slippers. *Probably a good day to make some arrangements. Call a judge, find a hall. Must have a large reception. Maybe some of the sourdoughs will come.* "If there are any left," she said aloud.

Later that morning, she backed the Plymouth out of the shed behind the house and planned to turn towards the courthouse in town. Instead, she found herself headed back to the high desert, back to the road that led to the strange shack in the dust.

Right about here, she thought, slowing down the car as she gazed over the land. Sage, low brush, not much moving. Hot, dusty critters finding a place for a mid-day nap. In the car, windows all rolled down, Kate could feel nothing that resembled a breeze. "This is going to be a zinger today," she remarked. She mopped her forehead with the sleeve of her shirt.

"Got to be here." She opened the car door and stepped onto the hot sand. "Got to be. I've got to find out if I'm losing my mind. It's got to be here…"

She walked maybe fifty feet before she saw it, a soft shape just ahead. Quiet. So quiet. The faint smell of dead underbrush mixed with the dry, windless expanse of nothing. Oh no, not *nothing*. Kate knew better. As dry and lifeless as the desert seemed, she knew that life abounded, small animals, latent insects, plants lying dormant waiting for a drop of rain, flowers waiting to bloom. It was all there. All it lacked was water…and time.

In a way the desert resembled the frozen land of the north. The Yukon Territory lay sleeping beneath ice and snow most of the year, then bloomed into glorious profusion when the sun returned, just like the desert that waited to bloom when the water came. Always life hidden where you least expect it. Always ready to bloom. If only for a brief time.

Kate didn't wait for the sun to move her into a stupor again. She walked…ambled…mosied toward the ramshackle building. She tried not to look excited, hurried. The shack seemed to lean more today than it did yesterday. Had there been a wind in the night? Or were her eyes bedeviling her with more trickery?

I'm fully awake now, not sun crazy or tired, she checked herself as she climbed the three steps to the porch and pushed on the door.

Again, the bright lights and the smell of coal oil, tobacco smoke and beer greet her. *This ain't right.* "This just ain't right," she says aloud.

"What's the matter, lady. Something wrong with your drink?"

"Don't have a drink," she snarls. "Could use one though."

"Hey, barkeep. Bring the lady a beer," the old miner calls. "That okay with you?" he turns toward Kate.

"Sure," she says.

"Coming up," comes the familiar voice. "Where you goin' to drink it?" the bartender asks in his low rich voice thick with a foreign accent.

"Right here...at the bar..." Kate feels hypnotized. She has lost all control over her body, her mind, can do nothing but lean on the bar and raise her glass. In front of her is Alex, her Alexander, with his dark eyes, a shock of unruly Greek hair, the grin that's aimed at whoever the eyes are aimed at. And at this moment, they are aimed at Kate, white hair, wrinkles and all.

"Here you are, ma'am," he courteously hands the mug to her. "Can I get you anything else? Beef jerky, popcorn?" His accent is thick and his voice is low.

"No." Kate swallows hard. "No, thank you." She knows she is staring, but she can't stop. Her great love, the man who filled her with soft pain, the face that pushed her heart faster and faster...right here in front of her.

"You here to see someone? Your husband?" Alex asks in his kindest voice.

"No...er, yes...I mean...yes, I'm here to see Kate. I want to speak with her. Has she done her number yet?"

"My Kitty?" Alex smiles. "She's getting ready to sing...the song, 'When You Wore a Tulip...'" He waves his arms and sways his hips in case his English isn't clear enough. "She's changing, backstage, if you wish to see her — for a moment."

"Thanks. I'll sip my beer first."

"When you ready, just go to that door and…"

"I know the way."

Kate is fighting herself — her real self — trying to shake the emotions that rage within her. What is surfacing is a mixture of adoration, confusion and anger. Alex doesn't recognize her, doesn't even find anything familiar about her. Surely she has retained something of her old self, enough for someone as intimate as Alex to have noticed.

Instead he is over there, making goo-goo eyes at that blond…she almost thinks *hussy* but amends it…dancer. She was here once, just like the blond, dancing sometimes, singing sometimes, and other times pushing drinks on the customers. Was she a hussy? She never thought of herself that way. She was a working girl, trying to make a living using the only talent she had, performing.

Still, they call me hussy in Homestead. I know they do; they don't even lower their voices half the time. It's just jealousy. They've lived their dreary little lives in one place and I've seen the world. Yessir, South America, New York, London, and the Yukon. Not another soul in Homestead, or maybe even Bend, has ever been to the Yukon, I'll betcha. Well, maybe one.

"Kitty's going on in about fifteen minutes…" the familiar voice breaks in. "…if you want to see her."

"Thank you." *Alex, if you only knew who you are talking to.* She watches as he returns to the blond and continues whispering sweet lies in her ears.

Through the saloon to the inner door to Kitty's dressing room, a knock and the sweet voice, "Come in," singing as she once did to

Alex. Only this time it is Kate, tall, graceful, and elegant, who enters.

"It's you again," Kitty speaks coldly, looking into the mirror.

"No need to get up." Kate feels slightly testy, again expecting the recognition of an old friend. Rather she is being received with the chill of the Yukon — from both Alex and Kitty. *Has she told him? No, couldn't have or he'd have recognized me. Besides, he'd never believe this!*

Still, she notices, Kitty has found a second chair. She sits down on it and watches the mirror to see her face being made up.

"Sorry. It's been a bad day," Kitty begins. "Alex and I had another fight. I want us to get married, for real, in front of a preacher or something. You know, legal like."

"I know. I'm getting married myself…soon."

"Alex says we're living common law, no need for a minister."

"Not unless there is property…or children…." She waits for a reaction.

"Well there's plenty of property. Alex and I own this theater and another over in Horse. We've invested in some property in Seattle and I have a small real estate business I started in Vancouver."

"And if you're married, there'll be a legal sharing, right?"

"Yes, I guess that's what it is. Or if Alex died, I'd inherit. Otherwise, I'm told I could lose the whole works. Women can't own things, unless their husbands will it to them."

"You've checked into these matters."

"Yes, last time we were in Seattle. Alex said we'd get married then, but we ran out of time and had to catch the boat back here."

"Nail him down, princess. Don't let him slither away from you. He's not about to give up anything, even in death, if he doesn't have to. He probably thinks that you could divorce him and sue for the property."

"I'd never, never, never do that. And he knows it. I'll never leave him. We're partners, in business and..." Kitty smiles, almost shyly, "and...in love."

"Look, girl, get your head on straight. He's Alex. He's going to play it his way. And there's nothing you can do when it happens."

"But I know he loves me, he..."

Kate's rage wells up and she wants to shake this child. "Wake up, Kitty. Wake up and realize that he's no good. He's a chaser. He's fool's gold, a phony. He'll love you and leave you, just like he does all the others." For a moment, she's preaching to Kitty as if she were her daughter, not herself. If only someone had shaken her up all those years ago.

"Hey, cut it out. You're hurting me." Kate has actually grabbed the girl's shoulders. She steps back, alarmed at her rage.

"I'm sorry, really, I'm very sorry. I just wish I could make you see who the real Alex is, a cheat, a rogue, a bounder, a cad..." She is running out of words. Not one to use obscene language easily, Kate is about as close as she can get at that moment. She has to make Kitty see.

Or does she? Kate sinks back into her chair. Is it her job to steer Kitty in a direction that she herself didn't take? This business of being with yourself and not able to change anything is beginning to weigh heavily.

Kate continues to fume as Kitty fusses with her hair. The dress she has put on is a blue gingham copy of a French gown, something to mix the siren with the country girl. Kitty knows she is every miner's dream, but in this outfit she is every man's dream.

"Don't worry, Miss Kate. I know how to take care of myself."

Kate takes a chance and suggests, "Maybe you don't." She nods towards Kitty's bulging waist seams. "Either you're eating too much seal fat or you're expecting a..."

"Shhh!" Kitty leaps from her chair and grabs Kate's arm. "Oh please, how did you know? Oh, don't breathe a word. Please, please, please," she wails. "He doesn't know. Nobody knows. I'll take care of this myself."

"But Kitty, my dear, you wouldn't..."

"No, I love children. And when I come back...I'm going to Seattle for a business trip next month. I'll just stay a few months longer. Then when I come back, I'll tell him my sister had a child and wants me to take care of it. He'll never know."

"You don't have a sister, remember?"

"Well, yes, but..."

"Then, wouldn't it make more sense to have it be your friend's baby? Maybe Flossie's. She's living in Seattle now and doesn't have a husband. You could say you're raising the child for Flossie...poor sick Flossie."

"Hey, you're good. I could do that. He doesn't know Flossie well, but he remembers she left because she couldn't take this cold air. Bad lungs or something."

"Don't count on him to marry you just because you look maternal with...Flossie's baby. He's still a jerk, a bounder..."

"I know. Don't start again."

I feel so helpless, Kate mulls the words in her head. *Why can't I get through to this child that she doesn't need Alexander, that she's about to lose him anyway.*

Kate wants to hug the younger woman, give her a maternal pat, but she settles for a sweet smile of encouragement. "You'll be all right," she says. "You'll land on your feet. Just keep your chin up and mush on."

Kate stays long enough to watch Kitty make her way to the stage and begin her song. She looks around for Alex — just one more look — but he has disappeared. So has the blond.

Then Kate again is outside, walking toward her car. "Mush on," she repeats. Good advice.

On the drive home, she nearly lost the trail a couple of times, thinking of Alex, how he looked and sounded after all those years. And he talked to her, right at her. "Course he didn't know who I was, but he talked to me, with respect."

All the years of hearing him talk down to her, call her names, question her mind and her sanity, consider her wrong if he considered her at all, all those years went racing across her windshield as she tried to stay on the narrow road. "Well, he's her problem now. I'm finished with him."

By the time she arrived home, she had decided to make another trip to Bend, stay at that grand hotel and enjoy a dinner at the plain little place called Andrew's Greek Restaurant.

Wedding Date?
What Date?

KATE FOUND AN ENVELOPE PINNED TO HER door. "Missed you. Gone to the hotel and will call you later. Remember, we have a dinner date tonight. Love, Warren."

"Ohmygosh! Is this Friday already?" Kate had forgotten that Warren was coming for the holiday weekend. But here he was. Booked into the hotel and waiting to come to dinner.

The phone rang just as Kate finished her bath. She wrapped a towel around herself and hurried downstairs to answer.

"I thought I'd come down early and help you fix that sticky door you've been complaining about. Where were you today?" Warren's voice sounded like a loving husband's.

"Oh, just around, you know my regular Friday chores. And don't worry about the door, I sanded it down and rubbed some wax on it myself. Works great now."

"Just can't do anything for you, can I, my darling?" He softened his criticism with sweet words. "The great Klondike Kate is self-sufficient."

"You sound bitter. Would you prefer a wife that's always leaning on you? Isn't that what you had?"

"Once in awhile it feels good to be needed."

"Warren, Warren darling," Kate cooed into the phone. "You don't need a reason to see me, early or not." She didn't wait for a reply, but launched her truth tale. "Warren, sweetheart, I couldn't get a decent cut of meat for tonight. Would you mind if we went out for dinner?"

"Of course not, Kate. I'll pick you up. About six. Okay? Can't wait to see you again."

"Me too."

"Kate..."

"Yes, Warren? Is something wrong? You sound strange."

"Kate...I don't know. I'm wondering...if...." He paused to clear his throat. "Am I reading things wrong? Do you...love...me?"

Kate wanted to respond quickly, "Yes, of course I do." But she took a deep breath before she spoke. "It's just...no, of course...you know that I...oh, Warren, yes. Yes, I love you..."

"But...what's the rest, Kate?"

Kate laughed then, gently, reassuringly for Warren. "Oh don't bother with me, Warren Thompson. Your bride has jitters, you know, the stuff that young girls get when they're faced with marriage."

Warren accepted her explanation, but added, "We'll talk some more when I get over there…my darling."

"Yes," said Kate.

Then silence. Two old people about to change their lives — again — were listening to the past while the telephone wire hummed between them.

Kate enjoyed dining out with Warren. He had an easy-going way of putting her at ease. When she was with him, she was an attorney's fiancé, not an ex-saloon dancer. She was the well-known Mrs. Kate Matson, not the infamous outrageous Klondike Kate. For those moments, Kate could feel safe and cared for. She didn't have to push the world when she was with Warren. As they sat in the dim candlelight of the Empress Room of the hotel, Kate and Warren seemed like an average set of grandparents enjoying their declining years.

"You look beautiful in candlelight, my lovely Kate." Warren smiled and held her hand.

"You're beginning to sound like a moony kid, you old goat."

"And you're beginning to sound like a reluctant bride. Tell me, what is going on?"

Could he have guessed she had been hallucinating in the desert? Had been preoccupied with make-believe? Had been talking to herself — in person? "Well…I, er…it's been a very strange week," she started. "Maybe you won't believe this, but…" she began her confession, then stopped. *No, he won't believe it. Neither do I. Let it go.*

"What won't I believe?" Kate had stopped in mid-sentence and seemed to be off in another world.

"Oh," she came back to Warren. "Oh nothing. I was just going to say something about the way I was treated at the grocery store, but that's water under the bridge."

"Have the biddies been in your way again?"

"Nothing I couldn't handle." Kate smiled gently at the picture in her mind, bathroom tissue and all.

"Is that it? Well now, we have to discuss wedding plans. Just what date have you set for our wedding? Didn't you tell me the twenty-fifth? When do you have the church reserved?"

"Church? Well...uh...I..."

"You don't have the church reserved."

"Well..." Now Kate paused to consider her words. "It all just seems so unnecessary. The ceremony thing. I guess that's what's got me jumpy. I just..."

"You're...jumpy?"

"Maybe that's not the right word. Maybe..."

"Come on, Kate. You're good with words. How many times have you told me about winning essay contests at the nun's school in Spokane. What's going on with you anyway?"

"Nothing," she said, perhaps too quickly. "I spent a couple evenings out in the desert, thinking. Maybe I've been in the sun too much. I'm beginning to feel like my life has been one long trip to nowhere. I'm wondering what I've done with my life...or probably what I haven't done."

"Kate, Kate, my sweet Kate. Just look at what you've done with your life. Look at all the folks you've helped, all the kindnesses you've done, all the places you've invested your money to help people, all the..."

"Not that, Warren. Me. I seem to have done everything for everybody…except me."

"Now now, Kate, you're just worn out. What you need is…"

"What I need is someone who listens to me. Warren, I'm falling apart. I can't keep my mind on what I'm doing." She took a deep breath and confessed, "I talk to myself, and…" She didn't know how to tell him about the apparitions. Then she recalled the old vaudeville routine and added, "…what's worse, I'm getting answers!"

Surprised at the sound of the old joke, they both laughed.

"Well, maybe I'm just imagining this. But, Warren, my sweet sweet friend, I've come to a crossroad and I'm having trouble choosing."

"Choosing? Is there someone else?"

"Of course not. No, my choice is with myself." *Between myself, actually.* "What's this life all about if it isn't for yourself? If we marry…"

"When we marry," Warren corrected.

"When we marry, I'll become Mrs. Warren Thompson…"

"I like the sound of that."

"All my life I've been somebody else. Does that make sense? I've been my mother's rambunctious daughter, the miners' Belle of the Yukon, Mrs. Floyd Warner, Mrs. Johnny Matson. Where am I? Who am I?" She had omitted the obvious, her relationship with Alexander.

"I know who you are. Surely you…"

"That's just it, Warren. I *don't* know who I am. All my life I've been Klondike Kate. I've played the same role for fifty years — and it is a role. But look at me." She pulled off the red chiffon scarf she wore loosely around her neck. "I even wear a piece of the old Kate costume. Did you know that? I finally cut up the old chiffon scarf I used in my flame dance and I wear one piece or another of it all the time. Just holding onto the past. Still, I'm not Klondike Kate anymore. Haven't been for years. Ye gods, for fifty years. I've been playing a part...and that part doesn't fit anymore."

"Hush, keep your voice down," Warren glanced about the room. People were looking in their direction.

"I can't hush much longer," Kate glared at Warren and waved the red scarf. "I can't keep this inside much longer. I'm past the age of consent and I don't know where I'm going, or if I'm going any place at all. We don't have many years left, my dear. We have to live them the best way we can. And if that is being married to each other, okay, fine. But if there's something else that needs doing, we may have to look at this wedding thing again."

"Check please." Warren's eyes pleaded with the waiter to hurry. He needed to retreat from the attention of the other diners. "Kate, let's drop this until we're alone."

Distraught from the day's experience and the evening's tension, Kate took a deep breath and let the tears come. Before they left the dining room, her cheeks were wet with the tears that flowed from her red eyes onto the red scarf.

By the time they reached Kate's house, she had stopped crying. Her voice told Warren she was fighting for self control. She strained as she told him, "Please drop over for breakfast tomorrow. We can talk some more then."

Unused to dealing with emotions, he accepted the easy way out. He kissed her goodnight, lightly, on her forehead, and escaped down the porch steps.

OVER THE NEXT FEW DAYS, WARREN AND KATE MANAGED to avoid the subject of wedding dates completely. They puttered about Kate's garden, repaired a window sill that had cracked and splintered, enjoyed long meals on the porch, in the backyard, even in the town park. They walked through the outskirts of town, arranged spring flowers into bouquets, even spent one sultry afternoon reading on the front porch. He had a copy of the new Hemingway novel, and she had bought the latest Woman's Home Companion magazine, with scads of good short stories.

"You have to read this one, Warren," she called over the top of the magazine Monday afternoon. "It's about this old couple who decide to take a vacation trip to New York City and get caught in a taxi strike and…"

"Umph," grunted Warren.

"…and they have to carry their luggage all over…"

"Sounds good." He wasn't paying attention.

"…and when the gorilla came up and offered them a ride they took it," she teased.

"Yes, dear."

"Warren. You aren't listening at all."

His head came up and he looked at her. "Sorry? What were you saying?"

"Never mind. Not important. Want some iced tea? Which reminds me…"

"Thanks, yes." He paused, then asked, "Reminds you of what?"

"I have to make a jug of Indian tea for the picnic tomorrow."

"You're riding in the parade?"

"Of course. Wouldn't be a Memorial Day parade without Klondike Kate sitting on the fire engine. Want to ride the hook and ladder?"

"Well, uh, actually, no. Thank you, but no, I'll decline. These old bones don't take well to discomfort. Besides, I thought you wanted to distance yourself from the Klondike Kate number."

Kate ignored the remark. "You can ride in the chief's car. Then we'll arrive at the park together for the picnic." Kate stood up and started indoors to make the tea. She filled the large glass jug with cold water, filled an over-sized tea-ball with aromatic orange pekoe tea and dropped it into the jug. Then she carried the container to the back porch and set it in the sun. An hour or so later, she fished out the tea-ball from the fresh tea and placed the container in the refrigerator to chill.

Warren already had felt the chill sitting on the front porch. He didn't mention Klondike Kate again that evening.

By morning the town was stirring to the sound of drums beating and horns honking. The high school band assembled behind the firehouse and its members tooted, banged and whistled their cacophony of warm-up riffs. The last of the veterans of the Spanish American War practiced lining up, some in wheelchairs. Added to the marching units were veterans from World Wars I and II, soldiers, sailors and marines, even a Women's Nurse Corps unit.

Homestead had contributed generously to the nation's wars and proudly paraded the heroes down Main Street whenever it could.

Kate arrived at the firehouse wearing her ivory silk Paris gown, still able to cut a svelte figure, even if both the gown and the figure were several decades old. At her throat was a necklace made of gold nuggets; in her ears were gold dust earrings. Diamonds and sapphire rings covered her hands, and on her head rested a dainty tiara set with diamonds, rubies and sapphires. Nestled in her snow white hair was a tiny red chiffon bow.

"Still a knockout, aren't you, Kate?" George, one of the firemen, offered.

"Gosh, Georgie, you turn a girl's head."

These were her friends, strong supporters, recipients of her generosity and the loves of her life. The sturdy young firemen enjoyed Kate's pampering. At least once a week she brought them a casserole, a cake or pie — usually their favorite red devil's food cake or Kate's Kiss-off pie.

"You still riding in our parade, Aunt Kate?" came a voice behind her. Kate turned to see Ozzie, one of the first firemen she knew.

"You bet, oldtimer. How many years has it been?"

"At least twenty, maybe twenty-five. During the Great Depression, remember?"

"If I recall, you were with the firemen when the old Methodist Church burned down. That was...let's see...1932."

"Things was bad then, wasn't they?" Ozzie stroked his chin. "Big old hot fire, that church must've been made out of dry tinder. Went up with flames 100 feet high, and the middle of winter. Cold?

Mygawd, I thought we'd all freeze that night, even with the fire as hot as it was."

The other firemen were gathering around Ozzie as he told his story. They all knew how it ended.

"Then just as we was about to freeze our...toes...off, there came Aunt Kate with her big pot of hot coffee. Lord, I thought she was an angel. Nobody ever thought to bring us nothing before that. But here was Aunt Kate..."

"And she's been here ever since," George concluded.

"Three cheers for Aunt Kate," Ozzie called out.

"Hurrah, hurrah, hurrah," the firemen answered as they piled onto the hook and ladder and started the engine. George held out his arm for Kate to climb aboard, someone pushed the siren button and they were off.

The official Homestead, Oregon Memorial Day Parade was underway.

Halfway down Main Street, as the fire truck approached the office of the *Homestead Courier*, Paul Benjamin pushed his way through the crowd and set off the flash camera. Kate dutifully waved at the camera, smiling her widest Klondike Kate smile.

Riding in the Fire Chief's car behind her, Warren nodded at the crowd, bewildered at the wild display of affection for his bride-to-be. "Over seventy and still going strong, ain't she," commented the driver.

"And ain't she pretty!" Warren agreed.

ANNETTE WAS TYPING THE LATEST VERSION OF HER STORY about Kate's approaching nuptials as the parade disappeared down the street and into the park. She got up to freshen her cup of coffee, then lit a cigarette as she reviewed the last few words she had written. "The wedding is planned for June seventeenth," she wrote, then wondered if that was the right date. Kate had seemed so reluctant to tell her. Oh well, she could always write a correction in next week's paper. Memorial Day or not, the weekly deadline was near. She had to get this thing out back.

She heard the Linotype machine stop, then Paul's footsteps clomp across the floor. He always wore his boots on pre-press day. "Hey, Marilyn Monroe, got that copy for me yet?" he yelled as he came through the door. "I'm about finished with everything else."

"Ready, boss," she replied as she yanked the page from the typewriter. "Kept it to eight inches, but you can cut it if you have to."

"Damn right I can cut it. I'm the editor, remember?"

"Thought you were the typesetter. Or are you the photographer?"

"Naw, the photographer has to wait until the typesetting's done. I'll fade into the dark room next. Got some great parade shots of Aunt Kate on the fire engine."

"Hard to know who I'm talking to around here."

Paul put his arm around her waist and grabbed the pages with his free hand. "Don't talk back to the…typesetter."

"Careful, Romeo, someone could be walking by."

"Naw, they're all at the park eating their picnic lunch, like normal people."

"What's normal people?" Annette mimicked a movie she'd just seen. "What's normal peoples like, Mr. Man?" she sang into his ear. Then she ruffled his hair and twisted out of his grasp. She stood still, feet spread apart, hands on hips and challenged him, angrily, "What do normal people do?"

Paul caught the shift in her attitude and offered a sullen whisper, "Who's normal these days?" He turned his back and left the room.

Annette listened to Paul at the Linotype as it began to clack away, then cleared off her desk and left, locking the front door behind her. Perhaps she could catch the last of the Memorial Day picnic.

Weddings of Now and Yore

THERE IT WAS, RIGHT ON THE FRONT PAGE, that familiar black and white picture of Klondike Kate wearing her fancy pink satin Paris gown and displaying her legs wrapped in green tights. *Maybe I ought to find another picture of me. That one's getting worn out.* Kate picked up the paper from her front porch and carried it inside.

"Klondike Kate To Wed, Again" read the headline. The story of the Memorial Day parade and picnic was accompanied by the photo of Kate waving from the high seat on the hook and ladder fire truck. Her marriage was front page news in this small town and she loved seeing herself in the newspaper — for whatever reason.

For fifty years, Kate had kept alive the legend of Klondike Kate. There were times it had been difficult to get any attention at all — the war years, and the days of the Great Depression. Who wanted to hear about a young sprout picking the pockets of gold miners at a time when everyone could use more gold in their own pockets? And there were times when she wished for less notoriety — the days of Alex's trial, her days of slugging out financial loss by working in a greasy spoon, the death of her "yam and yelly" man. She often wondered how people could earn their living writing about the misfortunes of others?

"This is a wedding, a happy affair," she remarked as she poured another cup of coffee and sat down to read about herself. A potentially happy occasion, even though Warren had returned to Portland wondering if it would ever happen.

"Don't fret about the ceremony, Warren," she had told him as she kissed him goodbye the day before.

"But I will fret, Kate, until we get this thing settled. When are we going to get married? That is, *if* we're going to."

"Yes, we're going to get married. June twenty-fifth. That's when." She had chosen her path. At least she thought she had, even though the newspaper said the seventeenth.

She held up the newspaper with its great headline and sipped her coffee. When she finished the article she let the newspaper slip to the floor as she lay back her head and closed her eyes. *June seventeenth. I'll have to have Annette correct that.*

Another wedding. Could she remember the others? The one to the handsome but irresponsible Floyd Warner. He was quite a man, handsome and willing, even though she discovered that *handsome and willing* don't make a marriage, only a wedding.

Then there was Johnny, dear loving devoted Yonny, who loved her more than he loved gold, or at least as much. The only time he left his gold mine was for Kate. Nothing else could bring him out of the frozen Yukon. Still, he couldn't leave it for long.

And always Alex. Well, no there wasn't a wedding, but it was like we were married. "Now there was a match," she said softly. "There was a match."

KATE BOLTED FROM HER CHAIR. "I'VE GOT TO CONVINCE THAT girl that Alex isn't right for her. She has to know. How can I get through to that twenty-year-old brain?"

Kate had decided to return to the desert shack. "But this time I'll bring her proof — proof that will show her I am who I am. But what? Gold nuggets? My bracelet? No, everybody in the Klondike had them." She was putting on her lipstick when the idea struck. "Red chiffon! She'll recognize the red chiffon."

Kate rifled through her scarf drawer which was filled with various lengths of red chiffon. Some pieces she would wind around her head like a turban, others she simply stuffed into pockets. There were bows of various sizes and twisted chiffon that resembled braids. Once they all had been part of a fifty-foot length of chiffon that flew through the air and tempted the men of the Yukon.

"Here, just the one!" Kate held up a square of cloth that she often tied around her neck when she went rock hunting. "Just perfect for desert wear," she announced in the voice of a fashion show commentater. "Just perfect." She wrapped the scarf around her neck and headed for the high country.

Soon she is back at the saloon in the desert. She rushes through the front door and pounds her way back to the dressing room, brushing aside Flossie to open the door. Flossie closes the door behind her, leaving Kate and Kitty alone.

Kate stands before the young woman who sits at her dressing table brushing her hair. There she is — Kitty, the youngster who loves the dangerous, daring Greek waiter, who loves her Alex because he promises her a life of excitement, delight, riches, success, attention — in short, the young woman who is looking for everything Kate herself had ever wanted.

Kate asks, "What can Alex give you that you don't already have?"

"Whoa, you can't just charge in here and start yelling at me," she says, staring at Kate. "I'm on in just a few minutes. I haven't time to talk now." The young woman seems to be less disturbed by Kate's visit this time. She continues to fuss with her hair.

"Let me do that," Kate offers. She grabs the brush and a few pins and starts to work with the familiar thick red hair, rolling it around her fingers, securing it with the large ivory pins, brushing a few locks around Kitty's face to soften it. "It's easier when you can stand behind and fix it," she laughs.

"Look, Kate, I appreciate your help, but really, I can take care of myself."

"No you can't!" Kate throws the brush on the table. It bounces and startles Kitty. Her shoulders hunch to protect herself — as if Kate were going to strike her.

"All right!" Kitty stands up and faces Kate. "All right. What's on your mind? Say it. Just say it and leave me the hell alone."

"You're making some mistakes. Some very bad ones. You have an opportunity you may never have again." Kate's eyes go to Kitty's bulging tummy. "Take it. Get the hell out of here, go back to Seattle, have your child and find work there. Then as soon as you can, take your child and move to New York. Your mother will help you. She'll love you for needing her. Start over in New York and become the actress you've always wanted to be — Kate Rockwell, star of stage, screen and radio, your name up in lights…"

"Stage, what and what?" Katie asks.

"Screen and radio, you know…"

"No, I don't. I know vaudeville, saloons, casinos. Sure I'd like to become an actress, but I seem to be going in the other direction. And now this," she pats her tummy.

"You'll lose your figure for awhile, but you can get it back. Besides, as a real actress you won't depend so much on your figure. Maybe that was my mistake, relying on something that didn't last."

Kitty and Kate look hard at each other. "Who are you, really?" Kitty asks, her eyes squinting at Kate. "How do I know whether you're part of my imagination or just some local dame out to scare me away?" Then Kitty throws back her head and laughs. "I know, you're really Alexander's mother, come to protect her little boy from the big bad girlie."

Kate's smile disappears. She knows she has to convince this slip of a girl that she is herself in about a half century. Slowly she unties the scarf from around her neck. She spreads it out across her lap before she holds it up to the crimson dress hanging on the peg on the wall. "Does this match?" she asks the young woman. "I brought it today to show you who I am so that I can convince you who Alex is. Do you recognize this piece of chiffon?"

Kitty takes a closer look as Kate waits. Then, catching her breath, she stares back at Kate. For the first time, the young woman sees herself in a body that creaks and groans, that is wrinkled and losing its tone, with hair that no longer sparkles like a glittering ruby, but has become a snowy opal of questionable color. She sees a woman who walks slowly, albeit gracefully, but who no longer twirls and spins, glides and leaps, slides and taps. Is this really going to happen to her?

At the same time Kate sees the vigor of her youth, the hope of new life springing inside her, the self-confidence of the young, the terrible longing to be seen, heard, and applauded. She sees a young woman who could become a great actress, who attracts attention easily, who loves the spotlight and yet is settling for the cheap glimmer of coal oil lamps. But more importantly, she sees a girl who is giving up her life to chase a man who doesn't want her. She sees that. And as she does, tears come to her eyes. This child is throwing away her own life to live the fantasy of another.

But before the tears flow, she has to try once more.

Kate gulps and faces Kitty. "Young woman, you're throwing away your life on that no-good, irresponsible...drifter who doesn't love you as much as he loves money, who will toss you aside when he's finished with you, who will find others to use, others who will help him get to the top. He'll step over rules, people, and anything else that gets in his way." Kate pauses for breath.

There is a long silence, a very long silence before Kitty whispers, "But he loves me, and I love him."

"Love! What do you know about love?" Kate shoots back. She fairly spits out the words. "What they holler from the audience? That's not love, it's men looking at a woman's body. All you know is that bunch of slobbering sailors on the way to Valparaiso who hadn't seen a woman for months. All you know is scurrilous New York promoters who got their kicks with ambitious young girls trying out for the chorus. All you know are the woman-hungry miners who put aside their digging long enough to spend their gold on you and whiskey before they return to digging. Those sourdoughs aren't about to give up their get-rich fantasies. Maybe it's time you give up your get-Alex fantasy." Kate grabs Kitty by the shoulders. "Take a look at life as real people live it. Real people get married, find real jobs, have babies and get up every morning and go to bed every night. They're not dancing and singing and carousing all night, but loving each other. There's real music in real love, whether or not you believe it."

Kitty stares as the the older woman gestures wildly and spews out the words. Then she glares at her and shoots back, "How dare you...how dare you come in here and tell me these awful things? You think you know how I feel? Well you don't! You haven't felt for...a long time...years and years. You think you can give me all this icy stuff about what I'm doing and where I'm doing it...well, you can't. You've forgotten. You've forgotten that you risked *your* life to come here. You got your kicks out of dancing in front of these men. And you fell in love with Alex. Fantasy? Fantasy? Don't you dare talk to me about fantasy when you've been living one for...how many years? And you're still living it. Why else are you here? Are you still hoping to get Alex to...love you? I have no doubt that Alex loves me.

I'm the one he comes home to every night. I'm the one he wakes up with every…most mornings. And what difference does it make if he's still dreaming big, making plans for the future? You can just bet your last poke that I'm in it!"

"Are you, Kitty?"

"Yes. I think so. Well, even if I'm not, Miss Kate, I love him," she says simply.

Kate takes a deep breath and pulls the red scarf around her neck and ties it. Wordlessly — she has used them all up — she turns and walks toward the door.

"You can give me a thousand reasons, but I'll never leave Alex," says the younger woman.

Kate knows that. She just feels better for having spoken what was in her heart.

"Klondike Kate To Wed," she repeated the headline. "Again. Still looking for that real person to love, aren't you, dear Eloise?" She sipped her coffee. It had turned cold.

The Lawyer

WARREN THOMPSON WAS A VERY VERY
careful man. He was a lawyer. He had to be
careful.

To the folks in Homestead reading the morning paper, Klondike Kate was going to wed "an
attorney from Portland." That sounded like hot
stuff, an image of a big-time officer of the court
winning huge settlements for the little people,
standing up for justice as he makes his case
against crime and underhanded dealings.

In truth, Warren Thompson was an estates
attorney who set up trusts for clients, handled
disposition of people's property and cleaned up
after executors. He had never handled an estate
that amounted to more than a few thousand
dollars. Most of his clients left this world with
settlements that usually just broke even.

He had heard of Kate long before he met her. After all, she had been embroiled in a racy love triangle with some big show business muckity muck. His firm had represented her when she was called to testify at the guy's trial. Kate was to offer testimony on behalf of the guy — what was his name? Pantages, that was it. Alexander Pantages. Apparently, some young actress had accused him of rape and Pantages needed all the help he could get.

Shortly after the sensational trial in California, Kate had stopped in Portland to take care of personal accounts handled by Warren's firm. He had heard she was in their law office, but couldn't manage to be around when she made her dramatic entrance and later an even more dramatic exit. Kate always announced her presence at the door and gave notice of her departure the same way — the pause to scan the room to make sure everyone was watching.

It wasn't until a couple days later that Warren first laid eyes on Kate that summer of 1932. Just a few years earlier Warren had become a partner in the firm. Within another two years he would be assigned to acquaint the firm with the new federal statutes dealing with something called Social Security. Up until then, he had been the firm's income tax expert; soon he would become the expert on other new programs of Franklin Roosevelt's New Deal.

The lawyer fell for Kate the first time they met. When the grief-stricken Kate Rockwell walked into his life, she was playing the tragic figure who bemoaned the woes of her beloved Alexander who was spending time in prison for indecent crimes against a young woman. She was the picture of distraction, managing only a slight sad smile when interviewed by reporters in the hallway outside his office.

"Will you be staying in Portland long, Kate?"

"Why didn't you testify on his behalf?"

"Are you in his will?"

"Has Pantages contacted you?"

"Will you be attending the next Sourdough's Convention?"

Poor Kate was beleaguered (if that is the word) by reporters whenever she came to Portland. Somehow, they were always tipped off when she was in town. But never mind, they still came to ask her more questions.

Kate was the dramatic figure as she entered Warren's office. Dressed in a pale green silk suit with a darker green blouse and wearing a wide-brimmed hat on her still-red hair, she lit up his heart. She passed him as he held the door for her and he caught the scent of...wonder...of a garden full of flowers...of heavens stretching to the skies...of a woman he could love. He knew immediately he had a crush on her — even though he was married.

Still, Warren Thompson was careful. Which made him hesitate before he took any steps — in court and in life. He assisted Kate in amending her will — such an odd codicil this time. Afterward he treated her to lunch in the Sand Room of his club (they were allowing women as guests of members by then) and he accompanied her to the police station where Kate could always count on a police escort to her car at the edge of town. At all times he maintained his poise. In short, he loved her from afar.

Strange, he thought, Kate could drive her Ford across Oregon, negotiate stretches of road that were barely more than paths, cross wobbly bridges that spanned rushing waters, brave the wilds of her countryside, but she balked at testing city traffic. Once in the early 'twenties, she had been the marshal for the Annual Parade of Roses and made a friend of the chief of police. When she told him of her fear of driving in traffic, the good man genially offered her a police escort any time she came to town. She took him up on it.

Besides, when the police escort was duly recorded in police files, it became a tip-off to reporters that Klondike Kate was back in town.

That day in 1932 when the lawyer's heart skipped a beat, he might have approached her, but he was a careful man. Warren watched Kate's comings and goings from afar, meeting with her only when she needed his legal assistance. Still, over the years the fire burned brightly in Warren Thompson's heart. If only he had been free...

But Warren was a married man, happily most of the time. His beloved Lillian had seen him through the lean days of setting up practice and had helped him enjoy the fruits of his labors, had helped him raise a lovely daughter Joan and a flighty son Willis. A decade later, in 1942, she died, after thirty years of marriage.

By the time another decade had passed, Warren was alone again. Joan had married Jeff Gillette, the son of one of Thompson's partners, just after he returned from the war in 1945. Two grandchildren followed soon after. Willis was frittering away his time at the local airfield, entranced with the new and exciting sport called barnstorming.

Kate walked back into Warren's life about a year after Lillian's death. Kate needed to change her will once again. Near the end of the war, Kate's husband, the old Johnny Matson, had died after ten years of marriage to his Klondike Kate. Back in 1932, shortly after Warren had met Kate, she just up and married that old gold miner, the one she called Yonny. The papers reveled in the love story of the smitten Swede from the Yukon who had carried a torch for Kate for thirty years, since the Gold Rush days. They printed excerpts from the love letters he wrote to her after reading about her beloved Pantages going to jail. The papers covered in full the gaudy marriage of the Northwest's celebrity to her "yam and yelly man."

Well then, one day Warren found himself in a new position, but still stalling. His Lillian had been gone nearly five years, Johnny Matson had been dead a few years, and Kate was alone again too — at least for the time being. Then one day she was in his office, changing her will once more, this time to arrange a bequest to the Homestead Fire Department. Following the main order of business, Warren cleared his throat, stood up from his desk, walked around to Kate and sat down in the dark leather chair next to her.

"Mrs. Matson...Kate...we've been friends for many years. I've been your attorney, you my client. I'd...well..."

Kate had seen that look on a man's face before. She knew what he was about to say. She smiled at him gently and helped him out. "Are you asking for a...date, Mr. Thompson...Warren?"

"Oh come now, Kate. We're too old for...dates." The very idea set his heart racing. He was still fighting for the right words to say things on his own to his Aphrodite.

"Well...yes...sort of.," he went on, gasping, lost in the depths of her sprightly gray-blue eyes. "What I mean is...what I'd like to…well, yes, Kate. A date." He gave up trying to camouflage his heart.

"Of course, Warren. I'd love to have…a date…with you. Please pick me up at my hotel at seven this evening. We can have dinner."

Didn't she turn the tables easily? There she was, setting up the…date. All he had to do was show up.

That evening, "…two people enjoying their later years dawdled over dinner in the elegant Waldorf Room of the Central Hotel in downtown Portland…" is the way the newspapers would have reported it, had they been there. But Warren had Kate all to himself — no reporters, no cameras, just two mature people talking away the evening, scarcely touching their food, gently touching hands.

However much Kate encouraged Warren, it still took him sixteen months to propose marriage. His words belied his actions: "We're getting on in years, Kate. We mustn't waste a minute of our time together. I'd be honored if you would marry me, you know, become Mrs. Warren Thompson."

Kate's answer was equally ambiguous. "I'd like nothing better than to become Mrs. Warren Thompson, but I don't want to lose Klondike Kate Rockwell. I'll make you a deal. I'll marry you, but I don't want to change my name."

"But you must. That's what brides do."

"Not this bride. I've changed my name before and found that Klondike Kate gets short shrift. I'll use your name when I have to, legally, but I'll still be Klondike Kate, Queen of the Yukon to the rest of the world. Those are my terms, Mr. Attorney Man."

Warren Thompson accepted Kate's terms and slipped onto her finger a twenty-four carat gold ring holding an auspicious diamond surrounded by sapphires. He barely could afford it, but he had splurged. Nothing was too much for his glorious bride-to-be.

Saturday With the Family

ANNETTE WHITTIER WENT INTO THE COURIER office on Saturdays partly because she had nothing else to do, and partly because she knew Paul would show up sometime during the morning. She sat at his desk, leaned back in his chair and idly picked up this week's *Courier*. "I did a good job on Kate this time," she thought. "Yes sir, a good job."

I wonder about that wedding date, though. She seemed reluctant about the seventeenth. Too soon? Too late to back out? There's a bit of reluctance in her. She isn't sure. That's it. She isn't sure she wants to do this again. My god, the woman is seventy years old. Why should she want to get herself enmeshed all over again? Especially when it's so clear she is still carrying the Pantages torch.

Is that me in fifty years? Am I going to be granting interviews and whining about how he done me wrong?

"No," she said aloud. "No way." Annette pushed back the chair and stood up. "Not this baby, not this kid. I won't become Kate Matson mooning over a guy she can't have."

A guy I can't have. A guy I can't have. There it was. Reality in its clearest form.

Annette looked at the picture of Kate again, snowy hair, enigmatic smile, the kind of smile that showed around her mouth but not in her eyes. She compared it to the front page picture of Kate as a girl. Yes, there it was, the smile that models and actresses wear when they appear in public. The kind of smile that men pay for, but that reveals nothing about the smiler. Was she happy? Ever? Did she *feel* like smiling, or did she do it just to appear happy to her public? Happy? What was happy anyway?

Women like Kate could be happy wearing the smile and not having to feel anything to back it up. Maybe Kate, like other models and actresses, feels something only when she's smiling at her adoring fans. That must be it.

But me? I'm different. I know I am. I'm miserable when I have to smile when I don't feel like it. "Guess it's because I don't have to do it much," she spoke to the picture. "I don't have to smile all the time. You do." The picture smiled back.

"A LITTLE TIME TO YOURSELF?" THE GROCERY CLERK GREETED Isabel Benjamin as she entered the store.

"You know it," Isabel waved back. "Only time I get to myself these days are my Saturday trips here. Kind of says something for motherhood, doesn't it."

"Mr. Benjamin put out another good newspaper this week," the clerk called after her as he picked up a copy to re-read the story about the town's most colorful character — Klondike Kate.

At home, Paul Benjamin sat with his daughter and played yet another game of Chutes and Ladders. Nonsense, repetitious, uneducational. No, wait! It teaches frustration, pointlessness, ups and downs. Maybe this is a test for playing the game called life.

"Your turn, honey," he called. The child was losing interest and had wandered off to find her doll. "Come on, Paula, Daddy just slid down another chute and it's your turn."

"You spin for me."

"I'm spinning the dial. See? Oh-wow, a five! You get a ladder. Come move up the ladder."

"That's okay."

"What's wrong, punkin. Why don't you want to play?"

"Dolly's sad, Daddy," the child cradled a pudgy half-dressed doll in her arms. "Dolly wants loving."

"Let's give her some loving then," the father agreed. "Come sit down here and let me hold you while you hold Dolly."

The two cuddled there on the floor, the board game forgotten. He smelled her delicious hair, the baby shampoo, the sweet smell of a child, and he felt blessed. "I love you, punkin," he whispered.

"I love Dolly," Paula returned, not moving except to pat Dolly on the bottom. "I love Mommy too. And I love you, Daddy." She twisted her face around to rub her cheek against his stubbly face. "Ooh, you're scratchy."

"That's because Daddy needs to shave," he said, moving to get up. "Now how about you playing with Dolly...put some clothes on her or something...while Daddy gets cleaned up? Then we'll have another go at something to eat before Mommy gets back."

Saturdays were father-daughter time as much as they were mother-alone time. During the week Paul didn't have any regularity in his schedule. Isabel was never sure when he'd be home, when he'd find time to get away from the responsibilities of running a small town weekly newspaper. Simply put, that was the plight of the small town newspaper editor.

Just after they were married, Paul's father had turned over the *Courier* to Paul, sort of a wedding present. The young couple had just graduated from college and Isabel was expecting their first baby. They retreated to the small town called Homestead where they could spend more time together, find fewer excuses for distractions. It all had sounded so appealing in the beginning.

But life in a small town wears thin all too quickly for a young couple brought up in the midst of city life in Seattle, especially during the exciting war years — servicemen coming and going through town, war industries booming, people flocking to the west coast Mecca from all over the country. Then came the heady post-war university days where young people, released from the strictures of war, found time to fall in love while they experienced an introduction to the world of knowledge.

Isabel had fallen in love with Paul during a literature class, while sharing a debate about the value of post-war literature. She maintained it had no place in a study milieu since it hadn't been tried and tested by time. Paul argued that good literature was good literature whether it was written yesterday or five hundred years ago. They knew something had sparked between them when they began to argue each other's points, backing up each other's contentions. The class howled at the turn-about. The teacher was unamused.

Isabel found herself pregnant just before graduation. They were married that summer and by fall they were packing up for Oregon.

"You must have a wonderful life, Mrs. Benjamin," the grocery clerk said as she sorted out her purchases. "I mean, married to a newspaper editor, something happening all the time, and that baby of yours."

"She's four now," Isabel broke into the soliloquy about her married bliss.

"Yes, she's a darling, a real sweetheart. Did you want two of these? They're on sale for just another couple days." The clerk held up a box of graham crackers. "Can't have too many graham crackers."

"No, one box is enough today. Thank you." Isabel wanted to get home, to spend some of that rare time with Paul. While she appreciated the shopping trip alone, she missed having time at home with her husband. She shifted her feet trying to give the clerk a hint. "I'm in a bit of a hurry," she explained.

"I'm going as fast as I can. I just thought…"

"Sorry. You're doing fine." All Isabel needed was an angry clerk. *Back off, girl, you'll spook the clerk. Or have you already spooked yourself? Paul at home. Me here. Doesn't make sense.*

She hurried out the door with her groceries, loaded the car and sped out of the lot. As she passed the *Courier* office, she looked over out of habit. Someone was there. Had to be that girl. Ye gods, she hangs around there all the time. Seems to have nothing else to do, no life of her own.

At home, Isabel pulled into the garage just as Paul came to meet her. Together they hauled in the groceries and began to unpack. "Ooh, smooth face," she said as he offered his cheek for a moving kiss.

"Just shaved. Gave way to Dolly and escaped to the bathroom." He nodded at their daughter, who was still pulling and tugging to put a shirt on her doll.

"Mama's home," Isabel called, but the child barely looked up. Nothing new about that. Mama is always home.

"Well, now that you're back, I guess I'll hike down to the office and catch up on the books."

Isabel stopped arranging cans on the shelf. Her high spirits fell. Calmly, she said, "Do you have to leave now? Your reporter seems to be there. At least I saw someone inside when I came by. Doesn't she have a life?"

"Oh?" Paul closed the refrigerator door and grabbed an empty paper sack. As he folded it, he started to explain, "I guess she's..."

"She wrote that piece about Kate, didn't she?"

"Er...yes."

"Good job. Hope you told her that. Kate's a hard one to write about...hard to find anything new. Wonder how she must feel living alone."

"She seems to get by. Hasn't been away from her family that long. Still enjoys it."

"I didn't mean her. I meant Kate…living alone and re-living a life that occurred fifty years ago."

"Never thought of it that way. But I guess you're right."

"I know that if some guy jilted me, I wouldn't spend the rest of my life re-living it. That *is* what she's doing, isn't it?" Isabel watched as Paul folded another grocery bag and stuffed it under the sink.

Was she talking about Kate? Paul wondered. *Or about Annette? Or about herself?* Paul wisely kept his mouth closed, letting her talk.

"And now Kate is getting married. Why? That's the only piece missing from the story. Why is she going to the altar again? It isn't as if she has to."

Gotta get out of here. "Wish I could stay and psychoanalyze Kate, but I'd better get down to do my books." Paul slipped into his jacket, hugged his daughter, kissed his wife and walked out the door. "I'm leaving the car for you," he called over his shoulder. "See you later."

The familiar walk from house to office was one of the joys of living in a small town. He could wave at neighbors. He knew them all. He could stop and chat for a moment with one of them out mowing the lawn or sweeping the sidewalk. He could drop in at the Homestead Drug Store and chat with the pharmacist about his reaction to the latest editorial in the *Courier*. He could stop at the bakery and pick up a bag of donuts, still warm.

"Morning," he called to Annette as he reached the office. "Isabel says she saw you here. Nothing else to do on a Saturday?" He sounded aloof, distant.

"I'd rather spend my time here."

"You know, Annette, I've been thinking. Maybe you ought to meet more people your age, I mean…"

"My age? You sound like you're ancient. I'm single, not a child. Besides, I don't need anyone else. I have you. And you're just my age."

"That's what I mean. Maybe you ought to try to find someone else…who…"

"Who what?" Annette sat back in her chair and stared at her boss. "Are you trying to get rid of me?"

"Great scott no. You're the best writer I've found yet."

"I wasn't talking about journalism."

"Well, what else did you mean?" He regretted the question as soon as he asked it.

"You know. You and me. Us. Maybe you don't realize it, but you love me." She swung around in the chair, stood up, and moved towards him. "Don't you?" This time she waited for his answer.

"Uh…well…Annette…you see, while I may feel something for you, I love my wife. I have to tell you that or I'd be lying. Sure we have our squabbles, our rough times, but she's the mother of my daughter. How you and I feel really doesn't matter…" He made a feeble attempt to push her away.

"Oh yes it does. There's no way I'm going to hang around and wait for you to discover that you and I are…are really something together." Annette faltered, her anger giving way to fear that she was losing the one man she had come to love in her short life. "We…we…"

"Come on, Annie, you know I can't…"

"What do you mean *can't*? Don't you mean *won't*?" She spit out the words.

"Annie…"

"Don't call me that!"

"Annette. You know how things are…"

"I know you're married and that you don't love her like you love me."

"Well…"

"You don't! You told me you don't!"

"Ann…Annette, please. Come here. You have to know that I…"

"Oh Paul. Sometimes you scare me when you seem so far away. Don't scare me like that."

"Come here, Annette." He held out his arms. Isabel and Paula had left his thoughts. Only Annette remained.

"Paul. Paul." She kept saying his name. Then the tears came.

Paul wrapped his arms around her and let her cry. "I'm sorry. Really and truly sorry. Of course I feel something for you, but I'm not sure it's strong enough to jeopardize my family."

Annette hated the sound of that word. Family. Damn the Saturday mornings at home. He always seemed so far away afterwards. Damn him and his family ties. *Why couldn't I have met him first? Why couldn't I have met him away from his family, his father, his…wife?*

Annette squirmed out of Paul's arms, grabbed her handbag and ran out the door. If she had stopped to find out, she wouldn't have been able to differentiate between her anger and her jealousy. She headed for her rooming house, but found herself walking up the hill towards Kate's house instead. Tears still streamed down her face and her eyes had puffed up. She turned her head away as she passed the only other person on the street, a woman carrying a bouquet of flowers from her garden.

Women in Love

ANNETTE REACHED THE OLD WOODEN HOUSE atop the Franklin Street hill and sat down on the concrete steps to allow herself another rush of tears. *He's gone. He's chosen her. He's not mine anymore. It's over. All over.* More tears, her body trying to catch its breath, her shoulders shaking with each attempt.

Kate was passing the upstairs window as she dust-mopped the floor. Was that someone sitting on her sidewalk? Appears to be a girl, and she's crying. Maybe she's hurt.

Kate leaned the mop against the curtain and slowly made her way down the stairs, holding tightly to the railing as she went. She crossed the vestibule to the door and went outside. Then she recognized the figure.

"Annette? Annette, is that you? What's the matter, honey?" Kate walked down the sidewalk to the steps, put her hand on the girl's shoulder and patted it. "Are you hurt? Did you fall?" she asked, looking about for signs of injury.

Annette shook her head and sobbed some more.

"Then it must be a man. Only a man can make you cry like this."

"Oh, Mrs. Matson, I'm so sorry. I shouldn't be here. I just walked and walked and…"

"No bother. And please, call me Kate. Come inside. Come on," she helped the younger woman to her feet. "We'll have a cup of coffee. Come with me."

The two walked slowly up to the house. Kate led her guest into the kitchen. Annette had begun to hiccough and occasionally shiver as the tears subsided and she fought for control.

"I'm really sorry, Mrs.…Kate. I feel so foolish showing up like this on your doorstep. I just didn't know where else to go."

"It's okay, honey. Aunt Kate knows just what to do." She poured a cup of her very strong coffee, steaming and black, and held it out to Annette. "Cream or anything?" she asked.

"This is fine. Thank you."

Kate pulled a pan from the oven and cut a slice of coffee cake. "Here, try this. Just baked it this morning. Too much for one woman to eat all alone."

At the word "alone" Annette broke into tears again. Kate let her cry for a bit, then asked, "Want to talk about it?"

"Yes…no…I can't."

"You mean he's married."

"Well, yes." Annette looked up through her red puffy eyes and saw that Kate knew. She wouldn't have to explain. This woman knew.

She sipped her coffee and nibbled on the cake as Kate busied herself at the sink. Then Kate turned and leaned against the sink as she spoke, rambling as she recalled the old times and what she had learned about life.

"Men tend to grab onto what's close by. In the Yukon, all those men, most of them were married, had a wife or girlfriend somewhere. But we were there, close by, in Dawson, not miles and heartaches away. That's a strong attraction for men.

"You're there, with him most of the day, sharing his successes and his failures, giving him a shoulder to complain on, a helping hand, a boost to his ego…. You're there."

"But I'm not there all the time, I mean, sometimes…"

"You're right, because when she's there, she's his helping hand, his shoulder, his ego boost." Kate could see the light dawning in Annette's eyes. "You see, this man doesn't know what he wants. He doesn't seem to feel any great abiding love for either of you. He can't make up his mind. Oh honey, I've seen it often. I've seen it happen over and over again. You know the song, 'When I'm not near the girl I love, I love…' well, you know it."

"What am I to do, Kate? How can I keep working alongside him, feeling strongly for him and knowing…knowing…"

"Knowing he isn't going to leave his wife for you?" Kate could say the words now. They didn't matter to her anymore.

Again tears filled Annette's eyes. She let the sob rise to her throat before she burst out, "But I love him."

Oh dear, she's got it bad. Remind you of anyone, Katie? Anyone you know sobbing over that son-of-a-bitch who married someone else while you were away? Remind you of anyone crying all night over some no-good cad who didn't love you enough to stay with you?

Now there was an illuminating notion. You can see it when it comes crying on your doorstep, but you couldn't see it when you were living it. Now it was Kate's eyes that welled up, tears forming in the faded sapphire gray eyes of a woman in love — still in love.

Kate poured herself a cup of coffee and sat down next to Annette.

The two women sipped coffee and let the tears flow for quite a while before Kate spoke again.

"What makes us do this?"

"Huh?"

"Give some man this kind of power over us." She pushed back her chair. "Look at us. Two intelligent, educated women crying over men who don't have the sense they were born with."

Annette nearly smiled. But she managed to add, "Men who don't know a good woman when they have one right under their noses."

"Are those pronouns mixed?"

Then they laughed, both of them. Annette because she wasn't aware that Kate knew a pronoun from an onion and Kate because Annette was laughing...and because she instantly recognized the truth of what Annette had said.

Again they lapsed into silence, this time more relaxed as they sipped coffee and watched a humming bird poke about the fuschia basket beyond the blue-checkered curtains at Kate's kitchen window.

"Like hummingbirds," Kate mused.

"What?"

"They're like hummingbirds. Ever notice how they just flit from flower to flower, sip honey until it's gone then move on?"

"Never much noticed hummingbirds, but I guess you're right."

After another spell of quiet, Annette ventured the big question. "Kate, did you really love that Pantages fellow? What was he like?"

Kate sat back in her chair. "He was...," she began, then stopped. "Not for print?"

"Not for print."

"He...Alexander was a man of little substance. I can see it now, although he had me fooled back then. He couldn't hold a job, or rather more likely, he *chose* not to hold a job. He wanted to move up. There was only one direction for Alex and that was up."

"But did you really love him? Or were you looking for something else too?"

"Well now, that's a question that deserves pondering. Guess I've had enough time to ponder it — he's been dead fifteen years — no twenty now." Kate got up to pour more coffee. She waited until she sat down again before she continued. She stared at her cup as she spoke.

"Alex and I had a working partnership. He had so many ideas for building his theater empire. I was the entertainer, yes, but I also had the capital. We called it *grubstakes* in the Yukon. I put up the cash and he followed through with the know-how to make it happen, you know, fulfilling the dream, his dream. Yep, his dream with my money." Kate took a bite of coffee cake and another sip of coffee before she continued.

"With the sourdoughs, you put up a grubstake, outfitted the miner and let him dig. With Alex, I put up the money and he built the theaters. We were partners." She put down the cup and watched the hummingbirds for a few minutes. "At least I thought we were partners."

"You were more than partners, the way I heard the story."

"Don't believe everything you hear, girl. You're a reporter. That's something you should have learned long ago."

"Oh yes. I've been taken a few times, had my ears turn red and my ego bruised. But I learned that lesson rather well. As a journalist, at least. Always check…"

"And recheck."

"Yes, check and recheck your sources."

Kate looked up at her guest and asked, "Do you, did you check my sources?"

"No, Aunt Kate. You *are* the source. I interviewed you. I let you tell me *your* story. That's different."

"Not really. What if everything I told you was a lie, a stretch of the truth?"

"But it's the story you've been telling for years. Nothing has changed. Except the introduction of this new man in your life."

"Oh, he's not so new. I've known Warren for years, twenty or so. He's not new. We're old friends. Old in every way."

The two women giggled.

"Is it?" Annette asked.

"What?"

"The truth. Or is your life made up?"

"My life? No, my life is not made up. Maybe the stories are, though."

Both women pondered that one for a moment as the humming-birds sipped and moved away.

"When you get to my…er…advanced age," Kate went on, "you begin to wonder about the memories, which parts really happened, which did you wish happened."

"You're one of the youngest old people I know," Annette put her hand over Kate's on the table.

"I feel young…sometimes." She patted Annette's hand with her other, then asked her own question of the reporter. "Ever wonder what you'll be like when you're my age?" She gulped before she asked, "Do you ever wonder what you'd say if you could meet yourself as an old…older woman?"

"Not really. I can't imagine even being thirty. Might make a good essay for the paper one day."

"Try it now. See if you can picture yourself at fifty." She looked sheepish, then added, "Sixty."

"Let's see. My hair will be gray, maybe a lovely white like yours. I'd like that. Maybe I'll be more plump — I have to work hard now to keep my weight down." She held up another piece of coffee cake. "I hope I'll have your wisdom and sense of humor."

"I hope you won't have my aches and pains or my heartaches."

"Why do you ask that question, Kate? Did you think about growing old when you were my age?"

"Oh my no. Nothing was further from my mind. It wasn't that I didn't believe I could get old, I just never thought about it. Maybe that's the blessing of youth. You can't — or won't — envision what's up ahead. But when you're old, you can sure look back and see where you've been."

"That's profound, Kate. Have you ever thought about writing down your story? You know, writing essays about what you believe, what you know?"

"Naw. Can't sit still for that long. I have to be out doing. When I get to musing, you know, thinking about the past, I get on my horse..." She laughed again, her throaty self-criticizing laugh. "I mean, I get in my car and drive. Used to have a horse, and riding in the desert was my thinking time."

"Just ride?"

"Yup. Just ride. Now I drive my car out there and sit on a log...or a stone, watching the desert critters slither and scamper around. When you sit real quiet they don't know you're there."

"Never tried that."

"Great way to relax. I sit, then I walk around and look for rocks."

"Rocks?"

"Yes, when the glaciers pushed those mountains up into that range," she nodded at the mountains barely visible through the window, "...or whatever happened, some of the rocks rolled down the sides, in the lower hill country and onto the desert. Look around," Kate got up and motioned for Annette to follow her.

"This fireplace, " she pointed as they entered the parlor. "Built this with rocks from the desert."

"Whoa, that's beautiful. You built it?"

"With my very own hands. Had a fellow stay with me for a spell. He taught me some mason's tricks." She walked to a corner shelf and pointed again. "Found these on some of my joy rides." The shelf contained more rocks, highly polished, in glorious shapes and sizes, some red, yellow, green, blue, orange.

"Kate, they're beautiful. They look like gems."

"Mother Nature did a right good job on these. I did the rest — polishing."

As the two women made their way through the many rooms of Kate's house, Annette saw more specimens of the work of Mother Nature and Miss Kate. One large stone that formed a doorstop in the hallway seemed to have been chiseled.

"Are you a sculptor too?"

"Naw, that was the work of an artist who stayed here once. He tried to make a figure out of it, but he didn't have his tools anymore. Hocked them, I think."

"You had roomers for many years, didn't you?" Annette asked.

"Yes. The only way a single woman could earn a living during the bad days, you know, during the depression. Even then, I put up a lot more people than had money. But we got along somehow."

Kate's eyes lit up with an idea. "Want to go rock hunting?"

"What do you mean?"

"Want to take a spin out into the desert and I'll show you a good place to find rocks. That is, if you don't have anything more pressing to do this afternoon."

"I tried to work this morning," Annette remembered what brought her to Kate, "but I don't have anything I really have to do. Yes, I'd love to go rock hunting with you."

"Come on then. You can leave your purse and stuff here. You won't need lipstick out there."

Annette, who once dreaded the idea of reaching her thirtieth birthday, followed Kate, past seventy, and for an instant considered the notion that growing old wasn't going to be so bad after all. To harbor all that wisdom, all those skills, to live a full life as self-reliantly and sure of herself as Kate seemed to be... yes, that was how Annette wanted to live her life.

The reporter who thought Kate was wasting her life mooning over a lost love had become aware that she, the reporter, was doing the same thing. Now she had found out that while Kate still had a soft spot in her heart for that lost love, she hadn't wasted her whole life over him. Hardly. She apparently was living her life the way she wanted.

"And you can't do that while hanging onto a man," she said aloud.

"Pardon?" Kate turned to her young friend. "Didn't hear what you said."

"Nothing. Didn't say nothing."

They both laughed at the double negative as they closed the door and walked arm in arm to the car.

It's Just an Old Shack

THE HIGH DESERT OF OREGON SITS HIGH above the Columbia River basin, just east of the segment of mountains known as the Cascades. A bit farther west is the snowy tip of Mount Hood, and on a clear, very clear day, from a vantage point, you can see the caps of other enormous mountains in the ancient volcanic chain.

On this bright day in early June, a scattering of clouds hid the mountain peaks, still allowing the glorious sun to shine on two women heading for the desert in a seen-better-days automobile. For much of the ride, they sat in silence, occasionally pointing to a jack rabbit or lizard dashing into the underbrush.

"This fella you're mooning over, anybody I know?" Kate asked at last.

"Promise you won't tell?"

"Naturally. You'd be surprised at the secrets I'm holding," she touched her chest. "Old Aunt Kate has heard 'em all."

"Even a silly reporter and her boss — married boss?"

"More often than you'd imagine," Kate smiled at her friend, looking away from the road.

"You don't mean…"

"Naw, don't know this particular boss and don't know that many reporters, but the scenario is familiar. I kinda thought it might be him. What's his name? Paul?"

"Yes." Annette took a breath at the sound of his name. "Did you ever fall for your boss?"

"Not them bastards…," Kate answered too quickly, then corrected herself, "…those bounders," a Canadian term she had picked up during her days in Dawson. "My bosses, the New York ones especially, all they wanted was a good time, if you know what I mean. Most of them were married only if they got caught, but most of them…no woman wanted.

"I remember a big, cigar-smoking guy at the old Star Theater in New York. Said I could work there if I put out…you know, gratify him…" Kate struggled with a polite phrase the young Annette would understand.

"Put out?" she asked.

"Uh, yes, *put out*. That's what we called it. Don't know what you youngsters call it these days — coming across, heavy petting, making love." As a part of the Yukon crowd, Kate could hold her own with words, but around her home she stayed away from coarse language.

"Did you work there?"

"Sure, I worked there. For almost the entire season, well three months anyway."

"Then you..."

"Not once. Not ever with that poor excuse of a man."

"But how then? How'd you manage?"

"Promises. Promises, my dear. Some men live on promises. I kept promising him his good time, but kept coming up with excuses. Too many people around, wrong time of the month, had a bad cold, my mother was picking me up, had to learn a new dance tune...oh, I kept coming up with some real smashing excuses, and he kept buying them. After a while it got to be a challenge for me. The other girls helped too. Most of them had...put...out..." she said the words slowly, "and he left them alone after that."

Annette was laughing. "Oh Kate, you're really something."

"I was, wasn't I," she agreed.

"And you still are!"

At last, Kate turned the car onto a narrow path and headed away from the road. She drove for a couple of miles before pulling up under what was either a small tree or a large bush. The women got out and stretched their arms over their heads.

"Look at the wild flowers," Annette called into the brisk wind that blew incessantly in the desert. "Every color. Oh they're beautiful." She set about to pick a bunch.

"Flowers are better left here. They wilt too fast. They'll be gone before we get home. Besides, we can enjoy them here, as long as you want." Kate pulled out her tobacco pouch and rolled herself a cigarette. As she put it to her mouth, she asked, "Care for one?"

"No thanks. I have my own. Never could get the hang of rolling those things."

"Only way to get tobacco in the Yukon. Roll your own, smoke a pipe, or do without."

"You're good at that. Did it take you long to learn?"

"Naw, I learn things fast." She inhaled deeply and stared off toward the mountains as she blew out the smoke. "Most things," she added.

Annette lit her own cigarette and stood at her friend's side. "Kate, when you saw Alex after all those years, you know, when he was in court, facing a jury, would you have taken him back if he had asked?"

Kate answered quickly. "No. Definitely no. I don't even have to think about that question. Sure, my knees went weak and my head turned giddy whenever I saw him — I could barely speak — but my brain was still working. I knew then he was a bounder, a cad, a no-good wretch of a man who used people, especially women."

"But you still felt something. What was it?"

"I don't know, honey. I truly don't know. But I do know it wasn't love. I also know it wasn't even lust by that time. Good grief, I was fifty...er, forty-something. I guess I'd have to chalk it up to a good memory that was still connected with my heart."

The two women sat down on a log and smoked their cigarettes as they watched a large hawk circling in the otherwise empty sky. After a moment, Kate offered, "As much as I loved him, as much as I knew he wasn't good for me, as much as I wanted him to suffer as I had suffered...I guess I invoked the Sourdough's Creed..."

"The Sourdough's Creed? What's that?"

"A fair deal. The Sourdough's Creed was an unspoken agreement all us sourdoughs respected. We were all in the adventure together, which meant we wouldn't steal each other's gold or mine prospects. It meant we'd support each other to our dying days. And it meant we wouldn't snitch on each other. Everyone in the Yukon had a secret. We were all hiding out from something or somebody. So our existence depended on us shutting up, wearing masks." Kate closed her eyes, remembering. "And it meant creating versions of ourselves to sell. In a few words, that was what it meant to live...to exist...in the gold mining region of the Yukon."

Again the women were silent watching as the hawk spotted a critter and dived into the brush, soaring back skyward with a small meal in its talons. They watched the bird and its victim until they disappeared into the bright sunlight.

"Yeah, that sounds like what I was going through when I came here, when I met Paul." Annette tapped her cigarette over the vast desert ashtray. "I was in love. The only way I could get past the old love was to seal it off and move on."

The sun was now high in the sky.

"I never told anyone, not even Paul, but my boyfriend and I went together...steady...through high school and half-way through college. I thought we were in love forever, but I was wrong. He found a cheerleader and I was history. Just like that. That's why I quit college." She snapped her fingers.

"So you fell...got up and moved here and then fell again...got involved with Paul on the rebound. Oooh, bad move."

"Yes. Paul actually reminded me of him...Ernie...and..." Her voice trailed off.

"Then look very closely at what you feel for Paul now. Can you name it?"

"Truthfully?"

"Yes."

Annette took her time. "Not love. Not lust. Not even friendship." She looked into space and ran more words past her brain. At length she turned to Kate and admitted, "Truth? It's not anything except memory…and wishes." She got up then, ground out her cigarette and raised her outstretched hands to the sky. "I don't need him at all." The young woman twirled in the sunlight as if to settle everything in sight.

"I'm glad…" Kate began.

"Yes, it's all very clear. I can see it all; I've got my memories for now…and I can accept the loss of Ernie. Oh god, this feels so good. I'm free. I'm free." Annette did a kind of dance around the desert, kicking tumbleweeds and stooping to gather a bunch of desert poppies. "I'm free," she howled, scattering flower petals to the wind.

Kate watched for a moment, then slowly put out her cigarette. She didn't believe that Annette had accomplished anything more than putting on a different mask. Kate pushed herself to a standing position and called to her young friend, "Come on. Got something to show you."

The real reason that Kate brought Annette out to her desert was to make a test. She wanted to know what would happen if someone joined her at the old shack. Would she still find the saloon inside? Would a stranger see it too? Was she hallucinating about the entire experience?

They walked east, the late afternoon sun warming their backs. Annette smiled broadly now, ready for a new experience, ready for a new life, if she had been honest with herself. A few hundred yards off the path, the shack appeared, dimly at first, then larger.

"See it?" Kate asked her friend.

"See what?"

Oh dear, she can't even see the shack. "Over there," Kate pointed. "Over there. Do you see that?"

"No, can't see anything but an old ramshackle lean-to. Looks like it's about to fall down."

"That's it! That's it! You see it."

"Well, sure, but what is it?"

"Come with me." The closer Kate came to the shack, the more cautious she seemed. Was this such a good idea? Would Annette think her crazy if she told her the story? Was there anything to tell other than the wild rantings of an old woman who obviously has lost her mind?

At the door, Kate stopped. "Just one of my old haunts," she lied. "Used to know an old sourdough friend who lived here for a spell, back in the Depression days. Brought him food once in awhile."

Annette walked slowly around the side of the shanty, staying far away from the walls. As she rounded the back, out of Kate's sight, Kate rushed to the door and pushed on it. The door wouldn't budge. She pushed again and again. Something was holding it shut.

"Careful, Kate, the whole thing could fall down if you push too hard," Annette called, appearing from around the corner. "Nobody home, that's for sure."

"Guess not." Kate picked her way off the tiny porch, missing half-rotted boards and avoiding rusty nails sticking out. "Bad idea. Nobody's home. Not anymore."

She never looked back as she and her new friend headed toward the car. *Bad idea*, she told herself over and over again. "Let's go look for rocks," she called to Annette.

PAUL WAITED AT THE *COURIER* OFFICE UNTIL LATE IN THE afternoon. When Annette didn't return, he dropped some papers into his briefcase, locked up and started walking home. At one point he was sure he saw Aunt Kate's old Plymouth speeding through town. Somebody with her, he noticed idly, but couldn't tell who because of the setting sun glinting on the windshield. Besides, at that moment he caught sight of his wife and daughter walking toward him down the street.

"Out for a stroll," Isabel said, bending over for a peck on the cheek from her husband. "Paula missed you. Thought we'd go looking for Daddy."

"Come here, my precious," he greeted Paula and scooped her into his arms.

"Get your books all in order?" Isabel asked.

Good god, I forgot all about those damned books. Now I'll have to do something about it on Monday. Damn and double damn. To his wife he said, "Oh sure, got them started at least. Too much for just one day. Maybe find some time tomorrow."

"Not on Sunday, pet. We've talked about that. The reason you're editing a weekly paper? Remember?"

"Okay, not on Sunday." Paula struggled to hold her dad's briefcase, Isabel linked her arm in her husband's, and the little family turned toward home. "What's for dinner?" Paul asked.

"WHAT DID YOU MEAN WHEN YOU TOLD THAT GIRL YOU weren't in love the day you met Alex in the courthouse? You gave her the impression you were 'too old.' Come on, Aunt Kate. Be honest with yourself at least. Too old for love?"

Kate paced in her kitchen, oblivious of her bad knee, feeling only the ache in her heart where the empty space was. Too old for love! Humph! She had been sipping a cup of coffee and smoking a cigarette. When she stopped to grind out her cigarette in the stone ashtray, her body went still. She stood for a long moment, seeing the pictures in her mind of a woman of twenty in love with Alex, then the woman at forty, even sixty. He was so much a part of her...how could she ever try to tell anyone she was "over" him. She should have told Annette that she felt something for this love of hers long after it was over.

"Ridiculous," she sniffed, turning abruptly and heading for the stairs. She made her way slowly up to her bedroom, but passed it by and opened the closed door at the end of the hallway. Inside, she hobbled directly over to a trunk buried under a pile of winter coats and mufflers.

She knelt slowly. Then she pawed her way down to the worn lid, pulled at the broken lock and opened it. Inside were neatly folded gowns that sparkled and shown through tissue paper. Gently, Kate lifted and moved them aside until she found a blue-checked gingham dress. She carefully withdrew it and closed the trunk lid.

She held the dress close to her body as she braced against the trunk to help herself back to her feet. She carried the treasure to her room and spread it out on the bed. Her fingers remembered the moves that changed her clothing into the girlish-styled gingham costume. She had to squeeze the middle buttons to put it on, but the dress fit her remarkably well. After all, she hadn't worn it in a half century.

Kate smiled at her reflection in the mirror. "Not bad for an old broad," she grinned at herself, turning to get a look at both sides and back. "Not bad."

Then she began to sway, moving her feet just enough to keep time to the music that had begun in her head. It began as "I feel pretty..." but moved back in time to "Daisy, Daisy, give me your answer do..." Aloud she continued singing the familiar old song, strutting back and forth in front of the mirror, gesturing with her arms and dancing simple small steps as the long full skirt swirled about her still-shapely legs.

"And you'll look sweet upon the seat..." a deep male voice joins her singing. Kate feels the stinging sensation in her eyes as she sees the shadowing reflection behind her. Alex! There, off-stage, singing along with her as she entertains the sourdoughs, is the most beautiful man Kate has ever seen. His dark eyes sparkle with mischief as he brushes the unruly shock of black hair from his Greek forehead. His mouth forms the words to the song as if they were warm syrup poured over freshly made pancakes.

That's how they had met. How could she have forgotten? She turns, half expecting the shadow to disappear.

But there he is, tall and young and very handsome in his starchy white shirt, bow tie and bartender's apron. No one else is in the room as Kate continues to sing the light ditty about a bicycle built for two. Alex sings along, but not as loudly as at first. Once he catches her attention, his voice relaxes under the sounds of the saloon.

Kate finishes the song and takes a long bow. A few gold nuggets are tossed on stage for this newcomer to the Yukon, mostly out of courtesy. The girl has sung her song and she's pretty enough, but she's new. The sourdoughs withhold their generosity until they know her better.

As Kate exits offstage opposite Alex, she slows her walk back to the dressing room, hoping he'll catch up to her. She is almost there when the strong arm shoots out in front of her, blocking her path. "Hello, Miss...Miss...didn't get your name."

"Kitty," she replies, her eyes on her shoes.

"You sing very well, Miss Kitty," his words stream from his mouth in low tones, the Greek accent adding flavor.

"Thank you, Mr....Mr....ah, I didn't get your..."

"Alex. Alexander..."

"As in Alexander the Great?"

"Precisely. But you may call me Alex."

Kate coos softly, "Well, Alex, as fine a singer as you are, and as friendly a fellow as you are, I feel it my place to tell you..." her tone turns stony as she concludes, "if you ever cut into my act again while I'm on stage, I'll have you fired. Do you understand me?" There is murder in her eyes as she tosses her red curls, shoves his arm out of the way, pushes open the door to her dressing room and slams it behind her.

In less than a dozen or so hours the two of them are strolling in the summer meadow that surrounds the mining town of Dawson City. They hold hands, gaze at each other, and speak sweet words of dreams and desires. They sit amid the blooming gentians and wild roses as Alex weaves a crown for her. He places it on her head before he pulls her toward him and kisses her willing mouth.

Ever after, even into her aching bones fifty years later, she would feel that kiss and know deep inside her that this was the man she would love forever.

THESE PHOTOS are of Kitty, the very young Klondike Kate. They may have been taken when Kate Rockwell was a dancer in New York, before she headed for the Yukon. Circa 1900. — Photos courtesy of University of Alaska Fairbanks. Photo at left from C. Waugamoin Collection. Photo below from Barrette Willoughby Collection.

KLONDIKE KATE'S GOWNS were expensive, most of them ordered from Paris. The dress above is believed to be the $1,500 gown she wore on New Year's Eve 1900 and again thirty years later to a sourdoughs' reunion celebration. The mummy wrap dress, at right, was a costume for a seductive dance where Kate was "unwrapped" by a happy sourdough miner.
—Photo above courtesy of the Deschutes County Historical Society, Bend, Oregon. Photo at right courtesy of the Yukon Archives, Whitehorse, Alaska.

EVER THE "PROPER" LADY,
Klondike Kate donned tights
and elegant costumes for her
provocative dancing. The outfit
at right was an elaborate
concoction of satin, pearls and
feathers. The costume below
was described as her Queen of
the Yukon dress. In 2000 it was
replicated for a display
celebrating the Yukon Gold
Rush Centennial at the
Washington State Museum in
Tacoma, Washington. Both
were considered daring for the
times. —Photo at right
courtesy of University of
Alaska. Photo below courtesy
of Yukon Archives and Alaska
Sportsman magazine.

SAUCY KITTY,
Queen of the
Yukon...

—Photos courtesy of Yukon Archives

...or sweet
AUNT KATE?

KATHLEEN ROCKWELL played out her role as Klondike Kate from her "crowning" in 1900 until her death in 1957. "Mush On and Smile" was her personal motto. —Photos this page courtesy of Deschutes County Historical Society, Bend, Oregon.

KATE WAS A PERFORMER — always on stage, especially when cameras were present. Above left was taken about the time of Alexander Pantages' trial (1929). Upper right is a typical postcard that Kate kept on hand for fans. It shows her "leading the band" at the first Eugene (Oregon) Pageant. Below, Kate is shown with Janet Blair, who starred in a movie about Klondike Kate. —Photos upper left and below, courtesy of Yukon Archieves. Photo above right is courtesy of Deschutes County Historical Society, Bend, Oregon.

KATE LOVED to display her gold, most of which she collected when she performed in the dancehalls in Dawson. Upper right, she holds her precious necklace of gold nuggets, with extras scattered in front of her. Below right she and last husband, William VanDuren, enjoy the jingle of the assayer's scale. They were looking for uranium on their property in Sweet Home, Oregon in 1956. Bottom photo was taken at the wedding of Kate and Johnny Matson, her "yam and yelly" man in 1933.

—Photos courtesy of Yukon Archives.

Iondike Kate Homestead near Brothers.

THE SHACK in the story was not all imagination. A bit of searching turned up these photos of Kate Rockwell's homestead at a place called Brothers, Oregon, near Bend. This site has long ago returned to sage brush, sand, wind and the little critters of the high desert. —Photos courtesy of the Deschutes County Historical Society, Bend, Oregon.

Klondike Kate Barn near Brothers.

It Takes Time For a Wedding!

NEARLY A WEEK PASSED BEFORE KATE thought again about the shack, other than a few passing reminders of the very-stuck door. Strangers not allowed, she had decided as she re-folded the gingham dress and placed it back in the trunk. The memory filled the void for a few days, then she busied herself with plans for Warren's next visit.

The groom came to call the following Sunday, bringing her a bouquet of roses and a request for a small quiet wedding...on the twenty-fifth.

"Nice article they printed about you," he said, picking up the latest *Courier* with Kate's radiant face smiling back at him. He put his glasses over his ears and read the story, start to finish, before looking over at Kate.

"Says here we're getting married on the seventeenth. That's next week. Misprint?"

"Dear me, did she get the wrong date in there. I definitely told her the twenty-fifth. Must be a misprint."

"Does that mean we won't have the public poking their noses in at our wedding?" he asked.

"Looks that way. They'll be ready to poke their noses on the seventeenth and we won't be doing anything special." Kate laughed her hearty laugh, but Warren continued to scowl. "Maybe they'll print a correction in next week's paper," she suggested. "Always love it when a paper makes a mistake. We get double the publicity when they have to print more about it."

"Kate," her fiancé looked at her and accused, "you planned this. You purposely gave them the wrong date."

"Who, me?" Kate tried to sound demure, innocent. "Little old me?"

"Don't pull that Yukon dancehall girl act with me, my love." The Portland attorney was smiling, but his voice had an edge of displeasure. "I've got your number."

"I'm sorry, Warren. We had talked about the seventeenth, but…"

"I'm not angry, Kate, just confused. What keeps us putting off the date? You want to marry me, don't you? You said you did."

"Of course, Warren. I said I did and I will."

"Aww now, Kate, nobody's forcing you. You don't sound exactly enthusiastic."

"Do I have to be enthusiastic?"

"Do you have second thoughts?"

"I'm trying, Warren darling. I'm trying to believe I'm doing the right thing. This has nothing to do with my feelings for you — you know I love you dearly. I'm an old woman, for crying out loud. I'm just not sure that you…"

"Don't you worry about me. I know it's right. We've known each other a long time. It's not as though we were marrying strangers. We get along, we have good times. Why not add the comfort of living together now that we have found each other?"

"Comfort? Comfort? Do you want to marry for comfort?"

"That's not what I…"

"Don't you want to marry for joy, excitement, adventure?"

"Er, well…" Warren's face showed his confusion. "Shouldn't older people be looking for comfort? I thought that was a very good thing to be finding."

"Adventure, yes, that's it. Let's have a marriage of adventure. We can discover new things about Oregon, about the world, about each other. We can travel and find out how other people live. We can…"

"Oh boy," Warren looked uneasy. "What is happening here?"

"I'm looking into our future. I see adventure and joy. What do you see when you look?"

"Well, I…uh…see two people enjoying each other's company, sharing our problems and our troubles. I see us as the patriarch and matriarch of our families."

"Whew! That's a tall order. I didn't know we had problems and troubles. And I'm not at all sure I want to be a matriarch." She stretched her neck and lifted her chin majestically.

"Kate, you're making fun of me."

"No I'm not. I just have been wondering if we have the same

picture of marriage in front of us. This begins to look like we don't."

"Of course we do. We'll go on living our lives. You'll make appearances as Klondike Kate and I'll go to my office and…"

"I don't think I want to make any more *appearances*. I may be about ready to retire the title, as they say."

"What's this?"

"I'm beginning to think I'd like to be a housewife, a community leader, someone who is regarded as somebody special rather than an oddity. Warren, I believe I'm ready to get rid of Klondike Kate."

Warren looked at her as if she had been speaking Russian. He had no idea what she was talking about. "Of course you'll be a housewife. We'll be community leaders together. And you'll always be somebody special. An oddity! My word, Kate, whatever are you talking about?"

Kate didn't answer right away. Maybe that was as close as they'd get to understanding each other. Maybe that was as much as she could expect.

"But I would like to travel a bit," she offered weakly.

"And travel we will. For our honeymoon, we'll go any place you'd like. Reno, Las Vegas, Phoenix, although I hear it's rather hot down there. Maybe the Grand Canyon."

"I was thinking more of Paris, the Nile, Athens or Rome. What do you think?"

"Hmmm. All right. Which? or all of them?"

"Can we afford all?"

"Not quite. Perhaps I could manage a tour around Europe, a few of the capitals, for two, three weeks. I understand most of the war damage has been cleaned up and they're letting tourists back."

"Oooh that would be wonderful." Maybe there was something to be gained by this marriage after all. "I'll call the paper tomorrow and get them to correct the date. The twenty-fifth of June."

When Warren left that night, he had promised to book a honeymoon trip to Europe. Kate had promised to secure a chapel, order some wine, food and flowers for a reception, and find someone to sing at the ceremony. *Maybe I'll ask Annette to be my attendant; And Warren can ask his brother to be the other witness.*

Kate knew this marriage to Warren was a good thing. It was just that when she was alone she kept having those recurring pictures of Alex. But after spending a few hours with Warren, she could convince herself this was her future — and a good one at that. Yes, she definitely would get going on the wedding plans...tomorrow.

Kate spent the early days of the week carrying out her marching orders. She found a small chapel at the Methodist Church with a basement room for the reception. She called three florists before she found one that would supply white lilies in June, and dickered with the church ladies to cater the food. "No wine in the church," they said, forcing Kate to cancel her wine order at the store. The punch would be made of sparkling cider.

It was Thursday before Kate thought again of the shack. She backed the car out of the driveway early in the morning and took off. She felt enthused, confident of the future, and eager to collect a few new rocks for a wedding present for Warren. She would work them into a monument for his garden, a small reminder of their wedding day.

The sun was becoming warmer faster these days and she rolled down all the car windows. The wind blew her white mop of hair about her face, and she threw back her head and sang, "Ta-ra-ra-boom dee-aye. Ta-ra-ra-boom dee-aye..." at the top of her lungs. Her free foot tapped at the floorboards, and her accelerator foot pressed on the gas pedal. Dust billowed in wide curls behind her, much like the chiffon in her flame dance dress. "Ta-ra-ra-BOOM..." she continued. One more chorus.

WARREN WAS HUMMING TOO THAT DAY, AS HE WALKED BACK to his office from a successful session with a new client. "Still snagging business for the firm. They can't say I don't pull my weight," he gloated, the freshly signed contract safely tucked into his briefcase.

Even the bigger picture of his life pleased him. After pursuing Kate all these years, she was going to be his at last. While he wasn't exactly sure what he was getting into, he felt a sense of accomplishment. New client, new wife. Maybe I'll even buy me a new tie...no, a suit...a new suit...for the wedding. Yessirree! If he were more limber, the lawyer might have managed a buck-and-wing, right there on the street. If he could sing, he'd have broken out with a chorus of "Ta-ra-ra-boom-dee-aye" all by himself.

Warren Thompson, groom-to-be, opted instead for the idea of a new suit. He'd make time tomorrow...or maybe Monday.

He had just finished translating his mental note onto his calendar when the buzzer on his desk sounded and the door opened, simultaneously. "Your son to see you," came the message over the intercom.

"What the hell are you up to now, old man?" came his son's voice as the young man burst into the room.

"Good day to you too, Willis," the father said politely.

"Damn your good day. What the hell does this mean?" the young man held up a copy of the Portland newspaper. Warren had to reach for his glasses, then scan the page before he found the item: "Portland Attorney to Wed Klondike Kate."

Peering over his glasses at his son, Warren asked, "And...what's your point?"

"My point? My point? What do you think you're doing, getting cozy with that money-hungry witch? All she wants is your money, and you know that."

Warren usually was willing to let a complainer exhaust his remonstrations before breaking in, but today he couldn't hold back. "Now see here, Willis. What I do is my own business...," he began.

"Not when it involves your estate."

"I'm not dead yet."

"I mean your lifetime savings, your house, your car, mother's memory."

"Ah, is that it? You think I'm defiling your mother's memory?"

"She's only been gone a short time..."

"Ten years. Willis, come here, son..."

"No, don't touch me. Don't work your wily persuasion on me. That money-grubbing witch is out to take you for all you're worth. Then she'll dump you. Like...like..." Willis couldn't remember the name of any of Kate's husbands.

"Kate has never dumped her husband. She's never taken anyone for their money...well...at least since she left the Yukon."

"You see? That's what she does...did. She fleeces guys."

"Willis. You've never met the lady..."

"Lady, hummph!"

"You've never met Kate. I think you'd actually like her."

The young man and his father faced each other stubbornly, their similar chins stuck out in pure Thompson fashion. "Tell you what," Warren began after a few moments. "I'll invite Kate here this weekend. Bring your latest tootsie and I'll invite your sister Joan and her family and we'll have dinner together, Sunday evening. How about it?"

"No. Definitely not. I won't be in the same room with her. I'd be afraid she'd pick my pockets." He turned away from his dad. Then he swung around and asked, "Tootsie?" The two men laughed then, and threw their arms about each other in an uncomfortable hug.

"Oh all right. But I'll show you she's out for your money."

"Will, what are you planning? Don't do anything you'll be sorry for after she becomes my wife."

"Just the sound of that. Your *wife*, Dad," Willis was almost whining. "Da-a-a-d!"

"Sunday night. My house. I'll have Mrs. Burkhardt cook us up a fine dinner. Bring your...new friend...and I'll call Joan now."

"Okay, dad. But I'm not promising anything."

Alone again, Warren picked up the phone and called Kate. She didn't answer. He dialed his daughter. She'd be home at this time of day, preparing supper for her family.

"Hi, Kitten, how're my favorite grandchildren?"

"Your *only* grandchildren, Dad, and they're fine. Jeremy fell on his bike and took some skin off his arm, but he's all right. Melissa is learning to help Mommy cook. Isn't that sweet?"

"Sweet. Yes. I'm calling to invite you, Jeff and the children to meet my intended."

"Your intended?"

"Oh, then Willis hasn't been in touch."

"No..."

"And you don't read the newspapers..."

"No. Dad, what's going on?"

"Well, I've asked Kate Rockwell to marry me. And she's agreed. And the wedding is set for June twenty-fifth."

"Dad, what a surprise. And who, may I ask, is Kate Rockford?"

"Rockwell, you know, Klondike Kate."

"Oh my god. Tell me you're joking."

"Joan! You too?"

"Willie doesn't approve?"

"He's withholding judgment until Sunday night. Will you and Jeff bring the kids and come to supper? Six o'clock, my place. No need to bring a brown bag. Mrs. Burkhardt is cooking."

"Dad, that was only once. And you'll never let me forget, will you?"

"Six o'clock. Bring your family and a very open mind. You'll love her. She's bright, she's beautiful, she's a peach."

"Dad, you almost sound like a man in love."

"Almost? I crossed the line long ago. Yes, I am in love."

"Then I approve."

"I'm not asking for your approval, but thanks. I hope the two of you will hit it off. I won't say you're a bit like her, but I will say that I think you'll get along."

"I'm sure we will."

"Your brother isn't that sure. Anyhow, thanks for the support."

When he hung up this time, he consulted his address book and called Mrs. Burkhardt to make Sunday arrangements. "Keep things simple, Milady," he urged, "simple but nice. I'm introducing my bride to my children."

"Congratulations, Judge. You deserve a good woman. Sorry that this one is all spoken for." Mrs. Burkhardt was a friend of Warren's late wife and had kept house for Warren since Lillian's death. She liked to call him Judge, just as he called her Milady. They were good friends, even though Warren had met her husband only twice.

"Too much excitement for one day," Warren declared about four o'clock. *Think I'll go looking for that suit, then go home. I'll try to call Kate again this evening.* As he tidied up his desk, he fingered the photo of his family, Lillian looking young and vibrant, Joan looking more like her mother than ever, and young Willis, still wearing knickers. "Weren't we a splendid family? Right out of Sinclair Lewis."

KATE KNEW THE WAY TO THE SHACK IN THE DESERT AS WELL as she knew the way to a man's heart. The sun was bright. After three choruses of Ta-ra-ra-boom-dee-aye, she hummed the throbbing refrains of Ravel, the music she heard when she did her exotic flame dance. Her body remembered every phrase and swayed with the music as she moved the steering wheel from side to side. An eagle flying overhead might have witnessed a Plymouth dancing in the desert.

Did I spoil things by bringing Annette here? She approached the turnoff. *Did I imagine the whole thing? How can a saloon from my past fit into a broken-down bunch of boards?* The questions raced through her head, questions she wouldn't have asked aloud because she didn't want to know the answers.

She still was humming when she parked the car and approached the shack. Apparition or not, Kate knew what had happened before was real. *Today is real. I'm alive.* She felt the warmth of the sun, smelled the rotting old lumber, and heard the screech of hawks soaring high in the clear desert air. *If all my other senses are working, why not the eyes too?*

At the door to the shack, she hesitated. But only for a second. She could hear the music inside and easily pushed open the door.

This time she walks past the bar, looking for Alex out of the corner of her eye, and not finding him. The light of the oil lamps shimmers amid the smoky haze, presenting a surreal picture of a very familiar scene.

Kate stands against the wall, taking it all in, shivering at its familiarity. After all, hasn't it been decades since she had lived it? Yet, here it all is, the smell of beer and tobacco smoke and burning oil and sweaty wool and...perfume. Real French perfume. She remembers the scent.

Something else is in the air that wasn't there before. Fir boughs are tacked to the walls and strewn across the stage. Warm cider? Does she smell cider?

The piano player begins a new set, starting with "Jingle Bells" and moves on to "Deck the Halls." As Kate watches, the miners settle into their chairs and become quiet. Approaching the stage is an apparition in white, almost like a goddess or an angel. She moves gracefully to the stage and begins to sing, "Adeste Fidelis, vidum triumphante...." The miners join in.

The waiters set out another round of cider and beer. The miners, the saloon girls, even the waiters sing "Away in a Manger." Eyes begin to find tears that had long been missing, frozen in the Yukon gold mines. The beautiful Kitty leads the singing from the stage, leaning over to sing directly to one miner then another, moving her slender arms as if to direct her motley choir.

Before the next song, an old miner climbs carefully onto the stage and motions for Kitty to lower her head. Between his hands he carries a crown of candles, set into a roughly-fashioned circle of tin. She bows, half-kneeling before him, and the old man, eyes red with memory, places it gently atop her red ringlets.

"Thank you, Yonny, my sweet yam and yelly man." Kitty kisses the forehead of the old miner then stands up, slowly, balancing the crown atop her head. More than fifty lighted candles give her flaming hair an angelic glow. The only sound in the room is a chair scraping and a husky cough, a lonely miner catching the sobs that well inside him. The vision of Kitty, all dressed in white and glowing with the magic crown, silences them all.

Then a single voice bellows, "Klondike Kate, Queen of the Yukon." And then the cries reverberates through the room. "Queen of the Yukon." "Our queen." "Our Katie."

Kitty grabs the moment and motions to the piano player. He

begins to play "Silent Night." Her cherubic voice rings out clearly in the warm smoky air. No one stirs, a few voices join her, and she nearly breaks into tears herself as the entire room stands to complete the song, "...Sleep in heavenly peace."

The piano starts up again and the next song is brighter, another chorus of "Jingle Bells." Now, balancing the crown of candles, she walks down the steps to where the men sit. She glides from one table to another, greeting each man, smiling and patting shoulders, shaking hands, wishing everyone a happy new year, 1900, a happy new century.

Just as she finishes her round, the piano player motions for her to take the stage again. Whistles and foot stomping from the crowd bring the mood back up.

"Merry Christmas, everyone," calls the girlish voice from the stage.

"Merry Christmas, Kate," comes the response from the audience.

"And Happy New Year," she calls. "Welcome to the year 1900. Welcome to the twentieth century."

A shout goes up from the floor. Hats are thrown into the air. The men grab the nearest girl, fighting each other to be first for a New Year's kiss, and the piano strikes up Auld Lang Syne.

The men dance then, some with girls, some with each other, and they drink whiskey and cider and beer, and they hoot and they cry and they tell jokes and they swat each other on the back and they dream of the riches that will be theirs during the coming twelve months.

From her vantage place against the wall, Kate watches it all…and remembers. Her hopes are as high as everyone else's for the future. Kitty swaggers over toward her, reeling from drink, excitement, the warmth of the room and the weight of the candles on her head. Kate catches hold of her hand and pulls her aside. Some of the candles have gone out. Others continue to burn, dripping melted wax into her hair. Her eyes tell Kate that the girl has had too much to drink and probably hasn't eaten in hours.

"Happy New Year, my ghost of Christmas Future," Kitty manages, giddy at the sight of the older woman. "Happy New Century!" She sways and then falls into a chair. Kate pulls up another chair and sits beside her.

"You're a mess," she tells the girl.

"Well, it's been a long night," the girl returns.

"Better slow up on the booze. Where's Alex?"

"Supposed to be working at the bar…but…" She puts her hand to her forehead and catches a drop of wax on her fingers. "These candles are ruining my hair. But I don't care. Did you hear what they called me? Queen of the Yukon. I'm their queen. Isn't that something! Queen of the Yukon, the whole damned territory."

"Kitty. Watch your mouth. God, you're really tipsy."

"Let's go find Alex. Letsh wiss him a Happy New Year. No, we'll *wish* him a Happy Happy."

"Let's just sit here a moment."

"I want to find Alex. Life is so good. We're getting ready to open a new theater. Did you know that? A new theater. Our wedding. Our…" Kitty pats her tummy, but won't say the words. "The new century looks pretty good for little Eloise Rockwell from Junction City, Kansas."

"Yeah, pretty good," Kate echoes.

Men file past their beloved Kitty and continue to wish her well. She greets each by name, squeezes their hands and plants kisses on their grizzly cheeks.

"Happy New Year, Johnny," Kitty whispers to the smallish man who crowned his queen earlier. He shyly takes her kiss. His eyes blink as he softly says, "I vish yew a happy year too, Missie. I vish you all da very best in da vorld." He can't take his eyes away from her face, framed in candlelight and glowing from too much wine.

Kate expels a single word, "Yonny," but Johnny Matson doesn't notice.

"Johnny's my yam and yelly man," Kitty teases, directing her comment to Kate. "We love each other, don't we Yonny?"

"Ya sure," he grins at her, then shyly beats a retreat.

Kate can't resist. "That's some fellow, Kitty girl. Why don't you snap him up? He's in love with you, can't you tell?"

"Ya sure," she mimics the miner. "Ya sure, Johnny Matson's a catch all right."

Kate sits with Kitty, remembering the revelry of that momentous night when the world turned into a new century. Such hopes. Such dreams. Such imaginations. People talk about flying through the air, about sending messages without wires, about wagons that have motors that don't need horses, about a new power source called electricity that will light up the world.

In Dawson, Yukon Territory, talk is more about shortcuts to finding gold, easier ways to get it out of the ground, better ways to bring in the gold, and better, faster ways to spend their newfound wealth.

Alex dreams of better ways to relieve the miners of their gold, of bigger dance halls, of theaters that offer bigger and better entertainment. Kitty wishes for Alex to acknowledge their relationship with a real wedding. Her baby will be born in this magical new first year of the century. What better promise than that to give a child?

Kate takes Kitty's hand and holds onto it. "You'll be all right, my girl," she says softly. Kitty nods.

"I know. I have Alex to take care of me."

"Ya sure," Kate grins at her. "You have Alex."

Then Kitty stands up, smoothes out her dress with her hands, pats her drooping red curls, straightens her crown of dripping candles, and moves off into the crowd, the flames wavering just a little as she totters ever so slightly. "Gotta see to my subjects," she calls to Kate over her shoulder.

Kate closes her eyes. Queen of the Yukon. Yes, she deserves that. She is good — at performing, at making the men feel relaxed enough to spend their money, at giving them respite in their hard lives. Wait a minute. Hard lives? Didn't they choose this? Didn't I choose this? We're having fun. We're enjoying ourselves.

Kate looks about the smoky room. The men slouch where they sit or shuffle across the dance floor with closed eyes or sprawl against the wall unconscious with drink. The few women are being pawed by drunken men, their feet stepped on as they dance, their gowns ruined by spilled drinks. Yeah, we're having fun.

And Alex is having fun too, with that blond new arrival, back in Kitty's dressing room.

"Yeah, we sure did have fun," Kate says aloud. The brightness of the sunlight and the heat on her face force her eyes open.

She stood in front of the old shack, the hot desert air swirling about her head. Dazed, she stumbled to the car and got in. She drove with all the windows rolled down, gasping for a breath of air. It was so easy to breathe in the far North. The air was clear and cold and...just the thought opened her lungs and she gulped in new air.

Queen of the Yukon, she mused. The prettiest, most glamorous, the perfect lady, a wonder to behold. Boy, I was something, wasn't I! She hummed, "Should auld acquaintance be forgot..." as she drove back to her home on a hill hundreds of miles south of Dawson.

KATE WAS PREPARING FOR BED WHEN THE PHONE RANG. Warren! She made her way downstairs. *He's calling to tell me the wedding's off. He's changed his mind. Well, that's okay. I'm not sure that I want to get tied down again either.* She picked up the receiver.

"Kate?" Warren's voice came through the wires easily. "Kate, you're still up. I've been trying to call you, some kind of trouble on the lines."

"Yes, I'm up, just getting ready for bed." He sounded so close over the phone, his voice nestled so close to her ear.

"Kate. How was your day? What did you do today?"

"Just the usual stuff. Gardened a bit, walked to the store, took a drive in the desert."

"A beautiful day for that. Wish I could have been with you. I know how much you love your desert. Find anything?"

"Why do you ask that?"

"Nothing. Just wondering if you found any more rocks to lug home."

"Rocks. Uh, oh, yes, rocks. Of course, don't I always?"

"Answering a question with a question?" He feigned an accusatory tone. "Sends off red lights to a lawyer."

"Did I?"

"You did it again." Then they both laughed.

"Was there a reason you called?"

"To hear your sweet voice." Warren was telling a half truth. "Well, not exactly just that…"

"Something's gone wrong." Kate held her breath and waited for his response.

"No, nothing wrong. Everything's right. I'm calling to invite you to dinner Sunday. I want you to get to know my little ones."

"Little ones? You have little ones?"

"They're not little anymore, but I still think of them that way. I mean Willis and Joan…and Joan's family, her husband Jeff Gillette and their little ones."

"Oh. Why, of course, I'd love to have dinner with all of you. Does this mean you're asking them to approve me?"

"No. You're not up for approval. I've asked you to marry me. They just want…" No, he was putting it badly. "I want…they want to…get to know you better."

"Well, in that case. I'd like to know them better too." Kate heard the sound of Warren's doubts. She wasn't sure she liked it. "Tell you what, I'll take a bus up on Saturday if you'll put me up. Then we can spend a nice long day together."

"A bus? I won't hear of it. I'll drive over and get you. Put you up?" How could he broach this subject delicately? "I have guest rooms in my home and you're more than welcome to…"

"Warren, darling, in a couple weeks we'll be married. No need to stand on ceremony." Kate spoke her mind when she wanted. This was one of those times.

"But for the children's sake…"

"Oh, for the children! Of course. I'll use the guest room."

Now it was Warren who sensed the edge to Kate's voice. "We'll decide that when you get here. No need to settle all our problems tonight. You sound tired. I'll let you go to bed."

"Yes. I'm tired. It's been a long day." She suddenly felt very old, very tired, and just a bit cranky. "I'll look for you Saturday."

"Until Saturday then."

She put down the phone, climbed the stairs, finished her ablutions, and crawled into her soft warm bed, stretching her achy limbs under the covers. Her mind still raced. *Guest room. Ha! Don't know how much mischief we could get into even sleeping in one bed. God, it's been a long time since I've felt a man beside me.*

WARREN SHOWED UP ABOUT NOON ON SATURDAY IN A pouring rain. Kate fed him a fresh ham and cheese sandwich and a cup of tea before they left for Portland. On the way out of town, she noticed the lights in the *Courier* office and two people standing near the door. Annette and her boss?

"You can't run out in this rain," Paul caught Annette's arm as she tried to escape.

"Oh yes I can. Watch me. I won't melt."

"Annette, please. Just hear me out."

"I've heard too much already. I don't want to hear any more."

"Annette, please." She tried to wiggle out of his grasp, but he just pulled her closer. "Annette, I can't lose you. You're everything to me."

"No I'm not. Your family is everything to you. And I'm a distraction, a dalliance."

Paul leaned his head to the side, "A dalliance? That's a word from the Roaring Twenties. Dalliance, indeed!"

"Dalliance. Indeed. Two words from the Twenties." They were close to laughing, but not quite. "We're even. Now let me go so I can catch the bus to Portland."

"You're not taking your car?"

"No. I don't want anything to remind me of this godforsaken place. Besides, I don't think it will make any more long trips. Not worth a thing to me. Nothing in this town is." She glared at him. His eyes pleaded with her.

"Annette, sit down. Just for a moment. Let me explain…"

"You've explained very well already. Isabel wants you to sack me. You want to keep Isabel. So, you give me this song and dance about respecting me and honoring me and wanting me to make the best of my life. Then you suggest I find work someplace else. That's explanation! Except that it doesn't explain why you can't keep your hands off me. Why we spend so much time together. Why we enjoy being together. Maybe even love each other."

Annette slumped into the nearest chair. She looked up at Paul, her eyes now pleading, looking for the glint that first drew him to her. "I just can't understand that. It all seems to come to 'Annette, look for another job. Annette, get out of here.' Well, I'm going." She stood up and headed for the door again. "And don't try to stop me."

She pulled open the door and walked into the rain. "Goodbye Paul," she called over her shoulder, hunched now to protect herself from the rain. Nothing, it seemed, would protect her from her feelings for him.

Paul hesitated before dashing out after her. "Annette, wait. Don't go. I can't live in a world without you. I have to see your adorable face every day or I'll go out of my mind. Please stay. I didn't mean all that. It's just that Isabel...I mean, I thought it would be easier on you. Oh, I'm saying this all wrong." He held her shoulders as they stared into each other's eyes, trying to find a solution to their dilemma. Then he added the words, "I love you, Annette. Please don't leave me."

The rain poured over them, making their skin glisten, their faces soft in the dim light of the storm. "I...love...you," he said again, deliberately, slowly.

"I'm sorry, Paul. I..." How could she explain what she was feeling, the longing for him mixed with the realization she didn't need him? How did Kate put it? "You don't need a man to make you happy. You only need to make yourself happy."

"I don't need you. I can be happy on my own. Go back to your Isabel and your kids and have some more and make them all happy. I'll be..." She didn't wait to finish her sentence before she turned and walked down the street to where her old jalopy was parked. The engine finally turned over and she drove back to her apartment.

By the time Kate and Warren reached Portland, the sun was setting. They stopped at a small restaurant just outside the city and enjoyed a Chateaubriand steak with mushrooms for two. They finished off a bottle of red wine from the Willamette Valley and made small talk. Warren talked mostly about his kids growing up, their antics, their missteps. Kate offered a bit of her growing up years, the mischief she raised in the school run by nuns, the pain of losing her father, the decency of the judge who became her new dad.

"You must have felt very lonely, losing your dad, then trying to accept almost a stranger as your father," Warren suggested.

"Never thought of me as lonely, but I guess you're right. I missed my dad, even if Mother didn't. The judge tried hard to give me things. Guess he expected me to come around and treat him like a father. He was gruff, as I remember. Didn't have much to do with children. But Mother loved him, or at least said she did long enough to get him to marry her." Was she suggesting that she herself was acting like her mother? Was she after Warren to marry her for some sort of old age security?

"When I was twelve — they sent me to a boarding school just outside Spokane. A very nice school, but strict. Run by nuns. Does that give you the picture?" She smiled at Warren who seemed to understand the plight of a girl being dragged into her mother's marriage problems.

"We were constantly playing tricks on them — the nuns — leaving stacks of linen in the chapel, turning off the hot water in the nuns' showers, changing the assignments on the blackboards... childish stuff, but it kept us amused."

"You didn't like school?"

"I hated it. They wanted me to learn stuff I had no interest in. I'd much rather have worked off my hormones in a game of volleyball. Or taken classes in French so I could travel. Or studied ballet and opera and...and...vaudeville. We were always putting on plays, but the Sisters didn't approve of our interpretations. I remember..."

"More coffee?" the waiter interrupted.

"No thanks," Warren told him. "We're about to leave. Shall we?" he nodded at Kate. "It's getting late."

Kate put out her cigarette, dabbed at her mouth with her napkin and gathered up her purse. "Off to see the wizard," she announced gaily as she took Warren's arm and allowed herself to be escorted through the restaurant. She smiled graciously into people's eyes as she passed their tables, just in case they recognized her and were too polite to say so.

At home, Warren carried Kate's small overnight bag to her room and deposited it on the bed. "You should be comfortable here," he said matter-of-factly. "This room catches the morning sun, if there is any."

"Where is your room, my love?" Kate asked, the glow of the wine adding warmth to her low voice.

"Just across the hall. If you need anything..."

"I need you," she said, suddenly wrapping her arms around him. She felt him stiffen, but she held on.

"Kate...we don't...you...don't..." His words wouldn't come out.

"You're not going to get all stodgy on me now, are you? After all, we'll be married very shortly. Don't you want to know who you're marrying? I love you, Warren. And you love me. What's more natural?"

"Kate, oh Kate." He was giving in. All his thoughts had been on what would the children say? Now they turned to his own feelings, his love for this woman. After all, they were grownups in his house alone...together.

"I'll give you a few minutes," he said, lightly kissing her forehead. He left her to prepare for bed.

Kate slipped into a silk nightie; she never wore anything other than silk to bed. She waved a matching negligee over her shoulders and walked boldly across the hall. "Get ready, mister, to spend the night with Klondike Kate, Queen of the Yukon," she whispered. Aloud, she called, "Warren, are you ready?"

When the morning sun entered the guest room, all it found was the still-made-up bed. Kate and Warren languished in the big bed across the hall, soothed by a night of love, sleeping in each other's arms.

Warren was surprised that he felt so good about having spent the night with Kate. She was someone special and now he knew why. As they dressed to go downstairs for breakfast, he was not thinking about his children.

It wasn't until after they had begun to eat breakfast he remembered. "I was supposed to meet them for church this morning. I don't even feel guilty for that," he told Kate sheepishly. "I feel wonderful. Oh, Kate, we'll have such a good time for the rest of our lives."

Kate had heard that phrase, "the rest of our lives," before. But she had never believed it. But here she was, nearing the "rest of her life" and planning to do something good with it. Was this what she had been looking for — a good man beside her, a friendly face to look at in the morning, a loving face to fall asleep with at night?

Kate held that picture for a moment. *The rest of our lives....* Then, where spaces of shadow had existed before inside her, the brilliant morning sun suddenly lit up and the shadows disappeared. She whispered his words back, "Yes, we'll have such a good time for the rest of our lives."

A Woman Is a Woman
After All

IN EVERY SOCIETY THERE ARE ALWAYS THOSE WHO LIKE to tell others how to behave. In the 1800s, it was Queen Victoria and her admirers. What evolved was a very staid, prim and proper society that combined dandy, elegantly turned-out men with fashionably corseted, well-covered women. Since clothes determine activity by their freedom or restriction, Victorian women were censored in almost every department. They could barely walk, much less sit. At rest, they crossed their ankles, rather than legs. They spoke softly, never drew attention to themselves, would never consider exposing any part of their body other than their lovely faces and graceful hands.

By the late 1800s, women were further encumbered by padding on their bottoms that resembled back porches and were called bustles.

For women to manage long, full skirts was difficult enough, but the bustles made movement even more difficult. Add to restrictive clothing the restrictive mores, and society bred a generation or two of very inhibited women, afraid to incense their husbands, families and neighbors, fearful of incurring the judgmental glances of everyone around them, longing to express their natural free spirits, and guilt-ridden for hating it all.

Kate Rockwell was a product of that era. By the time she had grown into an old woman, society had shortened women's skirts, had gotten used to women exposing their arms and legs in public, and had weathered one generation of bob-haired flappers, followed by another of jitterbugs and war workers. Women, who thought they had been released from societal restraints following each of two world wars, however, soon found themselves back in the apron pockets of someone called Emily Post. Dictates of post-war society became more stringent than an army manual and twice as detailed.

Things like placement of silverware on the table, forks-to-the-left stuff, and who introduces who to whom, and who invites whom, how and when, were made to seem important. Kate had read one of those etiquette books once and couldn't understand a word of it. Since she was educated in some of the West's better schools for girls, she should have picked up some of the finer points along the way. Perhaps she did, but simply chose to ignore them.

However she approached the rules of society, Kate was the one who broke them most easily and probably most often. She cared not a whit for what others thought of her, as long as they admired her looks. She enjoyed men looking at her. She didn't care much about what women thought, mostly because she knew she was more elegant than most of them and more beautiful than all of them.

When she was young, during those Yukon days, the clothes Kate wore were always designed for men to admire and women to envy. They were not cut to expose her body, nor to entice men, simply to play up her soft curves and tall frame. When she left the Yukon, riding horseback to her homestead in Oregon, Kate took with her the only clothes she owned, those fabulous costumes she wore for the miners. It was just a short time before she packed them away and opted to wear clothes that were comfortable.

But suggest that Kate dress up for an occasion, and she pulled out her trunk full of Paris gowns, gold and diamond jewelry, and put them all on. At first, it didn't even take a special occasion other than the one in her head. Have you ever seen a woman grocery shopping in a satin gown of haut couture, diamonds dangling from her ears, gold dripping from her wrists? Kate loved showing off her dazzling Yukon wardrobe.

Still, she knew when to soft-pedal herself. That day, in Warren's home, about to meet Warren's grown children, was one of those times. To meet her new family she dressed in a simple teal blue dress that buttoned to the throat, covered her arms almost to the wrist and had a skirt that fell mid-calf. She combed her softly waved hair away from her face and attached simple gold earrings to her lobes. She dabbed on her lips only a tinge of rouge. Warren and his family would find her acceptable or she'd go down trying.

WARREN'S DAUGHTER AND HER FAMILY ARRIVED FOR DINNER about three o'clock — Joan and Jeff Gillette and their children, Jeremy and Melissa. While the children bounced in and hopped all over their grandfather, Joan stood at the door waiting with her husband to be formally introduced to Kate. Joan was impressed with the tall, graceful white-haired woman smiling at her and could see how her father had fallen for this woman.

Willis, on the other hand, arrived a bit later and glared at Kate, the woman he had called hussy, the woman who was taking his father away from him. He stiffly offered his hand for shaking and he bowed, a caricature of an English nobleman. His eyes looked at her as a lord of the manor would regard his servant. "How nice," he said.

"Well, aren't you the image of your father," Kate responded, holding tight to his hand. "Are you studying law too?"

Willis cleared his throat and tried to retrieve his hand, but she held on. "No. I'm...I'm...an accountant. I tried law school, but...didn't care for it." He tried again to pull away his hand.

"Willis, how nice to meet you at last. Your dad's told me so much about you, I feel I know you already." Kate smiled sweetly. "And your...friend. Warren said you were bringing your...friend." Willis could tell from the way she paused that his father had recounted their last meeting.

"Penny. Oh yes, Penny." Willis used his free hand to point to his friend and offer introductions.

"Penny, what a nice name. Short for Penelope?" Kate smiled at her, but continued to hold Willis' hand.

"Just Penny. I find that nobody knows how to pronounce the

Penelope when they see it spelled. I saw you in the Rose Parade when you were marshal. I'm pleased to meet you."

"So..." Kate looked back at Willis without ackowledging Penny's extended hand. "This is Willis, the accountant, with a friend named Penny. Seems appropriate. I'm going to enjoy being part of this family." She looked deliberately into Willis' eyes and dropped his hand as she turned back to Warren.

The older man reached over the heads of his clinging grandchildren and took Kate's arm. "I think Mrs. Burkhardt is ready with dinner. Let's find our places." Jeremy and Melissa held his legs as he pulled them into the dining room. Kate walked by his side, elegantly leading the parade. She managed only a few words out the side of her mouth, "They're not so tough, Warren."

Kate never had a tattoo. But she might as well have been covered with them that Sunday in Portland. Willis and Joan glared at her throughout dinner, at the ease she moved about their father's house. She was darned if she would try to explain to them that Warren had picked her up the day before and that she was staying in the guest room, and that she wasn't pulling their father into perdition.

Instead, she used all her finishing school tricks to convince them their father had found himself a catch. She crossed her ankles instead of her legs, she sipped coffee with her pinkie in the air, she took tiny bites and never, never spoke with her mouth full. She was the quintessential lady.

She only guffawed once, when Jeremy piped up and asked, "Is Klondike Kate going to dance for us?"

The child's question and her responsive laugh silenced the family dinner. Heads turned toward Kate, seated at Warren's side.

"Kate doesn't dance much anymore, son," she smiled at the boy. "Perhaps you'd like to dance for us."

Willis guffawed this time. "Boys don't dance for girls," he said jovially patting his nephew on the head.

"But I'm not a *girl*, Willis," Kate corrected him. "Haven't you noticed? I'm a woman. And many a man has danced *for* me and *with* me." She spoke deliberately, in slow husky tones as she looked deep into his eyes. She pronounced each word carefully, as if explaining something to a child. "I used to be a dance hall singer, or didn't you know that?" Willis wiggled uncomfortably in his chair. "I used to earn my living dancing and singing. Why, in one week I could earn several thousand dollars. During just one summer I collected more than a hundred thousand dollars in gold dust and nuggets. The audience threw it at my feet. I had enough money to buy anything I wanted: fine Paris gowns, diamonds — real ones — and pearls. I bought real estate, lands and buildings, and opened my own theater — a couple of them. In case you didn't know, Willis, they called me Queen of the Yukon."

Willis turned his head sheepishly to his sister, asking with his eyes for help. Joan was engrossed in Kate's story. When Kate paused, Joan said, "Imagine, Willie, she's on her own. Doing all those things. Having fun."

"Great way to live your life, isn't it, Joan?" Kate grabbed the opportunity. "Can't imagine being stuck in some stuffy office and working your life away at some grinding job that isn't fun." She glanced at Willis, whose mouth was slightly open.

Warren said nothing, just sat back and watched the jousting with glee. He wouldn't interrupt Kate's moment for anything.

"Tell me again, Willie, about your job." Kate smiled sweetly at the younger man.

"My uncle works in a counting office," young Jeremy piped up. "He's a book man."

"How nice," Kate kept smiling. To Willis she asked, "You keep books for other people, count *their* money." She emphasized the word *their*.

"Er, yeah. That's my job."

"And for fun, what do you do?"

"I golf." He relaxed a bit and went on proudly, "I golf, just like General Eisenhower. Got my game down in the nineties. Go out at least once a week, sometimes twice in summer." Willis blinked. It seemed clear all at once that he lived a very boring life. Keeping other people's books and golfing.

"I never could see the sense of hitting a little ball around a field," Kate dismissed the conversation and turned to Joan. "I do hope you'll bring your lovely children to the wedding. Some people don't like children at such an occasion, but I assure you I'd be delighted. It would mean so much to your father as well."

"Yes, Kate, we'll all be there."

In a spontaneous moment, Kate asked, "And would you be my matron of honor?"

Joan gasped, looked first at her father, then at Willis. Her father smiled. Willis was still lost in a newly discovered resentment for his life. He shrugged his shoulders.

"I'd like that very much," said Joan.

"No fancy gowns, just a pretty dress. Maybe we can get Warren to buy a new one for you."

Willis cringed. He thought to object to his father spending anything more on this woman, but his father spoke first. "Would you be my best man, son?"

"Why, I…well that's…" he sputtered. "Okay. I'll do it."

"Then it's all settled. Our wedding will be a real family affair." Warren had seen his children succumb to Kate's charm. He called out, "Mrs. Burkhardt, is there a dessert in there? I think we're ready."

Fresh strawberries and cream topped off their meal. Afterwards, Warren took Kate aside and said, "I think we've won over Willis. I know we've convinced Joan."

"Joan is a lovely young woman, Warren. You can be very proud of her. She's a good mother and an intelligent person. But I wouldn't count on Willis just yet. He's going along, but I'm not sure he's convinced. He still attaches money to whatever we talk about."

"He'll come around. Who doesn't love you?" He kissed his bride on the forehead and led her out onto the front porch just as Joan appeared.

"You sit down, I'll be right back." Kate excused herself as Warren sat down on the porch swing. The old chains creaked as he pushed himself gently with one foot.

"At last, alone," Joan said, closing the screen door quietly behind her. "Wanted to talk to you alone." She seated herself next to her father on the swing. He stopped rocking.

"What's up, my dear?"

"I'm not sure how to say this. I…we…Jeff and I love Kate. She seems very…nice, very…er, talented…but…"

"But…but what?"

"She isn't like us. She doesn't fit in. Come on, Dad, a saloon singer? Willie says…"

"Willie? Good grief! Kate hasn't performed in thirty years."

"But she did once. Don't you see? What kind of influence will she have on my children?"

"She seems to be doing a good job with that." Warren pointed to the side yard. Kate had used the side door and joined the kids in a game of catch. Melissa and Jeremy and the white-haired woman tossed the ball to each other, ran imaginary bases and cheered each other on.

"But Dad…she's…"

"Not another word. Not one more word, Joan. I love that woman, have for years. If you must know I loved her when I was still married to your mother. Now I'm in a position to do something about it, and I'll be danged if I'll let you and Willis and your selfishness keep me from my Kate."

Warren left the swing to his daughter and moved to the porch rail where he could watch Kate and the children. Joan went back inside the house.

The Thompson children had made it clear they didn't want their father to marry this wild wild woman from eastern Oregon. They were convinced she was looking for a meal ticket in her old age.

"Now if I had been twenty years younger, even forty years younger, they might have accepted me, is that what you're telling me?" Kate asked as Warren drove her back to Homestead the next day.

"It isn't your age, Kate darling, it's…"

"What? It's what, Warren my love?" Kate spit out the words, her anger rising.

"I don't know, Kate. Darn it! They're protective. They're my children. I've raised them, cared for them, given them…values…" he hated that word.

"Values," Kate had caught it. "Values. What does that mean? I'm not good enough for you? Not good enough for a lawyer from Portland?" She was building up a head of steam.

"Kate, maybe we ought to slow down, take our time…"

"Time! We don't have a lot of that, or haven't you noticed. Do you want to marry me or not?"

There is was, right out in the open. Now who was waffling? Kate waited.

Warren took his time to answer. When he did, he had pulled the car over to the side of the road. As the engine idled quietly in the background, he took her hand and said, "You're too good for the likes of me, sweet Kate. I'm your lawyer, remember. I know how you spend your money. I know your generosity, your anonymous gifts to charity. I know who you are, maybe better than anybody else. And I love you. I wish I had my children's blessings, but…"

"You think you know me. You think you know who I am, this giving Aunt Kate from over the hills, this flashy Klondike Kate from up in the gold hills. But is that who I am?" She was talking more to herself than to Warren. "Am I a caricature of a woman, an image dreamed up by a press agent? Maybe they're right. Maybe your kids can see something we can't. I don't think you know me at all. Hell, I don't even know myself."

Kate fell silent, staring blindly at the view from her window. They were in the mountains now and the greenness of it formed a soft backdrop to Kate's mood.

Warren was silent too. Did he, after all, know this woman who sat beside him? Was she the gentle caring motherly Kate who ministered to the down-and-out, who gave generously to her community in an effort to sway their attitudes toward her, to make them accept her? Or was she the selfish, self-centered showgirl basking in the spotlight, demanding attention by stamping her foot…and getting it?

"Maybe we ought to wait," Warren murmured as he shifted the car into gear and continued the drive to Homestead.

At Kate's house, he pulled into the driveway. They sat there in the car, alternately talking and just sitting in silence. Kate could plainly see that Warren was as smitten with her as she was with him. After about an hour she kissed him lightly on the cheek and said, "I love you, you crotchety old goose."

Warren had long ago decided to stay with and protect Kate. His family would have to get used to it. He spent the night there, this time sharing Kate's bed. By the time he left in the morning, plans were underway for their wedding on June twenty-fifth.

"IT'S THE TWENTY-FIFTH. WE HAVE TO PRINT A CORRECTION," Annette waved a copy of the newspaper at Paul.

"I hate printing corrections. Write an update on last week's story. Just write that the date's been changed. Give her a call, get another statement."

"Okay, but take it easy. You'll blow up or something."

Paul had been edgy and moody ever since the weekend. He'd tried to call Annette; she hadn't answered. She had sat watching the phone ring, hoping he would be afraid she'd left town. Let him suffer, like I'm suffering. Let him worry about whether I'm still around.

Paul had even gone to her apartment, knocked on the door until he saw a neighbor peek through the curtain. He left. The rain and clouds didn't help his mood either. As long as he was miserable, those around him suffered. Isabel had gone so far as to ask him to leave the house if he couldn't sweeten up.

In the end, Annette decided to return to work, but keep her distance from Paul.

A weekend without seeing each other had put both Annette and Paul in cranky moods. Now they fumed about the newspaper. Soon they'd fume about their office habits, "Your desk needs clearing." "Don't hang your coat all over the chairs." "Stop tapping your pencil." "You're squeaking your chair again."

By noon they had sent most of the next week's paper to the composing room. "Let Hank do his part before final galley proofing. Come on, Annette. Let's go get a sandwich," Paul offered.

"Can't. I'm working on a new piece for next week."

"Do it later," Paul shouted. "We've got some talking to do. Are you coming or not?"

"No need to shout. If I don't go with you, you'll be talking to yourself." She reached for her sweater as she stood up. "You're buying!"

At Millie's, they sat in a back booth and ordered chicken salad sandwiches and Cokes. Paul had tried to sit next to her, but Annette pointed to the seat across the table. "Anybody could walk in here. Don't want to give our readers the wrong idea about their newspaper editor and his reporter now, do we?"

"You're sarcastic. What do you have to be upset about? I'm the one who spent the weekend worried about you. Where were you? I called. I went to your apartment. I couldn't find you. Do you know how crazy that makes me?"

"Paul, I just..."

"Crazy. That's the word. The exact right correct word. I'm crazy about you, over you, with you, I..."

"Paul, what's the use? Where are we going with this? We don't have a future together, and you know it. She's not going to give you up. And I don't think you want to give up your family."

"I didn't say I would, I just..."

"You want everything, family...and...me?"

"Well, yes...no..." He lowered his head onto his arms on the table for a moment. "I don't know what I want, Annette. I know I want you." His head remained buried in his arms as Annette patted the top of it.

"Poor Paul, poor pitiful perturbed Paul."

"Don't make fun of me, especially not alliterative," came a muffled order.

"Why not, you're pitiful." Annette tapped his head lightly, a kind of cuff behind the ears.

"Ow!" He raised his head. And when he saw the way she was

looking at him, his heart warmed and his complaints were forgotten. "Let's not fight anymore. Let's not fight ever again."

"Were we fighting?" Annette raised her eyebrows innocently. "I don't fight." She paused, then added, "I get even."

"Don't threaten me," Paul was serious again. "Never make threats to me. Do you understand?"

"What?" She was surprised at the sudden vehemence of his voice. "You're angry. Really angry."

"I said, never threaten me." He glared at her.

"I wasn't…we were joking…I'd never…" she couldn't find the right words.

Just as quickly, his eyes softened and he took her hand. "I don't like anything that even sounds like a threat."

"Okay. That's understandable. I don't either."

Millie brought their sandwiches and they set to eating, Annette still confused about the way he had turned on her.

Paul hoped she didn't notice his rush of anger. That threat incident had been years ago, he hadn't thought of her in years — Carol, or was it Karen? He couldn't even remember her name, but he felt he should explain.

"I'm sorry," he said quietly. "There's a reason your threat turned me into a raging idiot."

"Well you didn't have to…"

"There was a girl back in college," he went on, "a girl who made a list of eligible men and sought them out. Karen, yeah, that was her name. Karen discovered that I'd inherit my father's newspapers and she came after me. Annette, she threatened to force a breach of promise suit. So when you started to threaten me, I thought, oh no, not again, not another gold-digger…"

"She must have scared you good," Annette said.

"Scared? I was petrified. If Dad had found out…" Paul stopped. "You knew?"

"Just a gut feeling. You forget, I love you. I'm getting pretty good at figuring out your moods, even your thoughts."

"That's spooky."

They finished their lunch, dawdled over their Cokes until the ice was melted, then paid the bill and walked back to the office.

"Everything's smooth again," Hank called to them. He meant the galleys were ready after he had struggled to make everything fit.

"Yeah, everything's smooth again." Paul smiled at Annette as they returned to their typewriters.

Reality Test

KATE MULLED ABOUT THE HOUSE, WATERING
plants, dabbing at dust. Her mind wandered
between plans for her wedding and her weekend
in Portland. *I shouldn't have sounded off to them.
I shouldn't have embarrassed Warren. I shouldn't
have ordered so much punch for the reception. I
shouldn't have chosen white lilies for the wedding. I shouldn't...too many shouldn'ts. What
should I be doing? What should I have done?
Kathleen Eloise, you're not thinking straight.
When in your life have you paid attention to
should and shouldn't? It's time to do something
for me.*

Kate picked up the phone and called the
florist, a gentle soul named Mavis. "Hi honey,"
chirped Kate when Mavis answered the phone.

"Mavis, sweetheart. I wonder if you'd be a darling and change my order for the wedding flowers...Yes, I ordered lilies...white...uh-huh...only I'd like to change that to roses. I want red roses, all red roses...never mind the cost, can't be that much, I'll pay it. A red rose at the end of each row, a large bouquet — let's see, three dozen — up front...uh, okay, on the altar. And another two dozen, no make it three, on the table at the reception. Thanks, Mavis."

Then she called the caterer and increased the sparkling cider order by two more cases. As she hung up the phone, she let out a high-pitched "Yahoooo!" letting it trail off through the house. *Good thing I live up here alone or I'd have the dogs howling about now.*

She was in the midst of preparing a sandwich for her lunch when another idea struck her. *I've got to test this new feeling. I've got to be sure I'm doing the right thing.* She packed away the sandwich with an apple and a jug of drinking water and climbed into her car. *The sun has returned to its rightful place*, she thought as she munched on her sandwich and steered toward the high desert. Yup! The sun's in its place again.

She stopped once on the trail just off the highway to relieve herself, squatting next to a small bush. She was pulling up her jeans when she saw the tiny eyes watching her, three baby rabbits, helplessly eyeing the monster human who had invaded their nest before they could flee. "Don't you worry, little bunnies. I wouldn't hurt you. I only attack full-grown children of Warren Thompson." And she let out a hearty laugh that lasted all the way back to her car.

By the time she reached the shack, her heart was singing. Was it the chance of seeing Alex again? Or was it that she didn't care anymore? In either case, the idea had lightened her mood. It seemed clear that the excitement she felt was not at stumbling across her old flame, but the opportunity to confront that young girl she was beginning to recognize.

She approached the shack and didn't hesitate at the door this time. She knew the way and she took it.

Inside, she marches directly to Kitty's bedroom upstairs. No music greets her ears this time. No din of miners frolicking in the smoke-filled room, no tinkling piano keys, only a smell of stale smoke and liquor. Early morning is always the one time of day when the clatter stops. The night revelers have fallen off to sleep, and the morning hazy-eyed survivors haven't arrived yet.

Kitty is still in bed when Kate bursts through the door. "Why don't you just come in and be comfortable?" she invites sarcastically and sleepily. Kate pushes some clothes off the chair and sits down next to the bed. "Kitty, I've got to get something clear with you. Something that's been bothering me for a long time."

"What's that?"

"You and me, or rather me, I guess. We…I… never had a plan. You don't have a plan. You get up every morning and do just what's in front of you. At night you go to bed without a thought for the next day. You keep on without direction day after day, letting things happen around you and to you, but never making anything happen yourself."

"Hey, that's not true. Alex and I have plans. We're going to build theaters…"

"But don't you see, that's *his* plan. Not yours."

"We plan together, him and me. We're partners. I finance his theaters and he builds them and runs them. We're planning on more too," she pats her tummy. "We're planning a family."

"Planning!" Kate snorts. "You haven't even told him yet, have you?"

"Well, no, but he says he loves children, and we're going to have a family and…"

"Okay Kitty, my dear sweet innocent Kitty-Kat." The older woman covers her face with her hands and bends over, trying to curl up into a ball. "What can I say to you?" she moans from her cocoon. "How can I reach you in time?"

Kitty kneels in her bed to get closer to Kate. "You say Alex isn't as keen on this family and our partnership as I tell you? Well, I refuse to believe that. He tells me every day how much he loves me. Why just last night he, we, well, you know. Right here."

Yes, Kate does know. She can still smell his scent in the room. She knows he has been there, wearing the expensive cologne she always bought for him.

"Kate, my dear," says the younger woman from the bed. "It seems to be you who have the problem here with reality."

Kate looks up at herself and grins. "Reality? Reality?"

They both laugh then at the absurdity of that word. But Kate has to ask. Only she doesn't use words, she just looks at Kitty.

Kitty scratches her head. "You're the one who tromps in here to tell me what's wrong with my life. Well, take a look at yours. What have you done with it? Did you have plans for some great course that you followed through life? And if you did, why are you here bothering me?"

Kate can't answer. She doesn't know what to say. She places her hands on her knees and tries to concentrate. *Plans?* No. *Direction?* No. That is precisely the problem. She was too busy living life, enjoying herself...chasing Alex. "Kitty, what you need to know..." she starts, but isn't sure where she is going. "What I want to tell you is..."

Why is she here? What can she gain? Surely Kitty isn't going to change her ways when she seems to be so happy on top of her world.

Me! The thought strikes Kate quickly and precisely, stabbing through her brain and shaking her entire body. *Me! This is about me, not her.*

"Kitty, you're a darling. You have put your finger on it...the problem...my problem...." Kate stands up and seems to dance about the small space, light on her feet.

"And what is that?"

"Well, it's...me." She waves her arms, then stops dancing. "It's...it's...just me," she ends lamely because she isn't sure exactly what else to say.

"Look, Kate, my old friend. You've come to the end of your...our life. You've done what you wanted, or at least I can suppose you have. Now you're trying to decide if you lived your life or..." She doesn't know how to end that sentence either. Exactly what *is* the alternative? "But now it's over. You'd like to start again. Am I right?"

Kate nods, stunned by the child's perception. "I'm not sure," she tells her alter ego. "I can see...I can remember how happy I was...when I was you. I don't want to change that. At the same time

I know what's coming…for you. And I am powerless to change that too. Right now I'd settle for understanding some of this."

Too much to press into one — or two — brains. Kate has heard what the younger woman has accused her of. "You need some answers for yourself instead of bothering me." Now Kate has to do some deciding on her own, for herself this time. *Not just what color do I want the flowers for the wedding, but do I want flowers at all? Maybe the better question is, do I want this marriage at all? Or, do I want Warren at all?*

"You see, I found this man who loves me…who really loves me," Kate begins.

"Don't they all? Do you remember the boys in Valparaiso…they all loved…"

Kate stops her. "I'm serious. This one does, and has for a long time. I married once, grasping at marriage and thinking I had another Alex in tow. Then I married Johnny out of pity, because I wanted to do something nice for someone. But now…Warren…he's different. He's an old friend and we have much in common, and at the same time not very much in common. Do you understand that? Am I making sense?"

"Sounds like someone very special."

"He is. He's sweet, he's protective, he's fun to be around. At the same time he lets me be myself. Yesterday, while his kids were raking me over the coals, he just sat there enjoying me holding myself in. And I think he actually took a deep breath when I let loose. He wanted me to be who I am, not some gussied up old broad who was trying to impress his darned kids."

Kitty's eyes fill with tears. "You see, my old friend. This may not be the passionate wild love I have for Alex...that you had for Alex...that, well, you know what I mean. But it sounds like your new man loves you...for real."

Kate toys with the bracelet on her arm, then draws her jacket tight about her and stands up. "You may be an apparition, but you're a damned smart one."

ISABEL BENJAMIN WAS FEELING QUEASY IN HER TUMMY AGAIN, just as she packed Paula off to play with her friend down the street. The child's mother had obligingly come around to pick up Paula, heading to the park for the first round of play. The two mothers traded places once a week to give the other R & R for a few hours.

That morning Isabel had plans. She didn't want anything to interfere. She knew all about the woman they called Klondike Kate, although they had never met. She knew she was also known as Aunt Kate, the old woman on the hill who helped people. She hated the idea of telling her problems to anyone, but this stranger with the odd ways seemed to be the least troublesome of any of Isabel's ideas so far.

The upset feeling in her mid-section wasn't going to keep her back, not today when she had some time to herself at last. She pulled on a pair of dark green slacks, buttoned up a smart white cotton shirt, tied her hair with a scarf and off she went. She'd walk. No need to risk Paul seeing their car chugging down the street. He didn't have to know where she was going.

Near the top of the hill, Isabel was puffing, her face flushed, her arms working to help her forward. The walk had calmed her stomach, but now she was out of breath. She paused at the cement steps, turned and looked down on the town. That's when Kate spied her out the window.

Company? Someone coming to see me this early in the day? Doesn't look like a salesman. Kate wasn't wearing her glasses. She seldom wore her glasses except to read. *No, looks like a woman. And she's coming here.* Kate hurried down the stairs and was approaching the front door when she heard a tap of fingernails. Tap, tap, tap.

She opened the door to find the young woman with her forefinger extended, about to add another set of taps. "Hello!" said the surprised tapper.

"Good morning," Kate answered. "Are you lost? Sick? Do you need help?"

"Well, no, no and yes." Isabel tried to grin, but she wasn't good at it. "I..." she didn't know how to say it. Maybe straightforward was best. "I've come to see you, Kate. I understand you may be able to help me."

"Come in. Don't know what you've heard." Under her breath she added, "Could've been anything in this town."

"I've heard you listen to people's problems and give them solutions." Isabel spoke purposefully, while her mind raced with all the words she wanted to use.

"And you might be..."

"Oh, I'm so sorry. You must think...I mean, I am so...sorry. Sorry." Her voice had risen from a sing-songy lilt to a squeak. "My name is Isabel. Isabel Benjamin."

"And I am Kate. Kate Rockwell Matson." Kate liked to use three of her three names. She thought it sounded more grand, and more homey at the same time.

"I know. I haven't lived in this town long, but I read about you in the paper. I've also heard how wise you are, how..."

Kate laughed. "Who's been feeding you that?" She laughed again.

"Well you are. I heard it." Isabel's voice remained at the high pitch, sounding more and more like a little girl with each phrase. Now she was adding a slight whine.

Kate led the young woman into the parlor. "Can I offer you a cup of coffee...or a sandwich?"

"No thank you. I'm not hungry...at all."

"Then, what can I offer you?"

"Advice. If you will. I have a problem, or I think I do..."

"You married?" Kate nodded at Isabel's tummy section. "That kind of trouble?"

Isabel looked down, then up, very quickly. "No, oh no, it's not that, well it could be, but no, I'm married. I mean yes...I'm married."

"Have you talked to your husband?"

"No, I can't. Not yet."

"Have you seen a doctor?"

"Not yet."

"Can't you talk to your doctor about...whatever?"

"Actually, no." The young woman was wringing the corner of her shirt now, moving her hands back and forth as she talked.

"What I came to ask was whether you think I should leave him?"

"Your husband? You considering leaving him?" Kate asked carefully.

"That's what I want you to tell me." Isabel looked into the older woman's eyes and pleaded. "Please tell me if I'm going to leave him? Or…" she looked down, "…is he going to leave me?" The last words were barely audible as the tears began.

"You think I can see into the future?"

"Can't you? I heard you knew…everything…and…"

Kate moved over next to Isabel on the divan and put her hand on her guest's arm to calm her. "There there," she cooed, "not to worry. Nobody has to leave anybody if you don't want them to." As soon as she said the words, she remembered how Alex had left her when that was the last thing Kate wanted. People leave people. Maybe that's what this woman needs to hear.

"Why would he leave? Or why would you?"

The tears bubbled in Isabel's eyes. Then they trickled over. "There's another woman."

Isn't there always? Kate knew the story. Lord, she had lived this one. She held the sobbing Isabel, patted her arm and waited.

"He works with her," she blubbered in that high-pitched voice. "They work together. That's a bond. She listens to him, he listens to her. They talk to each other. We don't have anything much to say to each other anymore. When he's home, all we do is fight…" More sobs. "…about nothing."

After another spell of crying, Isabel reached into her pocket, found a handkerchief and dabbed at her face. She sat up and calmly tucked the hanky back into her pocket. She spoke confidently. "I'm not going to cry anymore. I need to find some answers." Kate heard the woman's voice drop several degrees into a more serious register. "What would you do?"

Somebody's put her up to this, Kate thought for a moment. *She's putting me on, teasing me. Some sick soul has sent her here to torment me.*

"I'd kick the bastard out..." she said, to test the waters. She watched Isabel's face. The shock she saw told her she'd made a mistake. This Isabel Benjamin was real.

"...then I'd look around for a new young buck and start showing up around town with him."

Isabel caught the silliness of what Kate was saying. Tears disappeared. She grinned. "Wish I could, but I have a child at home, a sweet four-year-old daughter...who needs her daddy."

The testing and the joke over, Kate turned to face her guest. "Does this 'other woman' have anything you don't? A third breast? A magic spell? A secret she's using to blackmail him?"

Isabel laughed. "No. She's just...rather plain actually. All she's got is him, during the day and parts of some nights. They share work. That's a very strong bond."

"Yes it is." Kate remembered the joy of working with Alex, the excitement they stirred up between them as they planned some new theater, some new show. "Maybe that's all they share together. Have you considered riding this out? Waiting for the newness to wear off?"

Isabel looked down. "I can't wait too long."

"On the other hand, you have one thing that she doesn't. At least we hope she doesn't." Kate peered at Isabel's stomach. "That's like a trump card."

"I don't want to use it. I don't want to keep him because he feels he has to stay."

"Oh yes you do. You want to keep him no matter what it takes. He'll get over this...this fling. He'll forget her in a very short time. He won't forget that little one. Does he know yet?"

"No. I'm still not sure."

"Get sure. Soon as you can. Then tell him." The calm in Kate's voice belied the urgency she was feeling. If only she had told Alex, if only she hadn't scurried off to Texas *on business* and if only she hadn't stayed away so long. Nearly a year. Time enough for him to find someone else. The old doubts had returned. If she had it to do over again...but she didn't.

"Find out. Then tell him." Now the urgency sounded clearly in her voice.

"Kate, you're a gem. You're every bit as good at...this...as I was told. I thank you. I just pray that someday Paul will thank you. I know little Paula and..." she patted her tummy "...this little fella will."

"Paul?"

"My husband. Paul Benjamin. You know, the editor of the *Courier*? He took over the paper for his father soon after we were married and now..." her voice jabbered on, but Kate wasn't listening. *Ye gods, this is Annette's boss, the one she said she...oh no. This is a mess, a real Yukon yam, as Johnny would call it.*

Isabel had finished her explanation and was standing now, smiling, ready to leave. "I'm so pleased to have met you at last, Kate.

You're a gem. I love to hear about all your adventures in Alaska. Can you believe it's going to be a state?"

"Yes, isn't that grand?" Kate answered quietly, still dazed by the wildness of the triangle she was witness to.

"I read the article in last week's paper. Do I understand you're getting married or something?"

"Or something." Kate was anxious to send the young woman on her way. She moved toward the door and Isabel followed. In no time at all, the composed wife was heading down the walk and off to schedule a doctor's appointment.

"Or something," Kate repeated as she closed the door. *What does that mean? Of course I'm getting married. And in just a couple of weeks. Actually next week...Sunday.* She sat back down on the divan and went back over Isabel's visit. She even dozed for awhile, dreaming of a spider laying her eggs all over the daily newspaper. A hand reached out and gathered up the paper, wadding it into a ball and tossing it into the wastebasket. Then another hand, a very small feminine hand with a gold bracelet dangling from the wrist, reached into the wastebasket and retrieved the paper. It carefully un-wrapped the eggs, but they had all turned dark, dead.

Falling Apart

KATE WOKE SLOWLY, DAZED AT HAVING FALLEN asleep in the middle of the day. "I need some cold water." She headed up the stairs, her mind scattered among a myriad of thoughts, sidetracked by the dream.

That's when it happened. Her foot slid off the step, she grabbed for the railing, but missed, and toppled back down the stairs. As she tried to get up, her leg crumpled under her and pain enveloped her body. Never had she felt excruciating pain like that. Tears filled her eyes as she lay back down, one leg folded under her body, and passed out.

When she came to, the leg was numb and her mind struggled to make sense. *Why am I lying here? Where is here? What happened to...* she tried to sit up, but the slight movement reactivated the sharp leg pain and she fell back to the floor. She realized that her head rested on the bottom step. If only she could grab the newel post and pull herself up, she could reach the phone on the hall table. She tried, but again the pain blacked out her brain.

Time meant nothing. It could have been hours, or just minutes, that she lay there, moving in and out of consciousness as the pain flowed and ebbed. She became aware of someone knocking on the door. She tried to call out, but could manage only a weak, "Who's there?" No one answered. She heard footsteps walking about on the porch, then someone tried the door. "Help," Kate's thin voice called out. "Come in and help me, please."

"Kate? Is that you?" called a familiar voice, but for the life of her she couldn't remember who it belonged to. "Kate...my god, what happened?" The voice burst through the door and came to her side.

"I fell."

"I can see that, but how? Never mind. Where's your phone?"

Kate pointed to the hall table, called out, "Alex?" then lapsed again into darkness.

When she awoke the next time, the pain had stopped. She was lying in a bed, presumably at the hospital, her white hair crushed under her head on the pillow. As her eyes got used to the white room, she became aware of flowers near the window, a chair, small bedside chest with a pitcher of water and a glass. She looked down at her toes under the covers and saw the strange traction machine, ropes and pulleys that held one leg in the air. Past the gear she saw the door, which now opened to admit a nurse wearing a starched white hat. "Ah, we're awake." She smiled at Kate. "You gave us a scare."

"Who are you? What's wrong here?"

"My name is Nancy. I'm your day nurse. You'll be here for awhile. Doctor will be in to see you soon."

"What's wrong? Tell me how bad is it?" She nodded at her leg.

"Doctor will be in shortly. Care for a drink of water?"

"Yes, but please tell me the damages."

"Sorry, doctor has to tell you. I'm just the nurse. Here," she held the glass with a bent straw. Kate took a long slow sip, her head raised just enough to grasp the straw. When she finished, she let her head flop back onto the pillow.

"How'd I get here? Who brought me here?" she asked in a frail voice. She vaguely recalled seeing Alex's large brown eyes before she passed out.

"Mr. Benjamin, from the newspaper. Says he went by your house to take a photo of you, or something. Found you on the floor. Seems you fell down the stairs. Nasty fall." The nurse offered Kate another sip of water, then put down the glass and walked to the door. "Don't go away," she joked, then disappeared.

"Don't go away?" Kate mimicked the lilting nursy voice. "Can't move my big toe and she's talking about me leaving. Silly silly woman." The patient turned her head back to the flowers near the window and let her eyes close.

"Klondike Kate," the voice broke through the darkness. "So the famous Klondike Kate has taken a tumble."

Kate opened her eyes to see a doctor in a white coat peering down at her, smiling through a bushy mustache, a shock of unruly brown hair falling across his forehead. "Uhmmm," Kate groaned.

"Are you feeling pain?" the doctor asked.

"No. Not feeling anything. Tired. Sleepy. Can't open my eyes much."

"That's normal. The anaesthetic is wearing off and the medication is kicking in. For now, sleep is good. Lots of rest."

"What's wrong, doc? What're the damages?"

"A bone near your left knee was broken, a clean split, but complete. We set it back in place, put a steel pin in there, but you'll be off your feet for awhile. These things take time to heal."

"You mean, I can't get some crutches and get out of this place?" Kate was waking up.

"Not a chance. Not for awhile."

"Oh that's impossible, doc. I'm getting married in just a couple of...next week."

"Sorry, not unless you hold the ceremony here. Now, I have no objections to being host to a wedding party, but there's no way you're leaving here for at least two weeks, more likely four."

Kate's moan could be heard clear down the hall. She tried to sit up, but fell back onto the pillow and let out a long groan. *What have I done? What have I done?*

OVER THE NEXT FEW DAYS, THE TOWNSPEOPLE CAME TO CALL on Kate, even the grocery store manager. "Missed your cheery self," he said and laid a basket of fruit on the bedside table. The firefighters came, in twos and threes, bringing her flowers and chocolates. Two of them — the firehouse cooks — even managed to sneak in Kate's favorite — meatloaf sandwich. For which both men shyly accepted Kate's outstretched arms for one of her famous hugs.

Annette stopped by often. Paul came too, wanting to explain what he was doing at Kate's house that evening. "I wanted to shoot a new picture of you, you know, for all the stories we're doing about you..."

"All the stories?"

"Sure, you know, your wedding and the Fourth of July and...everything." Paul had heard about Isabel's visit and wanted to know the details. At the sight of Kate's pale face before him, he thought better of it and stopped himself. "Sorry, Kate. We'll talk another time. Get well."

"Thank you for finding me," Kate extended her hand weakly. "Don't know what would have become of me if you hadn't..."

"Oh, somebody would've found you sooner or later. Glad I could help." The newspaper editor left then, working over the phrases he would use to report the incident in next week's newspaper: "nasty fall down the stairs...fortuitous visit by newspaper editor...pre-wedding photo...the famous Klondike Kate injured in fall...falls to injury...injured in fall."

THE STORY APPEARED IN THE NEXT NEWSPAPER, ALONG WITH A photo that Paul took in the hospital. When he mentioned his visit to Isabel that evening, his wife quickly changed the subject.

"Something going on, Isabel?"

"No."

"Kenny said he saw you up at Kate's the day she fell. Was it you?"

"No, er, well, yes, I guess it was."

"Really? Why? What were you doing? I didn't know you knew Kate?"

"I don't, or I didn't. I just...uh...wanted to meet her and..."

"Come on, Izzie, you're talking to me. What's going on? You didn't push her, did you?"

"Heavens no!" Isabel shrieked. "Why would I..."

"Well then, why were you there? What happened?"

"Nothing really. She was fine when I left."

"Okay. I accept that. Now tell me why you went there in the first place."

Isabel stood up and walked over behind Paul's chair. She knew she had to tell him and she couldn't look at his face.

"I saw the doctor today."

"What doctor?"

"How many do we have? Our doctor, silly."

"And why did you see the doctor? Are you sick? What's wrong?"

"Nothing's wrong. In fact, things are right, very right." She slipped her arms around Paul's neck, partly out of love and partly to be sure he stayed still. "We're...going to have another baby."

"How's Kate?" Annette asked as Paul entered the office.

"She's doing okay. Strange to see her so quiet when we're used to seeing her galloping around town." Paul sat down at his typewriter and looked for a sheet of paper.

"Did she mention our little trip out into the desert the other day?" Annette asked cautiously.

"You too? Does everyone hang around Klondike Kate? Don't tell me you were asking her advice too?"

"Too? Was someone else asking for advice? You?"

"No, not me." Paul kept his eyes on the paper coming out of his typewriter. He waited a moment, then added, "Isabel."

"Isabel? Why her? How do you know? What would she be doing there?"

"That's what I wanted to know. Kenny the mailman said he saw Isabel coming out of Kate's house earlier that day. I called Isabel and asked what the hell she was doing over there, and she told me, 'I went to get advice.'" He tried to squeak like Isabel.

"Advice about what?" Annette was sorting notes to file with press copy. Her head was down so that she didn't notice Paul's face begin to darken. Something in the tone of his voice made her look up at him. At first she thought he was blushing, then she saw the anger, the frustration, the fury forming behind trapped eyes.

He took a deep breath and spit out the words, "She's pregnant. We're expecting."

Annette stopped sorting her notes. "You're what?" she exploded inside while trying to control her voice. "She's what?"

"Isabel is pregnant."

"But how could that...how could you...? You mean you've been sleeping with her while you're romancing me? Come on, now. What kind of..."

Paul dropped the paper he was trying to insert into the type-writer and grabbed Annette's arm before she could swing at him. "I'm sorry, Annette. Really sorry. It just happened. But that doesn't mean..."

"Doesn't mean...what? That we can't just go on, you having your fun with me, then going home to do it with her too? What kind of monster are you? When were you going to mention this to me? This is the last, I mean the very last straw! Kate was right. You are just...a ...a man." She spit out the words at him, snarling like a hurt animal, wanting to strike something, but what? She considered herself, after all, a lady. Somehow she felt she'd be within her rights to take out a gun and shoot him, or twist a knife in his innards, or bash him on the head, but not to hit him. Instead, she stormed out the front door and headed for her car.

Automobiles are one of the nation's most useful all-around multi-purpose tools. Cars serve as homes, bedrooms, trysting places, child-care modules, pet pens, dining rooms, entertainment centers, even offices. They also have become a venue for exuberant emotions: a place to joy ride when elated, a solitary place to meditate when moody, and an opportunity to risk death in the face of disillusion, hopelessness or anger.

Annette faced her hopelessness and anger with the windows down, her eyes staring at the spinning road, not seeing clearly through tears which contorted the scene. She raced the car through town to the country road and barreled along much too fast. The angels had gotten used to such scenes and were prepared to dip their hands into still another tangle of steel and torn clothing and hubcaps and bleeding skin and gas-soaked upholstery and cracked bones.

"How are we this morning?" Nancy chirped as she brought in Kate's tray.

"Not so bad. Can I get out of here today? I'm supposed to get married next week."

"Sorry." Nancy busied herself, arranging the tray on the bedside table and refilling Kate's water glass. *Funny old woman*, the nurse thought. She said, "Still, as bad a shape as you're in, you're still not as bad as that poor woman they brought in last night."

"Oh?" Kate was beginning to take notice of life around her.

"Car accident. Out on Mountain Road, near the old Goodman place. Took that Dead Man's Corner at fifty or sixty miles an hour. Didn't make it."

"Anyone from here?"

"Why yes, as a matter of fact. It's that girl reporter, down at the *Courier*. Sweet young thing…"

"Oh my, she's dead?"

"No, I meant the car didn't make the turn. She's alive, but what a mess she is." The nurse turned and left the room before Kate could comprehend.

"Annette? Is it Annette?" she called after the nurse. No answer.

When the doctor arrived later that morning, Kate asked him, "How's that girl they brought in last night? The reporter?"

"She's doing as well as can be…"

"Don't give me that guff, doc. Give me the real stuff. She's a friend of mine. How's she doing?"

"Not well, Kate. She was banged up pretty good, but not too many head injuries. Seems she covered her head with her arms when she saw she was going over the side. The car rolled, and the steering wheel and flying glass took care of most of her injuries. Those darned cars. They go too fast. Just too darned fast."

The doctor finished examining Kate, then left. Kate settled back on her pillows, helpless to go find out anything, just waiting until someone else came to visit. She'd get to the bottom of what happened before too long.

It was the night nurse who gave Kate the lowdown. Seems that Annette had driven off in a rush to meet some guy in Bend and failed to make Dead Man's Curve. "Seems the guy had gotten her in trouble, if you get my meaning," the nurse winked at Kate. "And little missy was going to give him what-for. She didn't make it. Now she doesn't have anything to yell at him about. Lost it." She leaned close to Kate's ear and whispered, "Miscarriage, about three months."

Kate closed her eyes as she put together the pieces of the story. She was right. The girl had been pregnant. And Paul must have pushed her away. *That's got to be it. Oh, the poor child. Why do men have to be such miserable goats?* She pounded the mattress with her fists. *Goats who go waltzing through life impregnating everything around them then deserting... Poor Annette. Maybe they'll let me see her. She needs somebody. Wonder if they've called her family?*

Kate slept restlessly that night, visions of creatures that kept cutting their hooves on the sharp edges of the debris and bleating...bleeding too. As she awoke she was musing about how alike those words were: bleating, bleeding. "Goats!" she said aloud just as Nancy the nurse entered to oversee Kate's morning bath.

WARREN POPPED IN AT THE END OF KATE'S FIRST WEEK IN THE hospital. Kate had finally called him and he headed for Homestead immediately.

"My darling, how are you?" he asked as he entered the room. He seemed to be suffering along with her, although he wasn't sure whether to be concerned or to be angry that she waited so long to call him. He chose concern. "I was so worried. I've been calling and calling..."

"My dear Warren. I'm okay. Just can't walk for awhile."

"What does the doctor say? Can I talk to him?"

"I busted my knee and I'll be out of here in no time."

"How long, dear Kate? How long?"

"Sorry about the wedding. Guess we'll have to postpone it."

"You sound relieved."

"Now Warren, don't start. You know how much I want to marry you. I've been planning nothing else for the past few weeks. We have the hall, the food, the..."

"Everything but the bride," Warren finished for her. "Now what do we do?"

"We wait, Warren. It's not like this is the end. I didn't die. I could have, you know."

Warren's eyes grew round and his face softened. He hadn't even considered that likelihood before. Now it overwhelmed him. Kate...die? Impossible. That just wasn't going to happen. Not yet.

He took both her hands in his and held them tightly. "You wouldn't dare," he smiled wanly.

"No, I wouldn't. That would displease you, and I don't want to make you unhappy."

They consoled each other for the next hour or so, then Kate waved her hand across her head and feigned sleep. "I'm worn out," she told him. "Maybe I better rest a bit."

"Of course, my darling. Anything you need?"

"Just one thing," Kate decided to try something. "Would you mind terribly going down the hall and finding the room of Annette...can't think of her last name. If they'll let you see her, would you tell her that I'm in here and that I'm thinking of her. Tell her I'll be down to see her as soon as they make me mobile."

"All right. I'll try. Annette?"

"Yes, sweet little Annette."

I'll Never Love Again!

ANOTHER WEEK PASSED BEFORE KATE BECAME
mobile. Warren had stayed three days to make
sure Kate was on the mend. Before he left, he
secured a promise from Kate that she would re-
schedule the wedding as soon as possible. Then
he returned to Portland.

"Here we go, Mrs. Matson," the cheery Nancy
suggested one morning as she pushed the empty
wheelchair into Kate's room. "Here we are. Ready
for a spin?"

"Anything to get out of this room," Kate answered. She held tightly to the nurse as she
prepared to go over the side. Yesterday she had sat
up on the side of the bed. This morning she had
dangled her feet, one leg in a cast, over the side.
Now it was time to get out of the bed.

"Upsa daisy," squealed the nurse, straining against Kate's weight. Then, "Downsa daisy," as she lowered her patient into the chair. The trip through the door seemed to Kate like re-entering the world.

"Can I visit my friend Annette?" she asked. "Annette Whittier." The newspaper account of the accident hadn't told the entire story, she was sure. Paul had written the article carefully, concealing any facts that might have attributed a motive for this *accident*. Kate had a brief moment wondering if it really had been an accident, or if there had been some hanky panky involved.

"Just down the hall, but I don't want you to tire yourself."

By the time they had found the end of the hallway, Kate was pushing the wheels by herself, her strong arms providing the steam. "Knock knock," she called out at Annette's open door as she wheeled inside.

"Kate," came a small voice from the bed. The woman could barely see the figure under the covers, only tubes and bandages.

"Annette, Annette, what's happened to you?" She wheeled to the side of the bed and surveyed the damage — both arms bandaged, one in a splint, the form lying still as ice to avoid messing up the stitching that held her torso together.

"It's gone," Annette whispered to her friend.

"Gone?" It took Kate a moment to receive the message. "Oh, I'm so sorry. But maybe…"

"Don't you dare say it's a good thing," came the voice from the bed.

"No, I didn't mean that. Well, maybe I did. If things had been different…"

Annette had no one else to talk to about her predicament. No other visitors understood the depth of Annette's pain, the loss she had undergone. No one else could offer the comfort that Kate could — and did.

The two women talked away the next hour, sharing their grief over Annette's loss, the long-ago loss of Kate and the loss they both experienced of men they loved. "This hurts too much to ever think about doing it again. I doubt I'll ever love again," said Annette.

"I've said that before too, and I never meant it. I don't think you do either. You feel that it's all over, but Annette, you're not even thirty yet. Your whole life is still ahead of you, as long as you grab hold of it and live it according to your rules, not some hungry, bored guy who sees you as a plaything rather than as a person. You may not believe me…"

"How many times have I heard that one?"

"It's true. You aren't about to believe me, but at least listen and remember. I didn't believe it when someone told me, all those years ago. But someday you'll hear these words and they'll mean something. You will live for many more years, and most of them will be happy ones. You will love again, and it will be a love worthy of you — if you choose it instead of waiting for it to choose you." Kate shifted in her chair, then added, "If I have learned nothing else in my…er…considerable years, it's that love keeps popping up. Look at me. After Alex, I married two more times. And I'm getting ready to make the trip to the altar again."

"You're different, Kate."

"Not so. We're all alike, my dear. All of us women carry gullible, cheating, caring, trusting hearts, always ready to welcome a new love."

"What's that old song? 'I'll never love again...'"

"...until I fall in love with you.' But that's not exactly true. I'd be willing to guess you haven't met the one true love of your life."

"Or maybe I have, and, like you, I just can't have him."

The two women, bandaged and fighting the pain that lay just under the anesthetized surface, mulled over their lives for a few moments, deep in memories.

"Oh, I loved him, that Alexander Pantages," Kate began at last. "I loved him with my whole soul. Still, he wasn't mine to keep. Sometimes I almost believe that if we had stayed together, we'd have killed each other before very long. We were both so passionate, both so immersed in each other. At the same time, I wouldn't give up having known him, not for anything else in this world."

"Yeah. That's what I feel about Paul. I'm glad to have known a love like this, but if I can face reality, I don't think we could weather a lifetime together either." Annette tried to smile gamely under her bandages for her friend. "But I sure wish I'd had the chance to find out." Then she turned her head aside and cried softly into her pillow.

Annette was about to explain the details of the loss of the pregnancy when the nurse entered to retrieve Kate.

"Almost time for your lunch," she hummed. "Say goodbye for now."

"Goodbye, Kate. My mom and dad are coming to take me home next week. I don't think I'll come back here to Homestead. Unless maybe for your wedding. Send me an invitation, okay?"

"Sure thing, kiddo. Remember my old Yukon motto: Mush on and smile! See you."

SOMETIMES LIFE HAS TO HIT YOU OVER THE HEAD TO GET A message through. Kate was sure that was what happened on the stairs that day — life had a message to get through to her. By the time she returned home, summer was in full swing at its hottest. July and August in central Oregon can hold sweltering breathless heat.

Something called air conditioning was beginning to show up in a few Oregon homes — automatic fans that were stuffed into partially-opened windows to grind out refreshing cool air. But in a large house with high ceilings, like Kate's, she'd have to have one in every room to make a difference. As it was, the heat rose to the second floor and Kate moved her bedding down to the divan in the parlor.

She also loved to sleep outdoors and often took to her bed under the stars on very warm nights. By mid-August, Kate had healed enough to drive the car again, although she still needed a pair of canes to aid her damaged knee when she walked. One sweltering night she took a drive into the night air to cool off, and ended out in the high desert.

"Just like old times," she addressed a skittering animal. "Just you, me and the stars. They sure are bright tonight. I've missed you all." Then she was silent. No need for words as she let the images sink in: peaceful space, dark comfort, limitless vision, memories of a life well-lived.

Still, the image that kept popping up continued to elude her. That girl in pink tights, the gleaming crown of candles, the silken shimmery gowns that enhanced the girlish figure, the love energy that filled a room like so much tobacco smoke, the hazy revelry that kept laughter alive until the wee hours.

Who was that girl? Why couldn't she reach her? Surely that young woman held the key to Kate's own doubts, the answer to Kate's questions. *Is she me? If she is, why don't I recognize her? Why do I act like she's a very young stupid alien from another world, someone I don't remember, much less ever knew?*

"What happened on that stairs?" Warren had asked.

"Put off her wedding, that's for sure," joked Nurse Nancy, innocently unaware of how close she may have been to the truth.

Might be something to that. An awful way to say, hold on a minute! But on the other hand, so much is going on with me that I wouldn't put it past that slip of a girl who keeps bursting into my head. She's a mischief-maker that Kitty. That much I recall.

Kate still hadn't convinced herself that this new marriage was right. *Maybe on the outside*, she reasoned, *but not on the inside, not really sure.*

Do I love Warren enough to marry him? Can I marry him if I don't love him enough? How much is enough? Did I ever really love Alexander? How can I measure love? Have I ever known how to love...anyone?

Kate kindled a small campfire and used her sticks to let herself down on a log. She pulled out a thermos of coffee, rolled a cigarette and stared into the flames.

"Oh, the tricks we dancers used to play on each other, eh Kitty. Flossie was the best one to trick. She'd fall for anything. Remember the time we ran into her room in the middle of the night and told her she was on stage in six minutes? Oh, did she scramble! Remember the look on her face when she got downstairs and not a soul was in the saloon?"

Kate smiles. "Even before that, Kitty, remember the tricks you played on the nuns at school? Although you could hardly count them — because nuns are so gullible anyway."

Kitty pulls over another log next to the flames. There she sits, one leg across her lap, peering at Kate. "You remember the trick you pulled on board the boat headed for Chile, the summer Mother whisked you away?"

"Of course." Kate smiles at the memory, then asks, "which one?" The two women howl with delight.

"Which one! Which one of so many pranks! Well, let's see, the time you told them you had seen a pirate ship shadowing our boat and the day was hot and you could see almost anything you wanted in the shimmers of heat on the ocean."

"And they swore there was a pirate ship and they called the captain." Kate laughs some more, attracting the attention of some critters there in the desert and sending others running for their holes.

"The poor captain didn't want women on board in the first place, but he let Mother talk him into taking the two of us. Wonder if Mom ever made it worth his while?"

"Kitty, bite your tongue. You know Mother wouldn't do such things."

"It's been too long for you to remember. Poor old Kate. Can't remember what your mother was like. She'd do anything to attract the attentions of a man. Didn't you ever wonder where you learned that?"

Kate shifts in the place where she sits, her canes resting on a nearby stone. "Maybe if I blink, this apparition will disappear."

"Come on, Kate, the years must have blotted out the memories. Surely you remember New York. Dear Mother insisting on accompanying you to the theater. Do you think she was trying to protect you? Or was she trying to find a suitable man for herself?"

"You're wrong, little girl. You are just totally wrong. Mother's been dead many years, but she was always looking out for me...you."

"Where was she when you were trying to snag Alex?"

"I didn't try to *snag* Alex. He was my love. I was his."

"Sure, but where was Mommy during that time?"

"She met him only twice and she liked him."

"Did she suggest ways for you to keep him? Or was she busy trying to use his connections for herself? Those dreadful days when you had to testify against him in that nasty court trial in California...."

"How do you know about the trial? It hasn't happened in your life yet."

"Didn't you tell me about it?"

"I don't think so. Maybe. But..."

"Mama said she believed he was guilty as charged..."

"...and that he deserved to die..."

"For hurting her little girl."

They are finishing each other's sentences, almost as if only one were speaking.

"Well, didn't he?"

"But what has that to do..."

"Mama didn't want you to stay with him. And she didn't want you to be hurt by him. She knew that you'd be hurt if you stayed."

"Kitty, you're making my head spin. When I went to his trial, I thought I had cleared him from my soul. I had married someone else, had built my life in Oregon, was enjoying my fame...by myself. But when I saw him in that California courthouse, after so many years, the good times all came back — our escapes to the wild flower fields, the trips to Seattle and Chicago, the dancing, the loving. And when I saw him here, the last time I was with you, it happened all over again."

"You see, Kate," the younger woman seems triumphant, but hates it at the same time. "You see! If you can still feel all this ...how many years later?... you're still carrying a torch for that man. Think how I must feel; I'm living that with him right now. It's as if we're married. We travel together, we dance, we take those trips into the hills during our hours off, we work with our heads together planning for the next theater. And we love. Oh how we love..."

A cool evening breeze rushes past Kate's head and clears away some of the ghostly memories. She shivers. The fire has died down and the night chill covers the desert.

"Let's go inside," Kate suggests, reaching for her cane.

"Whatever you say, Kate."

The old dancer hobbles across the familiar sand, skirting the tumbleweed brush as she looks for hard ground to place her walking sticks.

"Sorry, Kitty girl. He's in your blood...my blood...our blood. The only trouble is that we're not in his blood. No one is. Alex has only one love — money."

The shack looms ahead. She approaches the door and turns to Kitty. "Money! If you can supply that, he'll be your friend. If you can't, he's gone. We can't get him out of our blood and we can't supply him with all the money he wants. Might as well accept that and get on with your life."

Inside Kate moves slowly back toward the dressing room, looking past the bar, and realizes for the first time what a dingy place she is in.

"You're going to be all right, Kate," Kitty says as they close the dressing room door and pull up two chairs. Neither speaks for a long time. Only the sound of the piano in the saloon keeps company with their thoughts. Then Kate begins to hum.

After several moments, the two women, seated together in the shabby dressing room in back of the drafty old Yukon saloon, strike up a chorus of "Hello my honey, hello my baby, hello my ragtime gal..." Injured knee be darned, Kate stands up and grabs Kitty. They manage some kicks and whirls, belting out another chorus. The two dance and sing together then, Kate recalling the steps she learned all those years before, and Kitty relishing the moment.

Flossie, walking past the door, hears the music and comments, "Kate is really belting them out tonight. Almost sounds like there's two of her in there."

Klondike Kate Reigns

KATE NEARLY MISSED THE LABOR DAY PARADE. She had planned to hobble down the hill, using her canes and walking slowly, but the boys at the firehouse came to pick her up about nine o'clock. They often did that, to try to repay her for the many times she had opened her house after a fire to serve the firemen coffee and sandwiches. Originally it was an attempt to win over the community. But Kate genuinely enjoyed the jokes and the horsing around that released the masculine energy around her house.

On parade days, and any time she needed a ride, Kate was chauffeured by the fire department. She became part of every parade, waving and cheering from her perch atop the hook and ladder truck, her shock of white hair framing the eyes that reflected a cloudless blue sky.

"You boys always know how to perk up a girl," she shouted as they drove slowly down the main parade route. Behind them the community band kept pace with "The Stars and Stripes Forever." Kate slapped her good knee to keep the beat. From her perch she could see all the way to the end of the parade. First came the unit of soldiers and sailors in uniforms from World War II, then those from World War I. Next came the few straggling heroes from the Spanish American War, the one that was waged while she was spinning gold in the Yukon. And bringing up the rear of the parade were the two aged G.A.R. survivors of the Civil War, riding in stylish gold Cadillacs and waving feebly to the cheering crowds who couldn't remember their war. The Korean War survivors hadn't come home yet.

At the end of the parade were horses and riders in their brightly colored harnesses and costumes, followed by a few politicians in Buicks and Cadillacs from the Central City Auto Dealers. No parade in a small town was complete without the politicians, especially in an election year. All the "Friends of Ike" and a "few Friends of Adlai" lounged in those highly polished convertibles that hot day in September 1952.

The fire truck made its way through the downtown Homestead streets, lined with folks waving small American flags. Youngsters sped up and down the sidewalks on bicycles, enjoying their last days before school opened, laughing and making the streamers on their handlebars stand straight out in the wind.

The parade wound up at the park, where many families had fired up the outdoor fireplaces and spread out bowls and plates of food atop checkered tablecloths. The smell of charcoal cookers joined the smell of wood smoke that billowed from the homemade brick outdoor stoves.

Then came the sound of the chink-chink-clink of iron horse-shoes along with the crack of a bat as it sent a softball spinning into the air. Little girls squealed, boys hollered, and mothers wiped the perspiration from their brows as fathers tapped the kegs of beer and prepared for a long afternoon under the trees.

Kate was tempted to join the Benjamins — Paul, Isabel and little Paula, but wasn't sure of her tongue. Maybe she'd be better off to stay with the firemen that day. Warren had promised to rescue her by mid-afternoon. As long as she could sit under the trees in the lawn chair provided by the firemen, she'd be fine. To tell the truth, after the exhilaration of the parade, she was feeling more like a forty-year-old than a seventy-year...er...sixty-year-old. Kate was getting so she couldn't even tell herself her own age.

"Aunt Kate, can I get you anything?" George Hanson asked.

"No thanks, George. I'm just resting up from the ride. I'll get something to eat later. Well, maybe a lemonade."

"Coming up."

BY THREE O'CLOCK, THE POTATO SALAD AND HOT DOGS WERE gone, the potato chips were disappearing and the Jell-o salads had melted. The ice cream container, insulated with heavy padding, was empty and the soft drinks were dwindling. Still the beer kept flowing from the old wooden keg.

"You look like the Queen of the Yukon," came a familiar voice behind her. Kate turned to see Warren, looking sharp in a straw bowler, open-neck sports shirt and summer jacket.

"You look like an I LIKE IKE poster," she told him. "Very dapper, my dear. You do resemble him." He leaned over and kissed her cheek, like an old friend or a long-married dutiful husband. "Nice trip today?" she asked.

"Without incident. Except some wiseacre kid tossed a firecracker at my car as I passed through some little town back there. Thought I had a flat tire."

The day had been long — the parade, the picnic, endless speeches by labor leaders, then the band concert. Kate was ready to go home. She bid her friends, the firemen and their families, farewell and let Warren guide her to his car.

"Let's talk wedding," said Warren as soon as they were comfortably seated at Kate's kitchen table, sipping iced Indian sun tea.

"Let's not. Let's put it off until tomorrow. I'm very tired. This has been a long day."

"Kate, are you wearing out on me? Or are you giving up on the wedding?"

"Tired, Warren dear. Just tired."

"All I wanted to say was that I thought we should just go ahead and have a small civil ceremony at the courthouse. We can drive over, get married, and drive back in just a couple hours."

"And miss the party? I don't think so."

"But Kate…"

"But Kate nothing. We'll talk about this tomorrow, when we're fresh. When we can think straight. Right now, I'm dead tired. But I'm hungry too. Don't know which is worse."

"Tell you what. I passed that new drive-in at the edge of town. Why don't we drive out there and get something to eat?"

"Eat in the car? At a drive-in? I don't know…"

"Come on, Kate. Where's your adventure?"

This was a turnabout. Warren willing to dare, Kate holding back. What was the world coming to?

"I'm hungrier than I have energy to fight you. Okay. We eat at a…drive-in."

That evening, two of the town's senior citizens drove to the edge of town, parked at a shiny new meter-like contraption and called in their orders: two hamburgers, French fries, milk shakes — one chocolate, one strawberry. Make those hamburgers with onions and pickles and lots of catsup.

WARREN SHARED KATE'S BED THAT NIGHT. THEY HELD EACH other as they dreamed their separate dreams, like old married people. In the morning, Warren tried to renew the talk of the wedding.

"Let's just drive over and get it done. Today maybe."

"Doc says I should be able to walk without the canes in another two weeks. Let's set the date at September fifteenth. Then, if the church is handy, we can do it there. If not, we'll go to the court-house."

"You got a deal, Kate, my girl," Warren almost danced around the kitchen. "Do you want to call the newspaper and tell them?" Something about printing things in the newspaper made them real for Warren.

"All right. I wish that nice Annette was back at work. She always wrote me up so good."

Kate called the *Courier* and talked with Paul. "I'll send over a reporter, Aunt Kate," he promised. "I just hired a new one. This will be a good chance to try her out."

"How's Annette?" Kate asked. "Have you been to see her?"

"No. It's too awkward. She doesn't want to see me. I'm sure she's doing well." Paul's voice sounded very distant. "Oh, and congratulations, Aunt Kate, on your upcoming nuptials." He sounded every bit like a newspaper reporter.

"Thank you Paul. Give my love to Isabel…and…that baby of yours."

"She's almost five now, not a baby much anymore." He had started to hang up, then put the receiver back to his ear and added, "Oh, and we're going to have a new baby around the house, very soon." He said goodbye and hung up.

Paul kept his word, sent the new reporter around that afternoon. She turned out to be a very efficient journalism school graduate who handled her notebook like a machine and rattled off questions like another machine. Very efficient, very thorough. And Kate loved telling her story all over again to fresh young ears.

When the newspaper was delivered Thursday morning, Kate smiled at the famous Gold Rush photo they had used, the one of her wearing the broad-brimmed hat, the soft satin Paris gown, dark blue, she recalled, with her legs showing, top to bottom, sheathed in pink tights. Her favorite. Well, the favorite next to the one showing her in the skin-tight shimmering pearl white gown that wrapped around her young body like a mummy casing. That was a pretty good picture too.

Kate had always been photogenic. Photographers found her a good subject, easy to pose, easy to shoot. Too bad all the film they had back then was black and white. Only a few photos had been touched up by colorists, to show off the vivid coloring of the young Klondike Kate.

Perhaps one day she should have an artist paint a portrait of the young Kate in her famous tights. Good place for it, over the divan in the parlor. Yes, good idea. She must mention it to Warren the next time they talk.

I'd Know
You Anywhere

THE INSISTENT KNOCKING AT THE FRONT DOOR
sent Kate hobbling as fast as she could, canes in
each hand. Still the going was slow. The knocking continued. "I'm coming," she called at last.
"Keep your shirt on." She didn't recognize the
figure behind the eisenglass, yet it was familiar.
*Who would call at this hour without phoning
ahead? Another admirer, a sourdough?* She
opened the door.

"You!" His voice sounded like home, like
the past, like Alex. The man standing in her
doorway even looked like Alexander Pantages,
only older. "You!" he repeated.

"Yes, it's me," Kate tried to sound short-
tempered, but her voice came out mellow, nostal-
gic as she recognized him, this man in his late
forties, maybe fifty. He had dark eyes and black

hair with a single lock of gray falling over his forehead.

"You come to my restaurant. You are a customer. My name is Andrew Koulakis."

"Yes, I guess I do know you, er, at least I've seen you." She covered her anxiety with a quip. "Have you brought me a nice moussaka?" She turned and hobbled toward a chair, inviting her guest to follow. He closed the door and held her chair as she let herself into it and placed the canes on the floor.

"Have you been injured?" he asked politely.

"Yes. A silly fall, on the stairs. Foolish of me. I'm fine. Healing well." She was jabbering she knew. Why was he here? Why had he come?

The man seated himself across from her and leaned forward, his hands together, his elbows resting on his knees, the gray lock falling into his eyes. He stared at her, as if to look deep into her and find something he needed.

"I'm sorry, where are my manners? My name is Kate…"

"I know. Kate Rockwell, known far and wide as Queen of the Yukon." He grinned the familiar grin, his black eyes looking straight into her. "I know more about you than most people. I've been looking for you for a long time. My name is Koulakis…Andrew."

"Yes, you said that. Now you've found me. But, as you pointed out, you didn't have to come looking. I've been to your restaurant." She took a deep breath and asked, "Why have you come?"

Now it was his turn to breathe deeply. He looked at the floor. Now or never. Just say it. "I'm looking for my mother," he said, his head turning back toward her, the eyes catching hers and holding them.

"Do you think she's here?" They watched each other carefully.

"I'm fairly sure. I barely remember her. She placed me with a family when I was about four. I remember she was beautiful, had bright red hair and lovely deep blue eyes that turned green when she was angry. She was easy to soft-soap." He laughed. "I know, I tried. And she played a mean game of peekaboo with those eyes. I can never forget them."

Kate felt her heart stop, then start up again, fluttering wildly. She watched him as he recounted his meager memories, letting the images wander through her own mind as he did. The chubby little boy, legs barely able to hold him up. Dimpled little hands that covered his large dark eyes before pulling away. Peekaboo! Black eyes, so unlike hers, yet as much hers as anyone's.

The man continued to talk. "I remember snow, much snow, and cold. But I also remember the warmth of my mother's arms, being handed around by old men who smelled of smoke and outdoors, who romped with me in the snow and fed me awful tasting things to drink. Were they miners? Did that take place in the Yukon?"

Kate's mouth was open as she listened to Andrew. He did remember. He hadn't been too small. They said he'd forget. But he remembered. She remembered too, that day when she loaded them onto the steamer that took them to Seattle, how they stayed at her mother's house overnight, then drove by carriage to meet the smiling couple who wanted a child so badly, who said they'd care for him as good as his ma. She saw again the look of curiosity mixed with fear and wonder as she handed him to them and told him to go with his new parents.

"I had a good home. My parents loved me and took good care of me," Andrew said, "but I always wondered about that red-haired woman who I knew was my mother." Andrew paused. He wanted to dash across the room and shake the truth out of her, but he only closed his eyes and asked, "Are you my mother?"

Kate blinked. Tears slid down her cheeks. "You poor kid," she began, then blinked back the tears and looked at this boy-man. "Andrew. Andrew." She repeated his name. "Andrew Koulakis."

Her body had begun to shake. Inside she could feel a volcano about to erupt, but she had to think straight. This man was looking for answers only she could provide. She had to make sure they were the best answers — for everyone.

"Andrew, I'm the red-haired woman you remember, or was…"

"I knew it. I knew it." He leaped to his feet and took one giant step towards her and kneeled in front of her chair. "I knew it."

"But…" she had to catch her breath and as she did she held her arms forward, fingers spread, palms outward. She was stopping him. This was more difficult than she could have imagined. The moment was what she had both looked forward to and dreaded all her life, one she had rehearsed, one she had played and played again in her head. She knew the lines: "But…I'm not your mother." Andrew rocked on his heels and sat down on the floor with a thud.

"You see, I was there, in Dawson when you were born. I knew your mother. Her name was Flossie, one of the best friends I had. We were both…entertainers…in the Yukon during the Gold Rush. Well, she found herself in…the family way. When she couldn't dance anymore, I took care of her. She stayed in my room and I made sure she ate right and took care of herself."

"Her name was...Flossie." Andrew grabbed snippets of what she was saying, trying to hold onto them, keep them in his memory.

"She was a wonderful girl, a true friend. She'd share her earnings with anyone who needed help. So when she needed help, I was happy to do it." Kate shifted in her chair. She was afraid this man would leap into her lap any moment.

"When you were born, Flossie wanted to take care of you, but she couldn't. She was too weak. She died when you were about two months old. She just couldn't hang on. That winter was so cold and lasted so long. She couldn't hang on." Tears flowed again in Kate's eyes as she remembered that dreadful time. Alex had ignored her, wouldn't come near her or the child. He sent a doctor to see her once or twice, but the poor man was usually full of whiskey.

"I tried to take care of you — after your mother died. I loved you, almost as much as she. My...partner...Alexander Pantages and I were planning to be married. I knew we could make a home for you."

"Do you know who my father was?" Andrew almost hoped it was Pantages, but he needed to be sure.

"Flossie was a good girl, but her heart was too big. She was an incurable romantic, and when spring came she loved to take long walks in the fields, pick wildflowers, meet young men and share her heart. We were all young...then...there in the north country. We were all just kids. No, I'm not sure who your father was. Flossie never told me."

"Go on. How long did you take care of me? You didn't marry Mr. Pantages. Do you have other children?"

The "other" passed without notice. Kate went on. "No, well, yes, in a way, Alex and I were more like partners, in life and in business. I was making good money in the dance halls, more than Alex made as a waiter. So I staked him to his first theater, there in Dawson, and helped him get the place going. Then we spent some of that money and traveled, to see what other theaters were like. We traveled all over. But that was after…" She shifted in her chair again.

…after we got rid of you, after Alex caused such a scene and insisted we travel as husband and wife, without a child. After he demanded that I find a family to raise you. After I took you to Seattle and found just the right people, a Greek couple — the Koulakises. After I held your little hand for the last time and hugged you and sent you into their arms. After I spent the trip back to Dawson crying tons of tears to mend a broken heart…

"…after I took you to find new parents in Seattle. They were friends I had met when I was in school in Spokane. Maria Koulakis came to visit me when she heard I was in town. Told me how she wanted a child but couldn't have her own." Kate held out her hands to Andrew and he took them as she told him, "You were loved. By many people. Your mother. By me. By the parents whom you have known all your life." She smiled at him then and added, "You must have been loved. Look how well you've turned out."

"You knew me then, when you came into my restaurant."

"Yes. And no. I knew the name. I wasn't sure until I saw those eyes that you were my Andrew…" She caught herself, then corrected, "…my friend's Andrew, the little boy I had cared for." She leaned toward him. "I wanted to keep you, Andrew. I did want to keep you, but it just wasn't possible. My life, our life, Alex and mine, wasn't a good one for a child. You needed a home, a yard, a place to grow up. And look what a fine man you've grown into." She measured his shoulders with her arms.

Andrew seized the moment and clasped her arms behind him as he wound his great arms around her. He held her, both of them reveling in that brief momentary hug that would have to do for a lifetime. She didn't think of *losing* him, only of having found him. And here he was hugging her.

They sat and reminisced then, he on the floor, she bending over him from her chair, laughing at small memories, instant visions of those few months together. No one mentioned again the fright of a young child as he was handed over to a stranger, nor the ripping apart of a mother's heart as she waved goodbye to her child.

When Andrew left, his step felt lighter. He had closed a door on a question that had haunted him his entire lifetime. He had confirmed what he had known in his heart, had placed a real live person into the photo he had carried around. She was older now, her hair not red anymore, her eyes without the youthful sparkle, but she was his. He had found his mother and he had hugged her.

Kate remained in her chair long after darkness fell, into the night. She had seen him, talked with him, held him in her arms again, that chubby little body all grown up into a lanky grownup man, so like his father, so very like his father.

All the Gold...

THE RESCHEDULED WEDDING WAS JUST TWO days away. Summer had lingered and September was turning into a scorcher of a month. Hot searing days, dusty and dry. Kate had become listless, tiring easily, not her usually peppy self. She almost longed for a cold brisk Yukon wind to come roaring through the house.

She took brief drives in the evening to cool off. She especially liked returning to that drive-in where they made a barbecued beef sandwich that had become her favorite. The young carhops all recognized her car and treated her as special.

Just two nights until the wedding, she thought. The old itch returned. She must take another drive out to the high desert, to the shack. Tonight. In the cool air, she'd drive out there one more time while Warren was still in Portland.

What had become so intriguing to Kate was the opportunity she was given to face herself, her younger self. The irony lay in being able to talk face-to-face with the girl she was and yet not knowing how to use this gift. What is it the young Kitty could teach her? What does that young thing know that Kate has lost? Perhaps, Kate's been given this chance to rid herself of the ghost who's haunted her for fifty years?

Yes, that must be it. Kitty's a ghost. Klondike Kate should be...a ghost.

Kate peered into the lighted road ahead of her car, carefully steering onto the desert path. She almost stopped the car when the idea struck. *That girl — Klondike Kate — has become my whole life!*

First it was my bitterness over losing Alex, my refusal to lose him, that kept me going back to Klondike Kate. For it was her that he loved, Kate, the girl of Dawson who caught his eye, and Kate, Queen of the Yukon, who he stayed with. When I started to have a life of my own, when I became a woman who could bear a child...don't, Kate. Don't.

The road narrowed and Kate stopped the car at last. She turned out the headlights. Her eyes adjusted to the dark quickly with the help of the full moon riding high in the sky, glowing in the day's warmth. She sat with the windows down to let in the evening breeze, dropped her head back on the seat, and saw that vision again, the beauty with the candles on her head. "Such a childish thing to do," she crooned to herself. *But then, it was all childish, the singing and prancing around the stage, the games played with the sourdoughs, the rewards of gold dust and the attention, all that attention.* "Which meant more, Kitty? Which did you covet more?"

"The gold, those shiny little bits of earth that could be turned into riches, turned into anything we wanted." The girl comes out of the shadow and appears softly lit in the full moon glow.

"But in the end they aren't worth the sand you're standing on."

"Aren't they? Those little nuggets bought champagne and fine gowns and diamonds and...and..."

"Fine suits for Alex, expensive cologne, silk shirts and ties, dollar cigars, and...theaters," Kate says flatly. "Theaters for a rogue to sign his name on, then take away from you. Theaters that formed the foundation of his empire, that became his life, that gave him such big ideas that you didn't fit anymore."

"You're mixing things up, old woman. You're forgetting the fun, the laughs, the music and..."

"And you're forgetting the tears, the fights, the ordering around, the words that hurt. I'll bet you've even forgotten the night he slapped you, hard."

"No." Kitty hangs her head. "No, I haven't. It was tonight. Just now. That's why I'm out here. We were quarreling. He didn't come back to our room last night. I guessed where he was and he denied it, said he slept in the bar, played poker with the miners, then slept it off there. I know better. I accused him...maybe I shouldn't...but I did. And he hit me. See?" Her cheek still carries the red imprint of Alex's hand.

Kate looks at that pitiful young girl, barely twenty, well educated in the rules of keeping men happy and avoiding life, but so ignorant about how to live her own life. "I wish I could teach you, Kitty darling," Kate whispers into the desert. "I wish I could teach you, but this is something you'll have to learn by yourself. And it's beginning to look like it's going to take you fifty years."

Just what does Kitty want?

Kate knows the answer to that. Kitty, at twenty, no twenty-six — let's face it, she was closer to thirty than to twenty — wants that baby, a family, a home. She wants the picket fence around it too, to protect what is hers, to keep all the happiness inside, untainted by the world around. She wants to grow her own flowers rather than pick them from the meadow once a year. She wants a warm fireplace to toast her toes instead of a hard floor where her toes follow a beat and hurt at the end of the night. She wants a kitchen to dabble in, maybe even learn to bake a cake. Instead she eats hardtack and boiled grub and drinks watered-down champagne all night. That's what Kitty wants — a home and fireplace — but she doesn't know it. And the wiser Kate can't tell her.

"Come on, Kitty, my dear," the older woman calls as she gets out of the car. She throws her arm around the apparition and marches her back to the shack. "Let's go talk to that fella you love so much, you know, the one who hits you."

Kitty holds back for only an instant, then walks alongside Kate. "He's in a rage, Kate. He's real upset. I don't know if..."

"You leave things up to me."

When they find Alex, he is hanging onto a dancer named Snaggly Gert. Or rather, she's hanging onto him. The elder Kate walks right up to them, disengages the girl's arms and tugs at Alex's sleeve. "Come with me, please," she invites.

"Who're you? Oh, that old battle-axe that comes to see Kitty. Well, I have no business with you."

"Oh yes you do. Come with me." She leads the dazed Alexander away from the crowd. She tries to find a private corner that is bright enough for him to see her. She wants him to face her, see who she is.

"Here," she grabs a candle from a table and holds it up to her face. "Look at me. Look at my face and tell me who I look like."

Alex squints, his eyes bleary from drink. "You look like...like...Kitty's grandmother. You look like my little Kitty's old lady." He slumps into a chair and closes his eyes.

"Well I'm not." Kate grabs his shoulder and shakes his eyes open. "I'm not., but if I were I'd have you horsewhipped for what you did to Kitty tonight."

The threat opens his eyes. He stands up and looks at her again, closely. "And just whose business is it what Kitty and I do?"

"Look at me, Alexander. Look at your Kate, your flaming Klondike Kate. Remember the flame dance?" She grabs the red scarf from around her neck and waves it around her head, swaying her hips back and forth, turning with an exotic slowness that can't help but jog the blurry mind of her long-ago lover.

"Hey, you do that plenty good for an old dame." Alexander staggers a bit as he turns to Kitty.

"You gotta watch yourself, sweetheart, or this dame'll take over your act."

"You better watch yourself..." Kitty begins.

"Kitty, meet me in your dressing room. I have more to say to Alex here."

Kitty steps back, then turns and rushes away from the pair.

"Now then, Mr. Pantages," Kate begins sternly, her finger pointed at his chest as she maneuvers him into the corner.

"You better believe it. Call me Mister."

"Do you know what Kitty calls you, called you a few minutes ago?"

"She calls me darling." He leers at Kate and tries to back away, but finds he has no place to go.

"Was she calling you darling after you hit her?"

"Ah, I didn't hit her, just tapped her a little…"

"You hit her."

"Hey, who the hell are you anyway? You can't talk to me like that."

"Look again, Alex. Look again and try to remember…"

Kate moves her face closer to his.

"Well, you remind me a little of…" He stares at the woman again. Closer. Directly in front of her face. "If you weren't so old… you dance like my Kitty. She does the…"

"The Flame Dance. I know. I know all the moves, because…"

"She taught you. Why, you're old and…"

"No, Alex. I know all of her dances and she didn't teach me. I know them because…"

"I need a drink. Get away from me."

"Alex. It's me. Kate. Your Kate. Except I got the chance to grow older."

Alex stares blankly. His head hurts. This vision of a grown-old Kate dangled in front of him makes him cover his eyes with his fists. He stands this way as Kate delivers her message.

"Don't you touch Kitty, ever again. Don't you ever strike her or lift a hand to threaten her. If you do, I'll come back and haunt you for the rest of your miserable days. I can't tell you to make an honest woman out of her, to marry her. That's her affair. But I can warn you never to lift your hand to her again. Is that clear?"

Alex nods helplessly, his fists still covering his eyes. His body is shaking, his shoulders slump. Kate saw him like that the day in California when the sentence was pronounced, sending him to jail for debasing another young woman. He cowered then, sobbing, a little Greek boy caught in mischief, trying to show contrition. Alex is not a contrite man.

He is also very drunk. As Kate turns to walk away, he takes a wide swing with his arm and doesn't even touch her.

Kate walks away.

"Wha' the hell," he mutters. "Wha's going on? You come back…"

Kitty is waiting in the dressing room. Kate smiles as she enteres, then sits down with a sigh. "He won't bother you again. I'm sure of it."

"But will he still see me?"

"Of course, Kitty. He loves you. For all his meanderings, for all his stupidity, the man loves you."

Kitty snatches that bit of hope and puts it into her heart. Her face shines with the radiance of a woman in love.

"But I'm still telling you, he won't marry you. He's not sure enough of himself to ask for himself what he wants most." Kate believes what she says.

Kitty doesn't. "Oh, he'll come around. He'll marry me," she coos.

Some Rocks Are Made of Gold

KATE RETURNED TO THE PARKED CAR, HAULED out her bedroll and built a fire. She slept deeply until dawn, dreaming of wide streams full of salmon surrounded by wider fields filled with forget-me-nots, buttercups, daisies and clover, miles and miles of wildflowers. "Proves we dream in color," she harrumphed when she woke. "That dream was in full Technicolor, just like in the movies."

She stoked her campfire and put on the coffeepot before wandering off to watch the sunrise, its rosy rays just climbing over the edge of the earth. Which is easier on the eyes, she wondered, the sun going down in the splendorous blaze of purple, orange and pink, or the dainty breaking of the sky in the morning when the light seems more delicate, more exploratory?

She picked up a rock that reflected the salmon pink hues of the sky, and turned it over in her hand before dropping it in her pocket. She found several more worthy of retrieving for her collection, stuffing them into other pockets, which made the walk back to the campfire a bit awkward.

Rocks were her passion. Pieces of the planet Earth that held secrets and security, wonder and knowledge. They were solid, reliable, certain, unmoving, forever. At the same time they were mystical, energetic, alive, potential. Like gold. Fingering the rocks in her pockets, she could sense the age of the planet, the billions of years in the making, just as she could feel its future, the ageless awe of everlastingness, eternity.

"Life goes on," she spoke to the cool air. "Life goes on."

Kate hobbled back to the campfire and sat down. She didn't need her cane early mornings in the desert when her bones hadn't yet had time to realize their age. *Guess that's why I get up so early. It's the nights I hate, when I feel every bone and muscle in my poor old tired-out body.*

Another woman in pain came to her mind — Annette. The girl's image sprang up in front of her. I'll stop to see her today. She may need uplifting.

Kate poured her coffee and sat chewing on yesterday's cinnamon bun and watched the sun creep higher in the sky, her face and the bun warming up as it did.

ANNETTE'S ROOM SEEMED BARE WITH ONLY A BOUQUET OF faded yellow roses in the vase near the window. Annette sat up in her bed, bandages still covering most of her body. Yet, she smiled as Kate arrived.

"Well, as I live and breathe — and I am still doing both — it's Klondike Kate," she greeted her visitor.

"Actually, it's Kate Rockwell. I'm coming to terms with my name…and who I am. Isn't that a hoot at my age?"

"It's still good to see you. Thank you for coming. It gets lonely around here."

"If it's lonely, then you must be feeling better."

Annette's eyes shifted away from Kate. "My body is healing, but I've lost…I mean, it's over." She placed her fingers on her abdomen. "I'm not…" and the tears trickled down her face.

"I'm sorry." What more could Kate say? This is for the best? Losing a child before it's born is a loss, a tragedy. She picked up Annette's hand and held it for a moment. "Has he been to see you?"

"Yes, once or twice," Annette nodded at the yellow roses. "He has his own problems now, at home." She smiled at Kate and brightened. "And at the office. I hear he's hired a new reporter."

"Yes, I'd heard that too. Well, I certainly hope he's helping with your hospital bills and such."

"Actually, yes, he is. Said he'd pay for the doctor and my medicine. My Blue Cross will take care of the rest. I'm still covered by my parents' policy. I'm lucky."

Annette didn't look lucky. Her insides had been a mass of wounds, her skin was still showing bruises where the damage was done. And the light in her eyes had darkened, not quite so sparkling. This young girl had undergone some serious life training.

"I'll be okay. Doctor says I may be able to go home and recuperate...maybe in another week."

"Where is home? I don't think I ever heard you talk about your family."

"Portland. We didn't get along well. That's why I chose a job out here. But now they seem to want me back there. So I'll go."

"And Paul?"

"You were right. We had a...thing...a fling...a whatchamacallit. I thought..." Her eyes were downcast again as she remembered. Paul had faced the window of her room just yesterday as he droned out the words: "Little Paula...responsibility...need to be a father...Isabel...new baby...parents...newspaper..." He had gone on and on, his back to Annette, giving her time to cry the tears of parting. He was telling himself, *she's smart; she knows what I have to do.* And Annette knew too that making a scene wouldn't keep him with her. The pain went deep, deeper than the wounds from the auto accident, deep into her soul. She would carry the scar the rest of her life.

To Kate she continued, "I thought we were in love. I still believe we were. But apparently not enough for him to choose me over his family." Annette straightened up in bed, smoothed out the coverlet, raised her chin and smiled at Kate. "But that's the way it's supposed to be...isn't it?"

Kate's voice was husky and quiet as she answered, "Yes, that's the way it's supposed to be." The two thought their own thoughts, brought up their own memories and cried their own silent tears for the men they would love forever.

Kate stopped at the newspaper office on her way home, ostensibly to pick up another copy of the paper, but also to get a look at how the new reporter was getting along.

"Hello, Paul," she greeted the editor. "Just came from seeing Annette. She's doing well, says she can go home next week."

"Glad to hear that," Paul swept a glance at the new reporter, who didn't seem to be listening. "Guess I should stop and tell her goodbye. Oh, and I have some papers for her to sign." He spoke self-consciously, eager to appear casual, yet displaying his concern. He still cared for Annette, no doubt about that. *How can a young fellow get himself into this kind of mess?*

"You do that," Kate tossed back at him as she walked out the door. "You go give her those papers."

When she reached her house, Kate went directly to the telephone and dialed Warren.

"Warren, sweetheart," she began. "I'm calling to make your children happy." She sounded flip. She wanted to.

"And how's that, my dear?" Warren sounded wary.

"I'm calling off the wedding."

Silence followed, except for the humming of the wires that spanned the mountains.

Then, "Oh Kate, no. No." Warren's voice cracked. She could picture him folding himself around the telephone as he tried to reach her. "Please Kate. Something's happened. What? What's wrong, my darling?"

"Nothing's wrong, Warren. Everything's right. I've come to my senses."

"If you were sensible, you'd have married me in June as we planned. Never mind my interfering children."

"It's not your children, Warren. Except that they're right. I have no business marrying you. You deserve someone who...who...." She didn't know how to finish that thought.

Warren did. "...who I can love, who I do love, who I want to spend the rest of my days with."

"That's not enough, Warren. And if you thought about it carefully, you'd see I'm right. We're both looking for someone to cling to as we head into the sunset." She imagined a grin on his face. He couldn't manage one. "We're facing a very limited future. I don't know about you, but I'm scared. All my old friends are gone, dead. Can't find many folks my own age to make new friends. Not many left, except you and me. So we cling to each other. Better to go down in twos. Is that it?"

Warren heard the flip tone of Kate's voice and knew what she was doing, knew that she was scared. "Kate...listen to me. You're absolutely right. This is scary, where we are. But why not ride out this...time...together? I can't bear to think of you frightened...and alone. Isn't it better to be frightened and with someone?" Warren wasn't a lawyer for nothing. He could put up a fairly good argument when he had to.

"Let's just say *postpone* then, if that makes you happier. I just can't go through a wedding right now."

"Kate, sleep on it. I'll talk to you tomorrow. I'll come down there and talk some sense back into your head."

"I'll sleep on it, but I don't think that will change things. It was last night's sleep that made up my mind."

"Besides," Warren added. "Both Willis and Joan have told me they can accept you as my new wife."

How kind of them, how generous, Kate thought. But all she said was, "That's nice."

WELL, THERE IT WAS. SHE'D DONE IT, SENT WARREN PACKING, even though he didn't go without a struggle. Kate pulled on her gardening gloves and went outside to what she called her weed patch. She knelt at one corner and pulled the rocks out of her pocket and placed them in the growing pile. She was arranging them in a kind of half-circle, partly to mark the edge of the garden, partly to hold back the weeds, and partly to form a tribute to...what? She had built so many tributes to so many dead things — a rabbit she found mauled by some larger animal, a couple of birds, a memorial to Mr. Matson, and an oracle similar to those she'd read about in ancient Greece. All about the garden were stone edifices that appeared like a combination of altars and headstones, all built of rocks she brought in from the desert and the nearby mountains. Anybody can grow carrots, but only Kate could make the rocks grow in her yard.

This one's for Warren, she decided as she piled the stones together, working in bits of mud to hold them in place. *These rosy-colored stones will mark his rosy-colored glasses, the ones that shut out everything but me.* When she was nearly finished, she made her way to the house and re-appeared a few minutes later with something in her hand. At the very top of the sculpture she added, inconspicuously, a gold nugget to catch the light, a glittering memento of their love.

Two hours later, Kate removed her gardening gloves, now covered with the mortar mud and rock dust. She stood up and wove her hands through her snowy white hair, pushing back a stray lock from her forehead. Her bones creaked more than ever and, as she entered the house, she was tempted to fall into a parlor chair. But she kept going, up to her bedroom. *Better get me a bath and wash the desert out of my hair.*

She was halfway up the steps when the telephone rang. She slowly went back down and picked up the phone.

"Kate? Klondike Kate? I'm calling from the Richmond Chamber of Commerce. We're planning a celebration here in October and we're wondering if you would appear in the parade and then speak at a banquet later that evening? We're remembering the Gold Rush Days fifty years ago. Do you do that kind of thing?"

Kate was used to such requests and used to a voice carrying on and on about what they wanted, even before making sure they had the right person.

"Yes, this is Kathleen Rockwell Matson," she said as demurely as she could manage.

"Yes, Klondike Kate?"

"I've been called that."

"Well, would you..." and the voice began all over.

When it had finished, Kate smiled — to make her voice sound less edgy — and said simply, "No, thank you," hung up, and continued upstairs to her bath.

"Could've used the money, I suppose. But I think I'm done playing Klondike Kate. Time to put her to rest. Maybe I'll build a shrine for her. Yes, in that space over by the garage. Maybe work in some more of those gold nuggets...for accents."

And I'll build another one next to it for Alexander. Time to put him to rest too. They can both rest together there, eternally at peace.

Kate removed her dusty clothes and wrapped herself in a robe of teal blue silk trimmed with ecru lace. She took note in the mirror of her body, not bad for a woman her age. My age, she mused. I haven't calculated that correctly for years, if ever. Let's see. Fifty-two years in this century, twenty-four in the last, seems to add up to...no, that can't be right...seventy-six? I'm seventy-six years old? I don't think so. She looked again in the mirror, turning to pose as Klondike Kate the dancer, entertainer, singer of classy vaudeville songs. She hummed lightly, "Casey would waltz with the strawberry blond, and the band played on...and on...and on...and..." Kate swayed just a bit as the song wound its way through her head.

The reflectors shone a light on her face and she could hear the gasps from the men, smell the stale smoke and whiskey, feel the applause and stomping of her audience. She sang, her voice stronger with each phrase, weaving back and forth in time with the music.

"And the band played on..." she sang. At the end she was startled to hear two hands clapping. Just two. She opened her eyes to find Kitty in front of her. Kate pulled her robe around her.

"You do that almost as good as I do," Kitty said as she continued to applaud.

"I've had more practice than you," Kate replied. She wasn't in a mood to confront the girl just now. "What are you doing here? Go back where you belong."

"This is where I belong. With you."

"Not anymore. I'm getting rid of you."

"Not that easy, Kate."

"And why not?"

"Because I am you. Took me awhile to believe it, but now I do. I'm you. You're me. We're stuck with each other."

"Well, I can unstick you if I want."

"Uh-uh. No way. I heard what you said downstairs on the phone just now, how you brushed off those people with that 'Kathleen Rockwell Matson' crap. Who do you think you're kidding? You wouldn't last five minutes without me."

"You don't think so? Watch me."

"I'd rather not. Look, Kate. Go draw your bath. We'll talk."

Kate picked up a towel and walked to the bathroom, Kitty following. She closed the door and opened the hot water tap.

"Don't you use bubbles anymore? I swore that when I got back to civilization I'd have bubbles in every bath. Have you stopped?"

"You're enjoying this, aren't you, you young..."

"Actually yes. I'm enjoying what you started. First you scare the daylights out of me by showing up where I work, in the middle of my love life, in the middle of Dawson in the Yukon, for god's sake..."

"No need to use that kind of language."

"Yeah, well, you have a short memory. We all talked like that up there. Remember?"

"But I never..."

"Oh yes you did. Boy, it has been a long time. You've forgotten. Well, I'm here to remind you."

Kate climbed into the tub...without bubbles...and began to

splash water over her arms. "I hope you don't mind if I go ahead with my bath," she snapped.

"You are in a bad mood. I can tell," Kitty snapped back. "I am too. I don't like the way you're pushing me out. Just when I was beginning to like this. Come on, fill me in. What kind of life have you really had? Tell me all. You're famous, I can tell that. I saw the newspapers downstairs, the big spread on page one about your upcoming nuptials." She spit out the word with all its syllables, nuptshee-ulls. "You get telephone invitations to appear here and there. You've really cashed in on my...our...little gig in the gold fields."

"People have heard about me, about the notoriety with Alex, the..."

"There! That's what I want to know about. You've alluded to it before. The 'notoriety with Alex.' What's that all about?"

"I don't think it would be right to discuss it with you. It's still in your future."

"Oh come on, Aunt Kate," her voice sounded condescending. "You can do better than that."

"I just don't think I should tell you how your life will turn out."

"Why? We can't change it."

"Well, yes, I guess...oh, you're confusing me. This isn't right. Why am I even talking to you. I'm trying to take a bath. Why don't you leave, go away, get out of here."

"Okay, I'm gone."

Kate pulled the washcloth away from her face and looked around. She was alone. "Goddam ghost is driving me crazy," she said aloud.

Kate finished her bath, pulled herself out of the tub, reached for the towel and began to dry herself. She replaced the teal blue silk robe and returned to her bedroom. The bed looked inviting after the night on the desert floor. She lay across it and closed her eyes, just for a minute.

"It won't work," came Kitty's voice. "Nope, you're stuck with me. So you'd best fill me in on how I grow up."

Kate moaned and turned over on her back. "You didn't…grow up. You stayed the same. Oh, your body aged, but you didn't."

Kate sat up then and faced her apparition. "You were twenty-two when you trekked north to Dawson during the Gold Rush of 'ninety-eight. What year was it when we met Alex?…when you started your romance? Let's see, nineteen ought two, which would make you about twenty-six. Pretty old for a dancer, don't you think?"

Kitty held her breath as she faced the older woman. "Yes, I was twenty-six, but I had such a baby face, everybody thought I was only eighteen or nineteen. Especially Alex, who…"

"I know what Alex thought. He saw a dancer doing well, saving her gold, a young woman ripe for the picking."

Kitty shook her head in protest, but didn't say a word as Kate went on.

"You had loaned Alex money to start his theater, it was open and running, and you were getting ready to take your little trip to Texas to…uh…what did you tell him? look for more opportunities? earn some extra money dancing? What was your excuse? I've forgotten."

"You know damn well why I went to Texas."

"Well, what year was that? Nineteen and two? three? And why the hell did you leave Dawson?"

"Who's swearing now? Don't get so het up. You'll lose your tinder. Calm down, Kate."

"Reality. That's what I'm trying to spark here. You were close to thirty years old when 'Frisco fell down in that earthquake. Remember. I'm just giving you a little face-the-music reality."

"This isn't like you."

"Or maybe it is. It's about time."

"Well go ahead. I went to Texas and I was pushing thirty. Alex still had no right to walk out on me, to take up with that child, that...that Jezebel! He had no right!"

"But he did, and you never quite got over that. You could never say, okay, that fish got away. Let's find another."

"Oh yes I did. I found another. Don't you remember Floyd?"

"Floyd! Ah yes, Mr. Wonderful Number Two. If anyone had more love for himself than Alex, it had to be Floyd. Still, he was handy to have around while I was setting up my homestead here. He was..."

"Diversion?"

"Okay, diversion. Anyway, he didn't hang around long."

"And how old were you then?"

"Do you have to keep...?"

"Let's move on. Surely we're closing in on what made Alex notorious? When was that? What was that? What happened?"

"All right. The papers were all full of it. Happened in the middle of what we called the Roaring Twenties."

"Of course you would have been in your roaring forties, wouldn't you?"

"Just shut up. The world went crazy after World War I."

"And I was only…"

"Don't interrupt. After the war, girls bobbed their hair." Kate patted her own. "We wore short tight skirts and some nice girls even began smoking cigarettes."

"That wasn't something new for you. I…you…always rolled your own." Kitty hadn't caught the implication that society took two decades to catch up to her.

"Life was gaudy, loud, free. Free love, that was what we called it. And Alex apparently got a little too free with his. Got caught manhandling some actress who worked in one of his theaters. She sued. He went to court."

"Did you go to cheer her on?"

"No. Well, I went, but as a witness for the prosecution."

"You would testify against him? Against your…my Alex?"

"I was ready to, but they didn't need me. Had a good time though. The press followed me around and made quite a splash over me."

"Did you see Alex? Talk to him?"

"We passed each other in the hallway one day, during the trial. He seemed surprised to see me and could only say a few words. He asked how I was, I think."

"Poor Alex. Poor poor Alex."

"Poor nothing. The man took my money, never paid it back, and became wealthy on it. Then he used that wealth to connive with every floozy that came his way. He…"

"Alex, wealthy?"

"Owned a string of theaters. That'll make you wealthy. Or it did for him. Vaudeville theater was big stuff back then."

"Or it will be, from where I sit."

"So there's your wonderful Alex. Never offered to help. He dropped me, never looked back, never acknowledged that I was alive. Once I went to him for help, walked right up to his great mansion and held out my hand. Know what he gave me? Six bucks! Six lousy bucks from a man who had millions. Well, thank goodness the judge didn't see all those dollars. He saw a philandering, arrogant, jackass who…"

"Did he go to jail?"

"Yes, but only for a few days. Then he appealed and the *actress* dropped the charges. The little hussy let herself get bought off, I'm sure."

"Where is he now?"

"You don't want to know."

"Yes I do. No, I don't. He's dead, isn't he?"

Kate nodded. They looked at each other, wondering how to comfort the other, wondering if they needed to.

After a moment, Kitty asked, "And then?"

"And then Johnny Matson."

"Johnny…you mean that little weasly guy who sits over in the corner and leers at me every night?"

"Yes, I guess I do."

"Johnny Matson! You married him? Why, he isn't your type at all. He doesn't drink or smoke. He barely speaks, and then none too clearly, all that yam and yelly stuff. That shy scared little rabbit of a man? You married...aw Kate. Why? How?"

"He wrote to me. Saw my picture in the papers during Alex's trial. Three years later...you know how valuable newspapers are up in the Yukon...he learned where I lived and wrote to me. The old sourdough!"

"And you answered?"

"Of course I did. He was an old friend."

"Friend? I don't remember ever saying more than a couple words to him. And he certainly never said much more to me." Kitty tried to remember. "I think we might have danced a couple times, but...marry him? Aw Kate, no."

"My Yonny was sweet, a gentleman, always courteous..."

"Sweet and courteous doesn't make a marriage. Compare him to Alex."

Now Kate was paying attention. Her body shivered slightly and she looked straight at her young self. "At forty..."

"Ah-ah. Isn't this truth-telling time?"

"Okay, fifty. When you're any age over twenty you can't be picky. That kind gentle man offered me marriage when I was...fifty years old. I took it. I knew he was older. I knew he was no great shakes in the looks department."

"Rich? Could he give you what you needed? Security?"

"I'm not all that sure security is what I needed."

"Think, Kate. You've been looking for security since you were three. And I don't mean the gold kind."

Kate's father, her real father, flashed before her. She was waving goodbye to him as her insides shook with dread. Daddy's gone.

Daddy's gone. I'm alone. I'm alone. The words repeated to the clickity-clack sound of the wheels of the train. Daddy's gone. I'm alone.

Kate's voice dropped to a soft low sound of truth. "You know, kiddo, I always figured Johnny had a huge stash somewhere. He never spent it on much more than a few dances at the saloon. He never drank, didn't eat much, never left the Yukon, didn't own more than his little digs. And he worked like a demon. Now if you work hard digging gold and spend little, for thirty years…" She couldn't finish the sentence. She didn't know how.

"You're right. What did little old Johnny Matson do with all his money?"

"He sure didn't leave anything in that cabin. Warren and I hiked up there after Johnny died. There was nothing. Some books in Swedish, some pots and pans, his bedroll and his digging tools. God, how did he spend his alone time?"

"Dreaming of me. He told me once. He'd lie down at the end of the day and picture me singing to him."

"Can you understand why I accepted his proposal? I knew he'd never leave the Yukon. And he agreed that I'd stay here, in Oregon. There were no demands."

"No demands, no benefits…"

"Except that I would be his beneficiary. He wrote that down."

"Yeah, except there was nothing to benefit from."

The two women were lost in thought. Then Kate looked at the ceiling as she sighed, "Yonny, my yam and yelly man, was a sweet little guy."

The young Kitty added, "With nothing to show for thirty years mining gold…"

"Except me."

Kate fell asleep then, stretched across her bed, still wearing her silk robe and thinking of her dear departed Swedish husband.

Love is Cool!

THE NEXT MORNING KATE WOKE TO A RINGING
telephone. She sprang from bed, but used great
caution going down the stairs. She grabbed the
phone and somehow knew it would be Warren.

"Hello?" She asked, out of breath.

"Kate? You all right?" It was Warren.

"Yes," she took a deep breath. "Just ran down
the stairs."

"Kate, I've told you about…"

Kate laughed. "Now, now, I'm just teasing.
You know dang well I won't take that risk again.
Besides I can't run anywhere."

Warren took a deep breath too. "I'm calling,
Kate, to tell you…" he was stalling. "…tell you
that I'm going to drive down there today…"

"What on earth for? It's very hot here. Wouldn't
Portland be cooler?"

"Kate!" he shouted so she would stop talking. "Kate, I want to come to Homestead so we can sit down and talk about our future. I'm…"

"Oh Warren…"

"Listen! For a change, listen to me, Kate." He paused to see if she would interrupt again. She didn't.

"I want to come there so we can talk about what's bothering you with our getting married. I know you love me. And I love you. And there isn't much else that really matters, is there?" He paused again.

"No, I guess not," Kate sounded like Kitty at that moment.

"Then it's settled. I'll be there in a couple of hours. Make some Indian tea and we'll find a breeze to keep cool." He hung up without waiting to say goodbye.

The air felt hot and lifeless that morning. Kate spent most of her time trying to find the occasional breeze that pushed through her high-ceilinged rooms in the house on the hill. The ceiling fan that she had finally installed stirred what little breeze tripped in.

It was just about lunchtime that Warren drove up in his post-war shiny four-door Buick. Kate fixed sandwiches, cut into some freshly-made peach cobler, poured tea over two glasses full of ice cubes and let Warren carry the tray to the front porch.

"I closed my office right after I called you, got in my car and drove. The mountains were cool, but this is stifling," he said as he settled himself into a wicker chair. He was ready to talk some sense into her head, but he waited until they finished their lunch. Kate carried the empty dishes back to the kitchen and refilled the tea glasses. The two sat on the front porch sipping tea and fanning themselves with cardboard fans from the hardware store, while the town below them moved slowly in the hot sun.

"Might have to go to the store today," Kate announced casually. "We're about out of tea."

"I'll go for you if you'd like."

"Maybe we could go together."

The lazy talk continued listlessly, but soon they fell silent, too warm to talk. Neither wanted to raise the question of the wedding. Was it on? Was it off? Since Warren had said nothing, Kate decided to stay away from the subject...for a time. Besides, perhaps there wasn't much to talk about after all.

Usually a very deliberate man, Warren's brain had stopped working in the heat. The drive down had been almost more than his aging body could stand. He had lost the vigorous plans that had been whirling inside him as he left Portland. And now, the combination of heat and years were dulling his thought process.

Which may account for what happened next. As if the warm air had sprung a notion into his head, Warren acted without thinking, perhaps for the first time in his life.

He turned to Kate, seated there on the wicker porch chair, and suggested, "Let's get married today."

Kate laughed her hearty laugh. "Ha! It's too hot."

"No it isn't, Kate." He stood up. "Let's just go do it, run over to the courthouse this afternoon and make it legal."

Kate had tried hard to ignore Warren, put him off, delay the wedding, keep things as they were. She had tried to warn him that she wasn't ready to marry. She had even tried to call it off — more than once. Hadn't she been postponing since May?

Today in the late summer heat, Kate was worn out from the effort. She couldn't think of any more excuses. Why not? She would probably enjoy being married to Warren Thompson. He was good to her; he obviously loved her. She didn't exactly need the security he offered, but it wouldn't hurt. She didn't give a rap for what his children thought. Maybe there weren't any reasons not to marry him. Or maybe she was just too hot to object anymore. Besides, if the ever-careful Warren Thompson was showing spontaneity, she'd better pay attention.

"Okay. You win. We'll get married...this afternoon."

It took Warren a few minutes to believe his ears. "Oh Kate, Kate, Kate." Warren smiled broadly and bent over to hug her. "You'll be happy. We'll be happy. You'll see."

He sat back and went on talking about their life together. "We can travel, see some of this country. We'll have the kids here for holidays. We'll make friends with some of the folks in town. I'll give up the practice in Portland and move here. You can stay here, Kate, right where you like to live. We'll take walks and go to movies and read together..."

"Read? Together? I haven't read a book in years. You want to read together?"

"I didn't mean...Kate, we don't have to read..." Then he saw she was teasing him and they both laughed together.

"Let's get one of those fancy new color television sets. I've enjoyed my black and white these last few years. I think I'd enjoy a color set. Do you have one?"

"No, but Joan does. She says she finds it rather entertaining. And the children like it."

"Well then, we must have one."

The two oldsters sat on the porch planning their lives together until the sun moved around and made the porch even warmer. They carried their empty tea glasses inside. In the kitchen, Warren took Kate by her shoulders then wound his arms around her and kissed her, a long loving husbandly kiss. She returned it with a very wifely kiss.

Soon after, Kate changed into her organdy dress, white with tiny purple and green flowers. She perched a wide-brimmed white straw hat on her head and wrapped a jaunty purple scarf around it. She stuffed something into her purse at the last minute, then announced, "Let's go get hitched."

Warren, dressed in a white Panama suit and straw skimmer, took her arm as he looked deep into her sparkling gray eyes. Off they went to the courthouse.

DOWN AT MILLIE'S THE NEXT MORNING, PAUL SAT OVER HIS second cup of coffee. He was working up his energy to go back into the heat and walk across the street to his office. Just as he asked Millie for the check, the door opened and in walked his new reporter.

"Hey, boss. You gotta grab your camera and get a picture of something."

"What?"

"You won't believe this."

"What won't I believe? Remember, I'm a newspaperman."

"Somebody phoned in to the office this morning and said there was something hanging from the Meriwether Lewis statue in front of the courthouse, the one standing next to Mr. William Clark."

"I know who the statues are," Paul answered in exasperation. "What is hanging from them?"

"Strange goings on in this town."

"Well, out with it. What is hanging on the Lewis statue?"

"I was just by there. Walked over to see for myself, and it's true. Hanging from the right arm of Mr. Meriwether Lewis, the famous explorer and naturalist, is..." she paused for effect.

Paul sighed and emptied his cup. "Okay, I'll bite. What?"

"A red chiffon scarf."

"Naw! Really?"

Millie threw back her head and laughed until tears streamed from her eyes.

"Millie, you know what that's about?"

"Sure do, Mr. Benjamin. I sure do."

It was several weeks before anyone had the gumption to remove the scarf from the statue of the explorer that gazed out across the Oregon desert. By that time there was a small item in the society column of the *Homestead Courier*:

> *Mr. and Mrs. Warren Thompson have returned from their extended honeymoon trip to Italy and are now entertaining friends in their Franklin Street home.*

Some Facts
About Kate/Kitty

EVER SINCE SHE WAS CROWNED QUEEN OF
the Yukon in her twenties, the real Kathleen
Eloise Rockwell traded on the title to keep her
fame alive. She even had a movie made about
herself in the 1940s. Kate created her image at
the height of the Gold Rush when she was
crowned Klondike Kate, Queen of the Yukon,
during a champagne-blurred Christmas Eve in
1900. She later created another image, that of
the homey Aunt Kate who cared for the unfor-
tunate of her community.

Kate was born in Junction City, Kansas, in
1876 to John Rockwell, a railroad telegraph
operator, and Martha, a waitress. Both were
divorced from other spouses, and five years
later from each other. Martha married another
divorced man, Allison Bettis, a former legisla-
tor, and they moved to Spokane, Washington.
Bettis became a successful judge and show-

ered his wife and adopted daughter with his wealth. Kate grew into a spoiled child, unrestrained and rambunctious, riding horseback and camping outdoors. When her parents noticed her increasing interest in men, they moved her to a series of private Catholic girls' schools — in Kansas, Minnesota, and California.

Judge Bettis lost his fortune in the recession of 1893, bringing Martha to yet another divorce. After she lost heavily in real estate speculation, she grabbed her daughter Kate and headed for South America to visit a son by a previous marriage. The naval voyage gave Kate another opportunity to entice young men — naval officers. When she announced her engagement to one of them (stories suggest she accepted diamonds from seven men), her mother stuck her in a Catholic school in Valparaiso, Chile, where Kate took to teaching other young girls.

Mother Martha, meanwhile, had run off to England on a romantic adventure. When she returned to New York, she learned her daughter had embroiled herself in yet another engagement — to a diplomatic attaché from Spain. Martha ordered Kate to take the next boat to New York. The fifteen-year-old Kate endured a scary three-month trip around Cape Horn and arrived penniless in New York.

It was Martha who prompted Kate to respond to a newspaper ad seeking chorus girls. "No experience necessary." The girl took to the stage and began her career as a dancer/singer. Martha imposed strict controls over her daughter as she moved from a walk-on part in a Coney Island honky-tonk to the chorus line, to legitimate vaudeville houses in New York, then to a not-so-legitimate variety theater in Spokane. It was there Kate had to learn to sit with customers after the show and push drinks (although she professed to drink only lemonade).

The excitement of the discovery of gold in the Yukon prompted Kate to quit the Spokane gig and head north. She settled her mother in Seattle, then entertained at a vaudeville house in Victoria, B.C. She even became engaged again, this time to a man ten years her senior. But she chose Alaska, and made the excruciating climb across Chilkoot Pass with a fairly respectable troupe of dancers. When the other young women were turned back at the border by Mounties who claimed the journey was too rugged for them, Kate, not to be stopped, donned boy's clothing and climbed aboard a scow to take the dangerous ride down the Five Finger Rapids.

Arriving in Dawson, she became a favorite soubrette, wearing expensive gowns and singing the favorite songs of the miners. She was treated royally, given special living quarters and the star treatment. The Yukon of the late 1890s was a place swarming with men intent on striking it rich. When they pulled a few nuggets from the ground, they immediately took them to town where they splurged.

Kate told stories about the large amounts of gold she accumulated. Speculation about how she earned it brought denials from Kate, who claimed she just listened to miners and their problems and entertained them. Apparently she had a talent as a good listener who could sympathize with the sad, lonely men. She also thrived on the attention of the men around her. At one time she reported she had pulled in more than $30,000 during her first year in Dawson, describing how the men threw gold at her feet when she danced.

Then along came a young Alexander Pantages, freshly immigrated from Greece and hungry for fame and fortune. Together they planned a life of getting rich by building theaters and presenting top-notch entertainment.

Kate's relationship with Pantages was based on their combined ambitions. Kate headlined at Dawson theaters and Alex invested in first one then another theater enterprise. Kate actually put up $4,000 of her own to open their first theater in Dawson — the Orpheum. When one enterprise failed, Kate would finance his expensive habits until he could find another. Together they later opened the Crystal, then the first Pantages theater in Seattle. Alex and his Kitty worked together and played together, living together openly and making plans to marry.

Some believe that Kate bore Alex's child during a brief trip to the States. She cared for an infant for a time, explaining that it was the child of a friend who had died in childbirth. Later she turned over the child to foster parents. While she financed a college education for the child, she never disclosed its identity.

Alex was as cold as Kate was warm. A self-taught man, he never learned to read or write, and kept accounts in his head. He seldom smiled and treated people with reserve. His head was filled with dollar signs. Kate, on the other hand, was a friendly, outgoing, trusting woman who believed she was destined to marry Alexander. The two toured the States, scouting sites for their planned theaters.

During one trip alone in 1905, Kate received word that her Alexander had married his protégé, a teen-age violinist from a prominent California family. Kate never forgave him. She went into shock, then filed a lawsuit seeking damages for breach of promise to marry her. The case was settled out of court for an amount reported somewhere between $5000 and $60,000. A distraught Kate returned to the vaudeville circuit, even attempting song-and-dance numbers on roller skates.

Through the years, the broken-hearted Kate kept up her vaudeville career, but distraught over her lost love, opted to hide out in the barren wilds of central Oregon, where cattle ranchers battled lumberjacks for power, and communities sprang up to satisfy the invading homesteaders.

Kate worked a homestead at Brothers, near Bend, Oregon, for four years before it was hers, grubbing sagebrush and piling rocks while wearing her ballroom gowns and high heels. In her 40s, she lassoed a 20-year-old cowboy named Floyd Warner, married him, sent him off to fight World War I, then divorced him upon his return. In 1929, when she learned that her beloved Pantages was being sued for raping a young entertainer, Kate was called to testify against him. She attended the trial in California, but never testified. Pantages was sentenced to jail, then acquitted two years later. He never fully recovered from his ordeal and died in 1936.

After the trial, the aging Kate, then nearing 60, re-connected with a 70-year-old sourdough admirer, Johnny Matson, and married him in 1933, choosing to live in Oregon while he continued to mine gold in Alaska. He died thirteen years later.

Between publicity generated by Pantages' trial and her marriage to the aged Matson, Klondike Kate was again in the news and in demand in the late 1930s. She often entertained at annual get-togethers of sourdoughs in the Northwest, survivors of the Alaska-

Yukon gold rush. Columbia Pictures in 1940 acquired movie rights to make a movie starring Janet Blair.

In 1948, Kate married her long-time friend and accountant, William L. VanDuren. Kate had rescued him a decade earlier when he was down-and-out and nearly blind. After she negotiated expensive eye surgery to restore his sight, he fell madly in love with her. They retired to the quiet of Sweet Home, Oregon, to live out their years. She died peacefully in her sleep in 1957.

In 1952, when this story is set, Kate had become a fixture in her adopted town, both the subject of derision by the uppercrust and a beloved icon by her lesser-well-to-do peers. She once ran a café and earned the title Aunt Kate by supplying public institutions with food. She became the one-woman auxiliary to the local fire department, serving coffee and cookies during fires and cooking meals occasionally to show her support. She gave gifts to children and handed out trinkets that reminded people of her days in the Yukon. She collected rocks and decorated her home and community with historic works of art. Her peace of mind came through her love of the desert, especially its sunsets. It was to the high desert that she often ran for spiritual renewal.

Ever the avid publicist, Kate had postcards printed bearing her picture and the phrase, "Smile and Mush On," and circulated them throughout her life in Oregon.

That much really happened. She must have wondered who was the real Kathleen Rockwell — Kitty, the saucy belle of the Yukon, or the warm neighborly Aunt Kate? That is what this story is about.

—Val Dumond and Babe Lehrer

About the Authors

VAL DUMOND HAS WRITTEN SEVERAL BOOKS, INCLUDING FOUR novels, but this is the one she's enjoyed the most. Some of what she has published: *Grammar For Grownups* (HarperCollins), *Elements of Nonsexist Usage* (Prentice Hall), *Doin' The Puyallup, An Airport for Tacoma* (co-authored for Leguilloux Press), and *Just Words* (soon to be published). She edits book manuscripts, leads a writing group, and became a publisher when the group recently published its own *The Sun Never Rises — A Rainthology*. She lives in Tacoma, Washington.

GRISELDA "BABE" LEHRER HAS RESEARCHED THE HISTORIC material and photos for this book. A strong supporter of the arts, she became fascinated with Klondike Kate while researching data for a proposed museum honoring Alexander Pantages, theater magnate of the early 20th century. Ms. Lehrer continues her avid interest in the theater and the arts. She lives in Tacoma, Washington with her husband Herman. Now both are retired from operating a successful ladies' ready-to-wear business in Washington and Oregon.

Acknowledgements

MANY THANKS TO THOSE GRACIOUS FOLKS WHO PROVIDED THE photographs to accompany this book. Photos are used with the kind permission of the following:

B. Willoughby Collection, Alaska and Polar Archives, Rasmusson Library, University of Alaska, Fairbanks — #72-116-334N.

C. Waugamom Collection, Alaska and Polar Archives, University of Alaska, Fairbanks — #91-116-01N.

Deschutes County Historical Society, Bend, Oregon.

Yukon Archives, Alaska Sportsman, March 1956.

Yukon Archives, Whitehorse, MacBride Museum Collection, Vol. II, print #3880.

Yukon Archives, Whitehorse, Rockwell, Kate Collection — 82/207 #38, #43, #66, #78, #450.

The authors also wish to extend their appreciation to Karen Westeen for her editing help, Lisbeth Wheelehan and other readers for their excellent feedback, Wolfgang Opitz for his title suggestion, Mark Ashley of Sands Costner & Associates for his creative cover design, and the friends of Kathleen Eloise Rockwell Warner Matson Van Duren in Bend and Sweet Home, Oregon, for their invaluable first-hand information.